Tomorrow Must Wait

Tomorrow Must Wait

To Roz and John,

Hope you enjoy

All best.

Martin

Oct. 2019

MARTIN WHITTLE

© Martin Whittle, 2019

Published by Martin Whittle

A CIP catalogue record for this book is available from the British Library.

Declaration

This is a work of fiction and although the events are historically correct all the characters, names and dialogues are entirely fictitious and of the author's imagination and any likenesses to individuals alive or dead are completely coincidental.

Details on raids, casualty rates etc are drawn from a variety of sources including books by M. Middlebrook and the internet.

ISBN 978-1-9996905-0-2

Book layout and cover design by Clare Brayshaw

Prepared and printed by:

York Publishing Services Ltd
64 Hallfield Road
Layerthorpe
York YO31 7ZQ

Tel: 01904 431213

Website: www.yps-publishing.co.uk

CHAPTER 1

Saturday 25th December 1943

At first Anne had not been too worried by the fact that Matt White, her Squadron Leader fiancé, hadn't called her on the 24th, the morning after the raid on Germany – he was often busy and always tired and she assumed he had just gone to bed and had forgotten to ring her. But when he didn't call on Christmas morning her fears began to increase as did her concern at the difficulty of finding out what might have happened. Many of the men she had known, who had been friends of Matt's in the squadron, had been killed or were missing and if she rang the airfield no one would tell her what was going on in any case – national security! And ringing Matt's parents might only cause them unnecessary distress. There was probably an obvious explanation. In any case, she had to go to work but resolved that if she hadn't heard by the end of her shift as theatre sister, she would ring the airfield in any case and try and get someone who knew what was going on.

She met with Jess, who was also a nurse at the hospital, during one of their breaks, and told her that Matt hadn't been in touch since the raid. Jess immediately felt apprehensive for her friend – she herself had already experienced the death of her own boyfriend in the Battle of Britain and she was careful with her words as the two chatted.

"Let's meet after work" she suggested. "Maybe go for a drink, something like that? It is Christmas after all!"

Anne nodded but she wasn't listening and all she was really thinking about was making her phone call to East Kirkby. She would try the adjutant, Squadron Leader Davies she remembered he was called. He had seemed a nice chap and he might bend the rules if she asked nicely. At least he would know if Matt was around.

The day in the operating theatre had been busy with many emergencies so that it wasn't until after seven o'clock that she was eventually able to make the call and her heart was thumping as she was put through, only to be disappointed by the fact that the adjutant was off duty. Instead she spoke to the duty officer who had no idea who she was and certainly felt it wasn't his job to say whether Squadron Leader White was there or not.

She slammed the phone down and ran down the corridor to her room, closed the door and fell on to her bed sobbing uncontrollably. *He's gone,* she thought, *I know it. They would have said if he was there.* She had been crying for a while before she heard a soft tapping on her door before Jess came in.

"Any news?" Jess asked nervously.

"No. I spoke to someone but they couldn't tell me anything. I think he's gone Jess. I just feel it somehow."

Jess sat beside her and gently put her arm round her friend who was crying pitifully again. There was nothing she could say to help so they just sat together until Anne became more composed.

"How about a cuppa?" she said softly "Nothing like a cuppa in a crisis, my mum used to say."

Anne smiled wanly "Your mum was probably right. Let's go and get something," and together they headed off to the canteen. Anne had lost her appetite and didn't want anything to eat so sat in silence sipping her tea as Jess worked her way through the hospital canteen's offering of a Christmas dinner.

When she was finished Anne said "I'm going to ring home again. I rang this morning to wish everyone a happy Christmas and didn't mention anything about Matt then, but mummy might have some bright ideas."

"They often do" Jess replied. "If it helps, come and find me if you need someone else to talk too."

"Thanks, Jess. I'll let you know what happens. I will try the adjutant again tomorrow."

She felt a bit more positive as she rang home. Her mother answered and seemed to almost immediately realise what had happened. "Anne you should come home. Surely you can get some time off? You work hard enough."

"He's not dead yet you know" Anne snapped back "And I can't just walk out of here." She was crying again and just put the receiver down and ran back to her room.

She couldn't sleep at first and just sat looking at the picture of Matt in his uniform which was on her bedside table and, although she eventually dropped off, when she woke in the morning her thoughts were almost immediately consumed by the possibility that Matt might be dead. She dressed quickly and went straight down to the operating theatre to prepare for what was going to be another busy emergency operating list. She felt dreadful but at least working helped to take her mind off what might have happened and, in any case, she hoped she could break off at some point to ring East Kirkby. She decided that if she couldn't get any sense out of anyone on the telephone then she would go to the airfield in person. At least then she would know for sure that Matt wasn't there.

The morning's list had been tough going and she found it difficult to concentrate so that by lunchtime she felt the need to get outside for some air but as she walked out past the porters' lodge one of them called to her.

"Hallo Sister Johnson. There's a letter for you. Came this morning. Delivered by hand it was."

He gave her the letter and a cold shiver went down her spine. It was Matt's handwriting on the envelope which she tore open and read the letter still standing by the porters' lodge.

My dearest Anne,

When you get this letter, it will mean that I have gone missing – hopefully I will be a POW but all that takes a while to come through. I wanted to say how much you have always meant to me and how much I love you. In another time we would now be married and be planning the rest of our lives together. But this is not another time – there is the war, the Nazis and Hitler to sort out first.

Should I not come back I want you to carry on your life, find someone else and settle down. All I ask is that sometimes you will find time at night to look up at the stars and think of me. I will be up there somewhere.

All my fondest love for ever

Matt

"Not bad news I hope sister?" she heard the porter asking her. She nodded and walked away from the hospital clutching the letter in her hand. It was freezing cold and she didn't have a coat but she didn't care. The man she loved was gone and as far as she was concerned her life was over. She walked for a long time and it was getting dark when she found herself back at the hospital and a different porter came out. "Are you alright sister?" he asked anxiously. "Only they was looking for you in theatre a few hours ago. God, miss, you don't look good. Can I get you anything? You look frozen."

"No, nothing thanks. Just had some bad news and I needed a walk" and with that she went back into the hospital. She went to her room and sat on the bed rereading the letter. *Maybe they just crashed and he will be alright,* she thought. *Lots of them end up as prisoners. And then he will be back home. Wasn't like Jess's chap – his parachute hadn't opened so he was obviously dead. Not like Matt at all.*

She desperately needed to get away from the hospital and she tried to find one of the senior nurses so that she could get permission to go. Sister Bryant listened carefully to what Anne had to say and then said stuffily that she couldn't possibly afford to let experienced nurses like her just walk out on a whim and, by the way, Mr Wright had been very annoyed that she had walked out of his operating theatre that afternoon. Then, when she said that Anne should have known better than to get involved with a pilot, she had to restrain herself from striking out. *Stupid old bat* she thought *What would she know about love and the possibility of losing the only person you ever cared for in the world?* In the end Sister Bryant relented and told Anne that she could have a few days off after the New Year so long as she worked until then. Anne walked out of the office and went to ring her mother again. She felt calmer now – the letter had at least explained why Matt hadn't rung and after a few more tears she arranged to go back to Worcester on the 3rd January.

* * *

As Anne squeezed herself onto the train at Lincoln, she accepted that this was going to be a terrible journey. The train was packed with servicemen, army and air force, and as it set off towards Peterborough the general drabness outside was made worse by the mixture of snow and sleet that was now falling. Anne found herself standing in the corridor wedged between a couple of RAF sergeants who, it transpired, were going on leave to Scotland.

"Bit tight in here, eh hen?" one of them said "where you headin'?"

"Going home" she said quietly "Back to Worcester. Where are you going?"

"Glasgow" the second one said "If we ever get there afore we have to come back, eh?" he chuckled taking a swig from his beer bottle.

Almost without thinking she said "My fiancé and I were going to go to Scotland when he next got some leave."

"Well it's pretty chilly up there just now lass, best wait 'til about May or June. Beautiful then you see if it isn't. Will he have leave then d'you think?"

"Don't know "she replied wishing she had never said anything in the first place. "He's just been listed 'missing' you see."

"Oh, sorry to hear that, hen. Still there's always hope isn't there?" And with that he turned back to his pal and they continued their conversation whilst Anne turned to the window and felt the tears rolling down her cheeks. It was snowing hard now and the grey sky just made her feel even more lost in her own misery, the only possible chink of brightness being the fact that she was going home to her parents.

The train eventually arrived in Peterborough and she battled her way through the packed corridor to the nearest door. She was almost pushed out of the train and managed, with some difficulty, to pull her suitcase out after her eventually finding the right platform for the Birmingham train. It was bitterly cold and once she realised that the train was not going to arrive for at least another hour she went to the station canteen to get a cup of tea. The place was heaving with people and it took her nearly half an hour to get her much needed drink. She wrapped her hands round the cup trying to thaw them out and was feeling a bit more comfortable by the time the train, engulfed in steam and smoke, wheezed and hissed its way along the platform. It was less crowded than the train from Lincoln so she managed to find a seat in one of the compartments and, as the train pulled out of the station, she began to feel a little better and after a few hours the train entered the dingy surrounds of New Street Station in Birmingham.

It was a long time since she had been to Birmingham and as she walked to Moor Street station to catch her train to Worcester, she was shocked by how much bomb damage there had been. Lincoln had only had the occasional bombing raid but the destruction here, close to the station, was terrible. She noticed that the people around her hurried along through the snow apparently oblivious to the devastation all around them, never seeming to look up or to acknowledge one another. *Maybe that's the only way survive all this,* Anne thought, *just denial.*

Her train was already in the station but before she got aboard she found a telephone box and quickly made a phone call home to see if her father could meet her. This time the train had very few passengers and she found a compartment all to herself. She gazed out of the window as the train left the station – it was mid-afternoon and already the light in the sky was fading but the snow had, at least, stopped and the feeble light from the late sun was breaking through the clouds, casting a yellowish glow into the carriage almost as if to welcome her home.

It was dark by the time the train arrived and the poorly-lit platform made it difficult for Anne to see if anyone was waiting for her but as she made her way to the exit she saw her father waving and she ran towards him. He held his arms open and wrapped them round her and held her as she wept against him, her shoulders shaking uncontrollably. He gently led her out of the station and into the warmth of his old Rover car and once she had stopped crying, he let in the clutch and they drove away.

"Your mother is so looking forward to seeing you" he said "Well I was too, of course." he smiled. "Let's get home and then we can all sit down for a natter. No news I suppose? Probably too early I imagine."

"No daddy, no news but I think that's good really, don't you?" she asked.

"I'm sure it is, dear. Been dreadful weather here, how's it been in Lincoln?" he asked trying to change the subject.

"Oh, pretty bad. It's so much colder over there you know. It's lovely to be home daddy. At the moment I wish I could stay forever."

There was still a lot of snow covering the roads but Anne's father negotiated them carefully and soon they were going down into their drive, in front of the house. Anne's mother was already at the door to welcome her and she hugged her once they were in and the front door was shut but there were no tears this time. Anne felt as if she had cried herself dry and after she had gone up to her bedroom, she tidied herself, just peeping into the room Matt had used when he had stayed only a few weeks ago, before she went down stairs.

"Cup of tea or something stronger?" her father asked. "I'm having a scotch myself."

"I think a nice cup of mummy's tea would be best just now" Anne smiled "Maybe later."

They sat round the table in a slightly awkward silence before Anne's father asked "Have you spoken to Matt's family?"

"Yes, I rang yesterday. They have only received an official telegram saying that he is listed as 'missing' and a letter from Wing Commander Squires saying what a good chap he was and hoping for the best" she added sarcastically.

"Well that's something dear isn't it?" her mother said "I suppose it could take quite a time to be certain what has happened to him" she added and then wished she hadn't.

"I think he is OK" Anne replied defiantly. "He was too good and kind to be killed" she added before breaking down in tears. Her mother put her arms around Anne and over her shoulder signalled to her father to leave them alone.

CHAPTER 2

Thursday, 6th January 1944

The end of 1943 and the beginning of 1944 was a difficult time for Bomber Command. The continuing raids on Berlin and the poor weather were taking their toll and many raids resulted in almost seven percent of the bomber force being lost, meaning that inexperienced crews were having to be used as replacements. It was a war of attrition, because German fighter crews were also suffering heavy losses as the two sides slugged it out in the skies high above Germany. The nature of the battle had changed from German fighters hunting independently for targets to now being directed to the bomber stream by ground radar, joining it and stayed there until they found a bomber to destroy. On the other hand, the Allies could identify the German fighters and shoot them down using aircraft, mostly Mosquitoes, equipped with new airborne radar. It was dog eat dog!

Bill Tucker, with his weary crew, trudged through the snow to the Sergeant's Mess. They seemed to have been travelling for hours from RAF Lindholme in Yorkshire where they had been undergoing conversion on to Lancaster bombers prior to joining their first front line squadron at East Kirkby. Tucker was twenty-two years old and had worked in a garage for three years before he had joined the RAF. He was a rather lanky six-footer with a shot of blond hair, striking blue eyes and high set cheekbones. As he opened the Mess door, he was amazed to see only about a dozen faces turn to stare at him. A slightly rotund, red-faced man moved towards the new arrivals holding out his hand as he did so.

"Hallo" he said "You must be one of the replacement crews. Welcome to you from us what's left."

"Er, thanks" stuttered Bill "What do you mean what's left? Oh, my name's Bill by the way."

"Mine's Frank. Well we weren't doing too bad up until a week or so before Christmas but since then they seem to be knocking us over like bloody ninepins. We've lost eight crews in the last two weeks, so we're stood down just now. It's been bloody slaughter. The Flight Commander only came to East Kirkby in November as a Pilot Officer, now he's bloody well in charge of us – Simmons his name is. Hey, come on in and get a drink down your neck" and with that he shook the others by the hand and wandered back to his friends.

Once they had all got a beer, they gathered round Bill. John 'Nobby' Clarke, the navigator, was the first to speak. He was the 'father' of the crew being the oldest at thirty years of age. His dark hair was thinning and he had brown, rather deep-set quizzical eyes and looked every bit the academic that he was, or at least, had been. A senior lecturer in physiology at Manchester University he had been teaching medical students before he joined up. He certainly took life more seriously than the others although he could still sink his beer with the best.

"Jesus, Bill I'd heard that things were bad but this sounds terrible."

"Ah, probably not as bad as he says, Nobby. Probably some are off on leave if the squadron's been stood down. This lot just haven't got anywhere else to go. Bloody orphans, they are."

Bill reckoned that Nobby had a tendency to worry unnecessarily and was certainly obsessional in some ways although maybe all navigators were a bit like that – perhaps they had to be. The others were joining in now and Jim Tanner the mid-upper gunner said that he thought there might be something in it since his mum had heard it on the radio. Lord Haw Haw was always going on about how many 'terror bombers' were being shot down by the German defenders. Jim was only nineteen years old, joined up directly from school and might have been called a 'spiv' in civilian life with his greased down black hair and his pencil moustache. He was quite short and had an odd way of speaking out of the corner of his mouth usually with a cigarette in the other side. "Well there you are then" said Phil Smith, who was the radio operator, "If Haw Haw says it, it must be true" and they laughed before moving over to speak to the others.

They all felt better after a few beers and were just beginning to relax when Flight Sergeant Spiers came into the Mess.

"You lot just arrived?" he asked Tucker sharply.

"Yes, Flight" Tucker replied "Just off the bus."

"You'll wish you bloody well stayed on it by the end of tomorrow. Report to the Flight Office at zero eight hundred hours. Flying kit – understood? And don't be late."

"Yes, Flight," Tucker replied as Spiers turned on his heel and walked out of the door leaving it open for the cold wind to blast in.

"Charming" he muttered "Is he always so friendly?" he asked Frank.

"No, that's him in a good mood!" Frank smiled. "He's OK really but not someone to upset. Have another."

"Actually, think I've had enough for now. We have been travelling all day and it sounds like we are flying tomorrow. Let's wrap it up for the night lads" he said to his crew. "Another night tomorrow – hopefully". And with that the seven walked out into the freezing wind which was now driving fresh snow into their eyes.

CHAPTER 3

Friday 7th January 1944

Tucker woke up with a start and for a moment was unsure where he was. It was icily cold in the Nissen hut and in the pitch black he could hear his colleagues snoring and snuffling away. He glanced at his watch – five o'clock – soon be time to get up, but to what, he wondered. He pulled the thin blankets back over himself and tried to go back to sleep but before he knew it an orderly had come in shouting "Rise and shine". The seven men gradually got themselves out of bed and quickly dressed before they got frozen.

"Bit bloody different to the HCU isn't it?" Clarke muttered "Don't they have any heating in here? That stove doesn't seem much use."

"Not exactly home from home is it?" Tucker replied. "Let's get over to the canteen – should be warm in there." And with that they headed out of the door. The snow had stopped but it was now freezing hard. Tucker looked up and noticed the planet Venus glowing overhead as they crunched their way over to the canteen which was steadily filling up with servicemen from all over the station. Frank and his crew were already in the line to get their breakfast and Tucker's crew sat down at one of the tables before joining the queue.

HCU – Heavy Conversion Unit

"To be sure the bloody food doesn't look much cop either" Dave Brookes muttered to Jim Tanner. Brookes was the bomb aimer and twenty-three years of age. Like Clarke, he was a teacher but at school rather than university. He was the comic of the group and over the time at the HCU he had kept the others going even when things got tough. Born in Dublin, he had a shock of ginger hair and sparkling blue eyes and was, everyone reckoned, full of the blarney.

"Yeh" Tanner replied "Looks like them eggs have drowned rather than been cooked!"

They moved over to their table and with the other five set about their breakfast, not entirely with enthusiasm.

"Well lads let's go and meet the boss." Tucker said as he downed the last of his tea and pushed his chair back. Together they walked over to the Flight Office to meet Flight Lieutenant Simmons, who they found talking to a very attractive woman in flying overalls.

Tucker saluted "Reporting sir. We came in last night from Lindholme."

"Good" said Simmons briskly "This young lady has just brought in a brand-new Lancaster – not yours you understand. You only get to use the older ones. You are flying P-Peter and I want you to get out to her now and get ready for a test flight. I will join you shortly. In the meantime, this young lady has to get off so she can bring us back another shiny, new Lanc."

With that he turned his back on Tucker and continued his conversation with the woman.

"Excuse me, sir" Tucker asked "Where will we find P-Peter?"

"Where do you bloody think?" he replied and then turned away again.

Tucker and his crew wandered out of the Flight Office and almost into the arms of Flight Sergeant Spiers.

"Good morning Flight" Tucker said quickly.

"Have you met Flight Lieutenant Simmons?"

"Yes, Flight. We have been given P-Peter but he didn't tell us where we might find her!"

"D Hanger. Go and get your kit and parachutes and one of the WAAFs will drive you there. I'd look sharp if I were you. Flight Lieutenant Simmons is not noted for his patience."

"Thanks Flight" and with that the crew went to the crew room to get kitted up.

They were driven out to the aircraft and once Tucker had climbed up into the Lancaster he began to feel more at home – the smell of oil and hydraulic fluid and the layout inside the cockpit had a familiarity which was somehow comforting. Dave Brookes clambered forward into the nose of the aircraft, Nobby Clarke settled at the navigator's table with Phil Smith on his left as Radio Operator. Smith, who was twenty years old, had started out as ground crew and so knew his way around the aircraft. He had a jolly face which went well with his disposition. His brown eyes seemed always to be smiling as was his wide, generous mouth. Charlie Barton, the flight engineer was already checking the dials and switches. He was a regular who had joined the RAF at the age of sixteen as an ordinary aircraftsman, four years earlier. He had volunteered for flying in 1941and trained as a flight engineer. He was from Leeds in Yorkshire and proud of it, as he kept reminding anyone who would listen!

The two gunners Jim Tanner and Bob Docker were getting into their turrets checking that everything was working and that they had sufficient ammunition – there was always a chance of a stray enemy fighter wandering around looking for business even on this side of the Channel. Bob 'Taffy' Docker, nineteen years old was from Cardiff, five feet 6 inches tall but broad shouldered and although generally considered a bit of a tough nut, he had a round, jolly face with a short beard. He had grown up around the docks and was the oldest of six children. He had started out in the army but after a year had fancied the RAF and had volunteered for flying duties. Since he had already been taught how to shoot by the army, being a gunner seemed a natural choice!

One of the ground crew came forward to speak to Tucker – apparently the aircraft had been quite badly shot up and damaged on its last trip and he explained what had been repaired and what possible problems they needed to look out for. The crew went through their checks and, once completed, got out and they all, except Clarke, lit up cigarettes. It was very cold outside with a fresh easterly wind but the sky was clear and it looked like it was going to be a nice sunny day.

"Well where's the boss then?" Brookes asked as he took a deep drag on his cigarette. "Bloody nippy standing around here just waiting for him to show up."

At that moment a car stopped in front of the aircraft and Flight Lieutenant Simmons jumped out complete with flying kit and parachute.

"You all ready then?" he asked "We're going up Sheffield back to Nottingham and then up to the bombing range and home. Navigator have you got the gen on the winds and the correct chart?"

"Yes, sir" Clarke replied.

"Right, well get on with plotting the course whilst the rest sort out the aircraft. Let's see, it's ten hundred hours I want to be back on the ground all tidied up by midday. Understood? Right let's see if you can fly as well as that ATA girl you were all ogling this morning"

Tucker smiled and led his crew back to the aircraft and one by one they clambered in.

ATA – Air Transport Auxiliary

Tucker and the flight engineer went back through their checks and fired up the engines.

Tucker confirmed with each of the crew in turn that they were ready and then called the tower for clearance to taxi. The Lancaster trundled to the end of the runway and when he got the green light from the control tower, Tucker opened the throttles and the huge aircraft started its take off roll. The tail lifted up and the aircraft was in the air more quickly than the clapped out one they had at Lindholme and they climbed quickly away.

"Course for Sheffield two-eight-five" Clarke said. "That should allow for the wind."

They were a good crew and Simmons noted that they worked well together with Brookes, the bomb aimer calling out land marks as they went along. After they passed Nottingham they headed towards the Wash and he got Tucker to climb P-Peter up to 15,000 feet. The view was breath-taking and, with the land covered with snow, the many airfields in the area stood out starkly. But they weren't here for sightseeing and once they were at altitude he called "Corkscrew port" to Tucker who first looked at him questioningly before realising he really meant it.

Tucker eased the aircraft to the left and down before turning to the right and climbing back to their original height. He called round the crew to make sure they were OK and everyone replied except the rear gunner, Docker, who eventually said "For Christ's sake Bill what was that about. Bumped my bloody head."

"Sorry Taffy, you OK though?" to which there was a grunted reply.

"Too bloody slow" Simmons was saying. "If it was for real the bloody rear gunner would be dead by now not just have a sodding headache. Didn't they show you how to corkscrew at Lindholme?"

"Well, maybe a couple" Tucker replied.

"Right, get out of that seat" Simmons said and got in behind the controls as Tucker slid out.

"Now the point here is that this is the best way of not getting shot down by a fighter. It will usually be the gunners who see the bastards first and they need to shout the direction you have to go, port or starboard, and if the turn is sharp enough the fighters won't be able to follow – well that's the theory. But you have to be quick. So, hang on everyone – rear gunner you shout port or starboard when you are ready."

"Port" Docker shouted and Simmons almost stood the aircraft on its left wingtip and into a dive and then heaved it to the right and climbed.

"See what I mean? You have to get her right over and down" Simmons asked "Now when you have a full bomb load everything will feel different" he continued "And while I remember, that applies to take off as well. She won't jump off the deck like today."

He handed P-Peter back to Tucker and they went to the bombing range and then back to East Kirkby. Simmons produced the usual trick for new crews of shutting down one of the engines on their final approach but Tucker and Barton managed things well and as Simmons got out of the aircraft he grunted a compliment to Tucker before walking back to the waiting car making it clear that they should fly P-Peter that afternoon and again in the evening.

"Practice, practice, practice. Can't beat it" he had added over his shoulder

* * *

Tucker and his crew finally finished flying by eight o'clock that evening. They felt exhausted as they filed into the crew room but were surprised to find Simmons still in his office and he looked up as they walked in.

"If you think that was hard, wait for the real thing. Today was just a walk in the park."

"Thanks, sir" Clarke replied with a touch of sarcasm. "When do we get to do the real thing then?"

"Five or six days I would think. At least you've got some time to practise, haven't you? Now, another couple of crews turned up today so I want all of you back here by zero eight hundred hours tomorrow, is that clear?"

"Yes, sir" they mumbled and walked out in to the bitter air.

"Who wants a pint?" Clarke asked

"Nah. I need some grub first" replied Brookes "Then maybe a pint. How about you Bill?"

"I'll just have something to eat, I think. Feel a bit knackered to be honest."

When Tucker finally got to the Nissen hut he found a couple of men sitting on their beds.

"Hallo there" one of them said and stood up as Tucker came into the hut.

"Evening" Tucker replied "You must be the new crews that Simmons was talking about."

"Yes, we just came in from RAF Waterbeach so just down the road really! What about you?"

"We came in yesterday from Lindholme – been flying all today. Looks like they mean business. So, both your crews in here then?"

"Yep. We are all sergeants – happy Harry told us that we can expect another lot in tomorrow. We have to meet him at eight o'clock tomorrow morning he said."

"Sounds about right. I'm going to get my head down so tell the others not to make too much noise. See you in the morning"

Tucker stripped to his pants and vest and got into bed and fell asleep almost before his head hit the pillow.

CHAPTER 4

Saturday 8ᵗʰ January 1944

When Tucker woke up, he was conscious of twenty-seven snoring, scratching bodies around him. The air in the hut would best be described as rancid but at least it was a little warmer than yesterday morning. He glanced at his watch and decided to make a move before the others got to the washrooms. He reckoned a shower would perk him up no end but as he opened the door of the hut an icy blast reminded him it wasn't going to be that pleasant.

Clarke heard the door shut and woke up with a start – he had been dreaming about a lovely girl who was being very friendly to him but once awake he realised where he was and that things weren't that great after all. He and the others had sunk quite a few beers the previous night before deciding to turn in and his head wasn't feeling too good. The others were stirring now and gradually the young men surfaced and began dressing. Apart from the smell, everything was damp from condensation and once they had tidied their beds, they all made off for the canteen and Tucker joined them as they were getting their breakfast.

"Bloody awful in that damn hut" Clarke muttered to Tucker. "If we could get that stove going it would be better. I'll see what they have in store for us this morning and if I get time I'll go and try to get it working properly."

Once the four crews had finished breakfast they made their way over to the Flight Office. Although it had snowed again in the night, the sky was clear now, promising a fine if bitterly cold day. Flight Lieutenant Simmons greeted them with a truculent glare, hands on hips, and then took them over to the briefing room. He was quite a short, well-built man and tended to strut rather than walk. His blue eyes looked suspiciously at the assembled crews and Nobby Clarke reckoned he had quite a chip on his shoulder, possibly one on each shoulder in fact – he had seen it all before.

"Right" Simmons shouted. "Now you lot have only a few days to get into shape. You probably think you know it all, but you know nothing" he emphasised by slapping his hands together. "Today I want the new crews to do a familiarisation flight with three pilots from 'A' Flight and then I want to see if you can all fly in formation because it's very important you get that right. It's even harder at night. Tucker we will get the formation flying started at eleven hundred hours but I want you to prepare a cross country exercise for tonight – you will leave here at seventeen hundred hours understood?"

"Yes, sir" Tucker replied, "Where will we be going to, sir?"

"Where I bloody well tell you. And in the meantime, get down to P-Peter and check everything is OK for later this morning."

Tucker and his crew walked out leaving Simmons to brief the others.

"That boyo seems like a man on a mission?" Docker muttered. "Can we go for a cuppa first? Got a mouth like the bottom of a parrot's cage this morning."

"Not bloody surprised" Charlie Barton replied in his strong Yorkshire accent "Eh, lad you nearly drank the bloody bar dry last night!".

"OK lads. Quick cup of tea, pick up our kit and then off to the aircraft. Nobby looks like you might have a few minutes this afternoon to try and fix the stove. Where will they send us this evening do you think?"

"Usually a tour of Britain – you remember that one we did at the HCU?"

"Bloody hell that took hours but that was during the day!"

"Well night is when we will be fly over Krautland so s'pose practicing at night is not a bad plan!"

* * *

The flights during the day went without a hitch including the formation flying which was remarkably difficult even during daylight. The crew of P-Peter gathered in the Flight Office at three o'clock to hear Flight Lieutenant Simmons explain their route for the night, which amounted to nearly nine hundred miles. They were to take off at seventeen hundred hours fly north to Edinburgh, south to Barrow in Furness and then back to East Kirkby. The forecast weather for the flight would be mostly clear but with a strong easterly wind.

"So, keep a good eye on your drift Navigator" Simmons warned "And remember colours of the day if you don't want to get shot down. Any questions?"

No one replied but they all felt suddenly anxious as they realised what was expected of them. They had never done much flying at night, let alone finding their way over a long distance.

Tucker looked at Clarke.

"You OK mate? Anything else we need to look at?"

"No. Think I have everything sorted out. At least on a clear night we should be able to see things out of the window" he smiled wryly.

They left the briefing, had something to eat and then set out for the aircraft.

* * *

P-Peter roared down runway zero-eight and lifted off into the clear night sky at five o'clock exactly. As the aircraft climbed away Tucker headed towards the coast which they crossed just north of Skegness. The plan was to follow the coast to just south of Edinburgh before turning inland and then down towards Barrow. As predicted there was a strong easterly wind trying to push them inland and Tucker had to lay off quite an angle to maintain their northwards course.

"Bloody wind is pretty strong up here" he called to Clarke. "How's it looking?"

"Not too bad so far." Clarke replied "H2S is working well for a change" This was a type of radar in the aircraft, which was particularly efficient when they were flying over areas where water and land were side by side. "Dave keep a good lookout – we should see the Humber soon".

"Will do" the bombaimer replied "Oh, it's coming up now Nobby – right on the nose."

"Good, that is looking good for timing Bill".

They flew on up the coastline and about an hour and a half later the bombaimer called that he could make out the Firth of Forth.

"On time. Come on to one-eight-zero for now but we will have to adjust for this wind"

Almost as soon as they turned Brookes called to say that he could no longer see the ground and that there were banks of clouds all around them.

"OK Bill just keep this course. We should be over Barrow in seventy minutes."

The aircraft droned on and there seemed not only to be a lot of turbulence but in addition Smith, the radio operator, called to say that he could see ice accumulating on the wing.

Tucker was beginning to feel uneasy – suddenly it felt very lonely up here. He needed to do something about the icing – if that got too bad the aircraft would just stop flying. Diving might take them into warmer air but also into the side of a mountain – there were hills all around them. Climbing was the only option and as they got to 20,000 feet the lack of moisture stopped any more ice accumulating. In fact, it all looked very beautiful with the moonlight shining on the tops of the clouds that were now way below them.

"Where are we Nobby?"

"By my reckoning we should be approaching Barrow – there in about five minutes."

"What do your toys say?"

"Well I can see a coastline on H2S but the only trouble is that it doesn't look like Barrow"

"Well what *does* it bloody well look like?" Tucker was feeling increasingly anxious and it showed in his voice. "Charlie how are we doing on fuel?"

"Fine just now Bill. About four hours left"

"Well, keep a close eye on it" he said sharply "We will be battling into a bloody strong wind going back so we need plenty."

"I think we are north of Barrow" Clarke said "This wind has carried us west. We should follow the coast for now."

"Not good enough Nobby. I need to know where we are for sure."

"OK I'll try and take an astrofix but with this turbulence it may not be too accurate."

"Well just do it anyway will you?" Tucker was beginning to feel the strain and there was sweat on his back even though it was freezing cold in the aircraft. *They had never trained us for anything like this* he thought. *Bloody RAF instructors what did they know!*

"OK Bill. I think I was right- the sight makes us about fifty miles north of Barrow so just carry on this heading for now."

There was no reply from Tucker who was clearly struggling

with all the issues. It was tough being the pilot – everything dropped on you. Clarke was also feeling pretty concerned and he was relieved to see the characteristic shape of the Isle of Walney slide on to his H2S screen.

"OK Bill, Barrow coming up. Get ready for the course change."

"Thank God for that" Bill replied "Sorry I was snappy. It's a bit different at night. Everyone OK?"

The crew all called in and Tucker turned P-Peter on to the new course which should, in a little under two hours, bring them back to East Kirkby.

Just as they turned Clarke was horrified to see that the H2S set had suddenly stopped working and he gazed in dismay as he tried turning knobs this way but and that, to see the screen still blank.

"Bill, H2S has packed in so were flying by dead reckoning for now I'm afraid. Should be OK to descend in about an hour and a half I reckon from now. Dave keep a good look out in case the clouds clear".

"Bloody hell Nobby. Is there nothing else we can do?"

"I think it will be fine. I got a good fix as we turned" he said trying to sound much more confident than he felt.

At the estimated time Clarke said that it would be safe to descend through the cloud so they could see where they were but as they broke through Brookes called up that all he could see was sea.

"Christ almighty!" shouted Tucker "Where the hell are we now Nobby?"

"Must be North Sea- maybe the wind has dropped and we are too far east. Suggest we turn west – should find the coast then."

Tucker heaved the aircraft round but all he could see was water. He suddenly felt afraid – if they couldn't find a landmark soon he would have to ditch the aircraft and with the sea temperature so low in the depths of winter they would all die for sure. Ditching wasn't that easy either, he thought. He checked the compass again to confirm they really were flying west and just as he was beginning to give up hope Brookes shouted that he could see a coastline.

"Looks like the Humber to me" he said "Good job we still have some moonlight, Nobby" he added cheerily.

Clarke came into the cockpit to check and agreed.

"Let's just follow the coast down to Skegness then turn right. That should take us home."

They eventually found the East Kirkby beacon only to be told to land on runway two-six.

"Bloody wind's turned right round" Tucker muttered. "No surprise we went adrift."

He brought the aircraft down to a gentle landing and taxied over to their stand, shutdown the engines and slumped forward in his seat. He felt exhausted but realised this had been an easy flight, with no fighters, no flak, no one trying to kill them.

Clarke came into the cockpit again.

"Sorry about that Bill. Not sure what we do if the wind changes direction like that – get lost I suppose" he smiled weakly.

* * *

The crew climbed wearily down from the rear hatch and clambered into the truck that was to take them back to the Flight Office. It was about eleven o'clock and they were amazed to be met by Flight Lieutenant Simmons.

"What kept you?" he shouted at Tucker. "Should have been back an hour ago. We were just getting ready to declare an emergency." Simmons was rocking back on his chair behind the desk and just as Tucker was thinking that there was every chance that he might tip over, he did. There was a crash and he reappeared from behind the desk his face red with anger.

"Should put you all on a bloody charge" he shouted. "I'm tempted to send you out right now to do the same trip to see if you can do any better. What a bloody shambles. Don't they teach you anything anymore? If that happens on an operation you're dead men, do you understand?"

Tucker was having some difficulty to stop laughing out loud and simply answered "Yes, sir."

Clarke, being older, however felt he had to say something.

"Sir, the wind direction changed right round and with complete cloud cover it was impossible to determine where we were especially after the H2S set went down."

"Well as far as I care Clarke you can tell that to the bloody Huns when you end up over there. I'm sure that they would be most interested in your explanation. Now you lot, report to me here tomorrow at zero seven hundred hours. Is that clear?"

Tucker nodded and saluted and the crew filed out of Simmons' office.

When they were out of earshot Clarke said to Tucker "You know Bill that's the problem with short men. They can't sit on their bloody chairs properly!" Both of them chuckled and Bill replied "He's a bit of a shit really isn't he? No sense of humour that's his trouble!"

They grabbed some food and a coffee before heading over to the Sergeant's mess for a few beers and then hit the sack exhausted by the night's experience.

CHAPTER 5

Thursday 20th January 1944

Anne's journey back from her parents to Lincoln was no better than the one to Worcester. She had had a nice time with her parents but everything and everywhere brought back memories of Matt and in one sense she was pleased to get away and back to work. When she arrived at the hospital the Head Porter saw her and said that she had a couple of letters.

One she recognised immediately was from Matt's mother and she rushed to read it in the privacy of her own room.

Dear Anne,

I heard today from the Air Ministry that whilst Matt is still listed as 'Missing' the bodies of five of the crew have been found. One other crewman is also listed 'Missing'. Perhaps you can give me a call when you have a moment.

Love

Flo.

Anne looked at her watch. It was seven o'clock so it should be OK to ring now and she went out into the corridor to the telephone. How often had she called Matt on that phone she wondered?

After she had spoken to Matt's mother she felt more hopeful than at any time since Matt had gone missing. The cockpit had yet to be located but the rest of the fuselage had been found and the five men were still in it or close by. It would be a miracle if he had survived but there was still a chance.

Although she felt better over the next few days, doubt gradually began to creep back into her mind. After all, how could someone survive a crash like that. Perhaps he just got thrown out a long way from the others or he was lying dead in the cockpit once they found it. It just wasn't possible anyone could live through that. In fact, rather than giving hope, the finding of those other poor souls might make it even more likely that Matt was dead. All in all, Anne was feeling very down when she bumped into Jess.

"Any news?" she asked.

"Well five of the others have been found dead so I think that doesn't look too good does it? It's not knowing that makes everything seem so difficult."

Jess put her arm round Anne's shoulders. "Sorry to hear that Anne. But you know there's still a chance that he will be found. Look why don't we go up to East Kirkby tomorrow night? There's a dance on and that might help to take you out of yourself for a bit. And you never know there might be some rumours around about Matt and the others. Maybe some inside info. What do you think?"

Anne hesitated "I'm not sure I'm ready for that yet Jess. Too many memories."

"Of course there are, but you need a bit of a break. Sitting around in the hospital isn't likely to help much either is it?"

"You can be very persuasive sometimes Jess. OK let's go but no trying to pair me off with someone."

"It's a deal" Jess smiled. "We'll catch the usual bus. I think there are about a dozen of us. It will be a laugh. You need that."

* * *

Anne decided to wear her black velvet dress to the dance – Matt had always liked her in it and it seemed to suit her five feet four inches height and her long auburn hair. Jess was wearing a turquoise frock which went really well with her ginger hair. Anne always had thought that Jess was stunningly beautiful and most men seemed to do so as well! They climbed down from the bus and walked the short distance to the base following the directions to the hangar where the dance was being held. As they went through the door Anne was immediately struck by how few men there were. At the dance before Christmas, which was the last time she had been to East Kirkby before Matt went missing, the place had been stuffed full of airmen. Jess looked anxiously at her friend and grasped her arm as they went in.

"God, Jess where is everyone?" Anne asked quietly.

"Well there are quite a few here really. It is a big hangar" she replied trying to be encouraging. She steered them towards a group of seven men who appeared to be one of the crews.

"Good evening ladies" Tucker said "Welcome to East Kirkby" and then he introduced the rest of the crew.

Clarke was the first to speak and asked Anne whether she had been to East Kirkby before.

"Oh yes" she replied "My fiancé was a pilot here."

"Was?" Clarke replied cautiously

"Well he went missing just before Christmas."

"What was his name?"

"Matt White, Squadron Leader White."

"He was Flight Commander of B Flight wasn't he? That's our flight."

Anne nodded and then began to feel very unsteady.

"I say, are you alright?" Clarke asked.

"I think I need to sit down for a moment" Anne said "I really don't feel too good".

Clarke went to get a chair and she slumped down. She looked very pale and Clarke noticed her brow was slightly sweaty.

"Sorry" Anne said "Any chance of a glass of water?" Clarke went off to the bar and Jess came over when she realised what was happening.

"You look like shit" she said to Anne "I bet you haven't eaten today have you?"

Anne nodded in agreement "Haven't really felt very hungry lately Jess, to be honest."

By the time Clarke arrived back with a glass of water she was beginning to feel better.

"Probably a vaso-vagal faint" Clarke said to Jess.

"Are you a doctor?" Anne asked.

"No. I'm a physiologist. I teach medical students – well, I did. I thought I should join up and then I volunteered for flying duties. I'm the navigator. Incidentally my friends call me Nobby."

Anne looked at him. He was about six feet tall and looked older than the rest. He had dark brown eyes and a kindly face – reminded her of her father in a way.

"When did you get here then?"

"Oh, only about a week ago. We have been out on exercises every day and some nights. Managed to get lost on our first night run. The Flight Commander wasn't very impressed!" he smiled.

"Who's that then? I may know him although looking around there seem to be so many new faces."

"Flight Lieutenant Simmons"

"Really!" she exclaimed "He was one of Matt's first new pilots when he was Flight Commander. Incidentally you haven't come across a spaniel called Scrap, have you?"

"I think one of the batmen, Barker I think, has a dog called Scrap. Where does he fit in? Before you answer would you like something stronger than water? You are looking a little better now."

"You know I would. How about a gin and orange?"

"Coming up" Clarke replied. "Anyone else want a drink?"

When he came back, he asked "So what about Scrap then?"

"Well, he had a rather sad track record. Each crew he was with came to grief in some way apart, I think, from the first who were Canadians who completed their tour and went back home. Matt, and Stephen his friend who was killed on one of the trips, looked after him. He was a lovely dog."

"Probably no one wants to take him on now" Clarke said. "Sounds like a bit of a jinx to me."

"Nobby, could you do something for me? Could you speak to Barker sometime, I'm sure he was the batman, and see if he would let me look after Scrap? It would mean a lot although I'm not sure how the hospital would view things."

"Sure. So, you're a nurse, are you? At the Infirmary I suppose. What do you do?"

"Theatre sister. Live in the hospital. It's good to get out I can tell you" she smiled.

Clarke and Anne chatted on for a while leaving the others to do the dancing and drinking. Jess seemed to have linked up with one of the officers and out of the corner of her eye Anne saw them waltzing around the dancehall. The time passed quickly and Anne found Clarke easy to talk to. Everyone gathered to catch their breath and have another drink when Anne looked at her watch.

"God is that the time? Here, Jess we need to get going or we'll miss the bus. It's been good meeting you Nobby and thanks for the drink."

"You too Anne. Here, can we meet up sometime, perhaps for dinner or a drink? It's always good to escape from here too. I'll try and find out about Scrap as well."

"Yes, OK but just for dinner you know" she smiled and with that the girls trooped out to catch their bus back to Lincoln.

CHAPTER 6

Friday 21ˢᵗ January 1944

When Clarke woke up the next day he felt remarkably refreshed. He had done little drinking because he spent most of his time talking to Anne and in any case having a chance to speak to another human being who was not someone crammed into this billet was a big relief. He got up, showered and went down to the Flight Office. It was still early and very cold with a keen easterly wind.

Once in the office he realised that Simmons was, as usual, there already but what really caught his eye was the Ops board. There had been a rumour that there might be an operation in the near future but it was a surprise to see that tonight was the night. It gave him an oddly mixed feeling of excitement and fear. He was just leaving to go back to tell the others when Simmons called out.

"Well Clarke let's see if you can find your way back tonight then. I wouldn't put too much money on it myself."

"Thank you, sir." Clarke replied "Your confidence is touching" and before Simmons could answer he left the office. Clarke had come across some difficult people in his time but he thought that Simmons came high up on the 'prat list'. Everyone was getting dressed when he got back to the hut.

"We're on for tonight" he shouted "Briefing is at fifteen hundred hours."

"Bloody hell" replied Tucker "Thought we would get a few more days to practice but there we are. Right," he said to his crew "We need to do an air test this morning so let's meet in the Flight Office after grub."

The air test went well and after lunch the crew rested before the briefing. *This was it* Clarke thought as they went into the hut which was gradually filling with the ten other crews due to fly that night. The four experienced crews, including Simmons's, took up seats at the back of the room leaving the front for the beginners. The atmosphere was smoky and tense and everyone stood up immediately as Wing Commander Jonathon Squires walked into the room.

"Good afternoon chaps" he began. "I know this is the first trip for six of you crews but you must remember that you have been well trained and you are flying the Lancaster, the best bomber in the world. The target for tonight is Magdeburg and it is important because of its synthetic oil works and this isn't our first visit there. There will be no moon which should keep the fighters off you and two diversionary raids have been arranged one to the North Sea for some "gardening" and another to Berlin. I will now hand over to the Squadron specialists for your navigation, radio, bombing and, of course last but not least, metrological information. Remember to take careful note of what they have to say."

The briefing finished and as the others filed out of the room Tucker and Clarke sat and compared notes.

"You OK Nobby? Got all that?"

"Yes, I think so. No moon so I hope everything works. I keep thinking back to that first bloody night exercise"

"Stop worrying Nobby. I'm sure everything will work out fine. Let's get something to eat and then head out. Take off is seventeen hundred so we better get cracking"

"Gardening" – Minelaying operations

The seven men finished their meal and six of them lit up cigarettes to contribute to the fug of the canteen.

"What you reckon then?" Docker asked Tucker "We got a chance boyo?"

"Yeh, we'll be fine. What can possibly go wrong" Tucker joked "The worst that can happen is that we get lost or shot down and Nobby will take care of the first and you and Jim will make sure of the second."

Docker took an extra-long drag, "You know what boyo, I've been thinking maybe volunteering for aircrew wasn't such a good idea after all" he said in his singsong Welsh accent. "It was OK while we were flying around over here, like! Quite nice really."

"Come on Taffy" Tucker said "You've only got to stay awake and keep those Jerrys off us. Right lads time to go."

They walked off through the freezing cold night to the Crew Room to get kitted out and pick up their parachutes, together with the all important coffee and snacks. Their truck drove up and once the crews got in they were off, first stop being at P-Peter sitting out there in the dark.

The crew climbed on board and all went forward except Docker who turned left to squeeze into the rear turret. It was very cold in the Lancaster and Tucker found himself shivering as he and Barton went through their check lists.

"All OK Charlie?" Tucker called

"Now't wrong if that's what you mean?" he growled back "Bloody cold though isn't it?"

"Warm compared with up there" Tucker replied pointing up to the sky.

"Everyone else OK?" he asked and all replied. "Nobby, everything working?"

"Yes, seems to be" Clarke replied quietly. Ever since the briefing he had felt himself becoming increasingly anxious – getting them there and back was down to him. It was true that recent exercises had gone well but the memories of that first night time one still haunted him.

Tucker and Barton went through their routine checks and with clearance from the Tower they started the engines, starboard inner first.

Clarke was making sure of the details of the route – runway zero-eight was in use so that they could take off into the brisk easterly wind. Right hand turn out and the climb to 10,000 feet over Southwold then climb to 15,000 feet to join the bomber stream. It sounded straightforward enough on paper, Clarke thought, but factoring wind speed and direction both of which would change as they got higher made it more complicated. In any case the Met man never got the bloody wind direction and strength right!

"OK everyone, are we all ready?" Tucker called "Here we go then."

The heavily loaded Lancaster slowly began to roll and Clarke forced himself to concentrate on his charts and dials. "Lord God, look after us please" he muttered.

The aircraft was rattling and shaking as it picked up speed and the tail came up but suddenly everything was smooth as the aircraft lifted off the runway, climbed away and banked to the right.

"Come onto one-three-zero Bill" Clarke called.

Just at that moment there was a huge flash behind and below them.

"God in heaven" Tucker said, "What the hell was that?"

"Looks like one of the aircraft crashed just after takeoff" reported Docker the rear gunner. "Can't see nothing else, bit cloudy, see."

Tucker already felt jumpy but this made him feel even more nervous and he gripped the controls tighter as he tried to concentrate on keeping the aircraft going in the right direction.

"One-three-zero Nobby, right?" he asked Clarke

"Yes. H2S is working OK, I think. We are going over the Wash just now. Can you see anything up front Dave?"

"Not a bloody thing" he replied "We're still in cloud. Looks like a foggy night in London town to me!"

"Down to you then Nobby. Looks like we are blind at the moment."

Clarke swallowed hard. 'Trust the dials' he said to himself. At least he could make out the huge bay that was the Wash with H2S and they seemed to be going over the lower edge of its mouth which looked about right.

"Should be over Southwold in twenty minutes" He could feel the sweat on his gloved hands which, he noticed were shaking slightly and his mouth was dry.

'*God this is the first trip. Not sure I can do another twenty-nine. Not if it feels like this every time. Haven't even got to Germany ye*t' he thought but concentrating on the dials and charts helped take his mind off things for a while.

"Coming up to Southwold now" he said "Turn left onto zero-nine-zero and climb to 15,000 feet. This should put us at the back of the bomber stream."

"Zero-nine-zero, 15,000 feet" Tucker repeated back to him. "OK Jim, Taffy test your guns and keep a bloody good look out. Here we go everyone, our first crack at the Germans."

As he spoke, the aircraft broke out of the clouds. '*The stars looked almost as if you could touch them*', Tucker thought. He looked out and could see other aircraft around them and some others below picked out against the cloud. In its own way, it all looked rather beautiful.

"Bill we are just crossing the enemy coast. About two and a half hours to go" Clarke said. "Looks OK so far."

Tucker felt a bit better now that they were out in the open above the cloud. Being in cloud was so claustrophobic somehow.

And at least joining the other bombers had gone alright – it was a really dangerous time. Someone's timing out by a minute or height by a couple of hundred feet could mean collision and the end.

"How're the engines Charlie? Everything looking good?"

"Yes Bill. Seem to be rattling along alright."

The explosion that occurred suddenly just in front of them was an even greater shock than the one they witnessed just after takeoff but this time it was so close to them that P-Peter shook like an angry dog before diving and falling over to the left.

Tucker struggled to get the aircraft flying straight again but the heavy plane just seemed to want to keep diving away.

"Charlie what's wrong?" he asked as he fought to get the aircraft under control.

"Port outer seems to have had it" he answered "I'm feathering the prop, that might help."

As far as Clarke was concerned his world seemed to have turned upside down. Bits and pieces were dropping off his chart table as the aircraft tumbled through the sky and he suddenly felt very afraid and death seemed very close.

"Christ, what's happening Bill" he asked but there was no reply. He looked around the corner at the radio operator who just shrugged his shoulders.

Tucker was gradually getting control of the aircraft but it felt as if something was drastically wrong.

"We need to jettison the bombs, Dave" he shouted "Just get rid of the bloody things. Don't care where we are."

"We are over Germany anyway" Clarke said recovering some of his composure.

"Right. Let the buggers go then Dave. And good bloody riddance. Give me a course to get us home Nobby."

"Bombs gone Bill." P-Peter's descent gradually slowed and the aircraft came up on to an even plane.

"Do we need to land soon as possible or can we get back to base?" Clarke asked

"Let's try for base, Nobby." She's flying a bit better now the bombs are away."

"OK three-zero-zero should be about right."

The strong easterly wind helped their return and after a while Clarke thought he recognised the coast around Ostend and with relief, about an hour later he could see the Orwell estuary leading up to Ipswich. *'Thank God for H2S'* he thought.

"Come on to three-three-zero. About thirty minutes to home."

Tucker turned the aircraft on to the new course and began to descend to about 5,000feet.

"Call them up Phil. Tell them we have some damage but no injuries."

The East Kirkby beacon blinked at them and Tucker turned the Lancaster on to the final approach to land. The touchdown was not the best he had ever done but at least they were back on terra firma. He taxied the aircraft to their stand and he and Barton did their shut down checks and soon all was quiet.

Clarke sat looking at the chart table for a moment. They were alive but they had failed. The trip wouldn't count towards the tour.

Once everything was tidied up the crew jumped down from the aircraft. It was cold and the easterly wind cut through them. Their wait for a truck was short but the WAAF driver drove them in silence back to the briefing room.

"What happened to you then?" the intelligence officer asked.

"Someone blew up in front of us, sir, and the aircraft became difficult to handle so we dumped our bombs and came home" Tucker said.

"Didn't you think about carrying on? How far from the target were you?"

"About hour and a half, sir" Clarke said.

"So why not keep going. We don't expect you drop your bombs just anywhere you know. Not the plan at all."

"No, sir" Tucker replied. "At least we got the aircraft back, sir" he continued trying to be positive.

"Not the bloody idea though is it? We don't send you off just to spray bombs all over the place. Old Man will want to see you in the morning. Buzz off."

Tucker saluted and the crew walked out disconcertedly and back to the crewroom to get changed.

"Bloody hell, Bill" Brookes said. "Feel like we've been told off like naughty school boys. I mean we could have parachuted out then they wouldn't have a plane, bombs or us!!"

"Ah well" Tucker sighed "Let's go and get something to eat and sink a couple of pints. The one I'm worried about is bloody Simmons, if he gets back that is!"

* * *

Tucker spent an uneasy night worrying about the inevitable confrontation with Simmons in the morning. He had not heard the returning crews and was surprised that the billet was empty apart from his crew and one other. He dressed quickly and made his way to the canteen for a cup of tea and something to eat. There were several bleary-eyed crews who looked at him with surprise.

"What the hell happened to you? We thought you was goners."

"We got knocked about when one of the aircraft in front of us blew up, Jim" Tucker replied. Our aircraft was all over the place so we dumped the bombs and came back. Was it a bad night for us then?"

"I'd bloody say it was. I think we lost five out of ten that came from here. Bloody shambles as usual. Cloud all over the target so

God knows where the sodding bombs went. But the really bad news is that Simmons got back!"

"Christ. Got to go and see him at eight o'clock. He'll be in great form, won't he?"

"Wouldn't say so to be honest. He was like a bear with a sore head in the debrief room" Jim smiled "Might have been better if you'd been shot down. You'd only have to face the SS then!"

"Thanks pal" Tucker said as he walked out on his way to meet Simmons.

"Come in" Simmons called out. Tucker and his crew walked in and stood to attention. Simmons looked very tired with dark circles under his eyes which stared out at the men in front of him almost as if he hadn't seen them.

"What happened to you lot then?" he asked almost inaudibly

Tucker explained and waited for the blast of abuse.

"Why didn't you carry on? You had three engines left didn't you? You bloody well managed to get back here."

"Yes, sir" Tucker replied. Here it comes he thought.

"Not impressed Tucker. But on this occasion and since it was your first sortie, I will overlook what happened but consider this your first warning. And, of course, this doesn't count to your tour, you know that don't you? Now buzz off. I don't think there will be any action tonight but keep an eye on the board. And report to Wing Commander Squires at ten hundred hours."

Once they were out of the office Tucker was the first to speak.

"Think that was a lucky break boys. He looked like shit didn't he. Probably why we are still in one piece."

"Yeh but we have still got to see the boss, haven't we?" Tanner said stuffing another fag into his mouth.

"Think it's routine" Tucker replied. "Mustn't let us think we can get away with turning back too often. Anyway, I'm going down to see the crate. Good to see for ourselves what the damage was."

"Well I'm off for a fucking cuppa" Tanner muttered and all but Clarke turned away to the canteen.

"Don't be bloody late you lot" Tucker shouted after them as he and Clarke looked for couple of bikes so they could go and see the aircraft.

When they got to D hangar the ground crew had already stripped off the damaged engine. One of the mechanics came over to them as they gazed upwards at the wing's leading edge which looked as if it had been attacked by an axe.

"You've had a lucky break Sarg" he said. "Dead jammy that the debris didn't cut anything really vital or you wouldn't be here now."

"Thanks" Tucker said and he and Clarke turned away to go back to the Mess.

"Well that's something in our favour" Clarke said "Presumably Simmons didn't know that."

"I wouldn't be so sure with that bastard" Tucker replied. "Anyway, let's see what the Old Man has to say."

Tucker's crew were lined up outside Squires' office and on the stroke of ten o'clock the adjutant told them to go through. They stood to attention in front of his desk and Tucker saluted.

"OK Tucker. I have seen the report on your aircraft. You were probably right to turn back but don't make a habit of it, understand? At the moment Bomber Command is about all we have to hit the enemy with and we expect every crew to make a maximum effort. At least you got the aircraft and your crew back. Now dismiss."

Tucker saluted and the crew marched out into the freezing cold and then back to the warmth of the Mess. It was a while before Tucker spoke.

"OK lads. Reckon we got off fairly lightly there, but Nobby here and I saw the damage to the engine and wing. Not a pretty sight but we made it back and even though this doesn't count to the tour, we learnt a lot and let's try and get through next time. I say we go down the Red Lion this evening and get rat-arsed."

CHAPTER 7

Saturday 22nd January 1944

"Sister Johnson there's a call for you. A doctor, he said, but I didn't catch his name."

Anne was clearing up after an appendicectomy and as she went to the phone she assumed it was going to be about some other emergency.

"Yes, Sister Johnson here."

"Hallo Anne it's me, Nobby."

"How did you get me here?"

"Well I said I was a doctor and I needed to talk to you. I mean I am a sort of doctor aren't I, so I thought that would be OK."

Anne smiled. "Well I would get shot if anyone knew this was a personal call. What is it about in any case?" Her heart skipped a beat as she thought for a moment that it might be about Matt.

"You remember when we were talking at the dance you spoke about Scrap the hound. Well I spoke to Barker and he is looking after him just now. What do you want to do?"

"I can't do anything just now. I have to go. Why don't you call me this evening – the porters will know where to find me? Bye for now" and she quickly put the receiver down.

One of the surgeons was walking towards her "Everything alright sister? You look a bit flushed. Not going down with this wretched cold I hope. Can't afford to have you sick you know" he smiled. "Are we ready to start that abscess. It looks pretty ugly."

"Yes, Mr Steed. Ready when you are" and she hurried away to get her surgical trolley ready.

* * *

Anne was writing a letter to her mother when there was a knock on her door.

"Someone on the phone in the corridor for you"

"Thanks Patricia – just coming"

"Hallo" she said

"Nobby again. You said ring tonight so I am. How was the operating list?"

"Not too bad. Nobby, John, please don't ring there again. It was very embarrassing and rumours fly round hospitals you know. Just imagine them saying, 'Oh she's just lost her fiancé and now she's taking off with someone else.'? Which is absolutely not true. I love Matt so much and I want him back here with me" She started crying and was tempted to put the phone down.

"I'm sorry Anne. I didn't mean to do anything to hurt you. It was selfish of me but I thought you would be pleased to know about Scrap – a bit of good news. It must be terrible for you just now. If it would help, perhaps we could meet for a drink – I could get the bus into town tomorrow evening. What do you think? Maybe it would help just to talk. Might help me as well – we had to turn back last night – on our first outing too. Powers that be weren't too happy especially our favourite Flight Commander."

"Well…. it would certainly be good to get out of here" Anne replied cautiously. "How about meeting tomorrow around midday. Mind the buses are pretty scarce on a Sunday but during the day should be OK."

"It's a date" Clarke said quickly "Where would we meet?"

"There is a Lyons Corner House. How about there?"

"See you around twelve o'clock then" Clarke replied and rang off.

Anne walked back to her room uncertain that she had done the right thing. Just sharing lunch should be OK and Clarke was probably a good listener. And perhaps she was a step closer in getting hold of Scrap.

* * *

Sunday 23rd January 1944

Anne hurried from the hospital afraid she was going to be late. She had not slept that well thinking about Matt and then the rights and wrongs of meeting Clarke. It was bitterly cold and the wind seemed to cut through her winter coat and as she walked briskly up to the restaurant, she saw that Clarke was already outside waiting for her.

"Sorry I'm late" she began and not really sure what to do next she reached out and shook his hand.

"Well, no rush really" he replied "Restaurant's shut – Sunday!"

"Oh God. I'm so sorry – how stupid of me. There is a pub just around the corner – they do pretty good lunches."

"Fine. Let's go there then. It's pretty parky out here isn't it?"

"Have you been waiting long? I feel really bad about things now. Let me get you a drink at least."

They dived into the pub which really warm and welcoming in contrast to outside. There was a log fire burning across from the bar with an empty table next to it.

"You go and sit down" Clarke said "What would you like to drink? Oh, I could order food too whilst I'm there."

"Gin and orange and anything hot, please. The cold has made me feel quite hungry. I'll buy the next round though."

Anne looked round the bar. The last time she was in here was with Matt when things were so different.

"Here we are. Food's coming soon. Hotpot but of what is not crystal clear I'm afraid! Have you had any news about Matt? There certainly hasn't been any word around the station."

"No, nothing. I spoke to his mother the other day but she has heard nothing else either. I pray each night John, that some sort of miracle will happen and that he will be alright. Not knowing makes it worse you know."

"It must do. Difficult to know what to say. Probably it might be a while before you find out if he is a POW."

"Well, here's to just keep hoping" and she lifted her glass in a toast. "How's it going up at East Kirkby? What happened on your first trip then?"

"We ran into some trouble and had to drop the bombs somewhere in Germany and come back. Flight Lieutenant Simmons wasn't over the moon."

"Why did you volunteer, John? I mean you could have carried on at the university, couldn't you? Teaching medical students is really vital."

"Wanted a change I suppose. Bit of adventure. Well that and maybe I thought it was the right thing to do. My bit for the war, that sort of thing."

"It is so dangerous though. I mean these young chaps look on it as a bit of a game, even Matt seemed to see it that way to begin with, and most of them haven't known anything else. But you have a professional life and a lot going for you and, well John, you are a bit older than them, aren't you?"

"True. Maybe it just seemed a good idea at the time. Have to tell you it didn't feel such a bright idea when the aircraft was falling out of the sky! But somehow it feels more worthwhile than sitting in a lab all day doing terrible things to rats. I mean that's what I do when I'm not trying to convince medical students that they really do need to know something about the circulation of the blood!"

Anne laughed, something she hadn't done for quite a while. Almost before she realised it she asked "Is there a Mrs Clarke then?"

"No, not at all. I was engaged to a girl at the university for nearly five years but then she pushed off with someone else. I reckon she didn't see much prospect of fame and fortune from marrying just a university lecturer!"

"Was that what tipped you into joining up then?"

"Well it certainly was a factor. She meant a lot to me at the time and for a while things seemed pretty empty without her. Bit like you and Matt maybe although at least Sylvia is still around somewhere. Oh, sorry Anne, shouldn't have said that."

Anne nodded as the hotpot arrived. "I'll get the next round".

They ate in silence and Anne suddenly felt less hungry but the food was good and she was pleased to get something warm to eat.

"Better than the grub at East Kirkby" Clarke said. "It's been a bit of a shock coming down here. Food at the HCU was really good. Perhaps they were trying to fatten us up – lambs to the slaughter maybe?" Anne smiled.

They finished their meal and had another drink before Anne said "Well, I better be getting back and I guess there won't be many buses going your way on a Sunday? Sorry about the muddle."

"God no, don't worry. It has been good meeting up. Hell, look at the time I must dash. What do you want to do about Scrap? Can you keep him at the hospital?"

"I doubt it. I was thinking of taking him home to my mum's. We used to have a dog so I suspect she will welcome another. I will leave it until I go home again probably next month. Is Barker OK to keep him for now do you think?"

"I'm sure he will be happy to do that, as much for you as the dog. He told me that he was very fond of Matt and he somehow sees looking after Scrap as doing something for him."

Anne had to catch herself from breaking down in tears. "Tell him thank you. I know that Matt thought a lot of him too. You take care of yourself, John." She reached up a kissed him on the cheek. "Take care."

CHAPTER 8

Thursday 27ᵗʰ January 1944

Clarke woke up to the shouts of the orderly, with rather a sore head. The crew had been down at the Red Lion and then made the fatal mistake of 'popping into the mess for a nightcap!' Phil Smith, it turned out, had been quite a good cricketer at school and had played for Hampshire in the junior county team. He and Barton got into an argument about the quality of Yorkshire's cricket and this steadily deteriorated somehow into a challenge about who could drink the most beer in five minutes. It wasn't a pretty sight!

"Glad we don't play much cricket in Wales" Docker was saying. "Rugby is our game boyo. Now that's a real blokes' game."

To this Brookes waded in with "To be sure, it depends on the colour of your shirt Taff. Them red ones you lot wear, well I'm not so sure!"

It was about two o'clock before the party broke up and the crew staggered back to their hut.

Clarke made a quick exit before the others got up and made his first stop the Flight Office. Simmons was in his office as usual but Clarke managed to peep in unseen and noticed to his dismay that they were on operations for the night. He made his way to the mess to join the line for breakfast.

"Morning Bill. Some moderately bad news. We're on for tonight."

"Christ" he replied "I knew I shouldn't have had that last bloody beer. We need to do an air test this morning Nobby – can you rustle up the others?"

Clarke managed to get some breakfast down, by which time the others had dragged themselves to the canteen. Everyone looked bleary eyed and a couple of them had not bothered to shave.

"We are on for tonight lads. I will get the aircraft ready for ten thirty."

"Piss off" Tanner said trying to light his next cigarette. "Can't they run the bloody war without us today?"

"Don't think so, Jim. And gunners are fairly important!"

Tanner muttered something and then wandered away.

'Worse than some of the medical students' Clarke thought smiling.

The air test went well and the crew were beginning to feel more human as they dragged themselves to the Briefing Room to be ready for three o'clock.

As usual Wing Commander Squires and his retinue walked in exactly on time.

"The target for tonight, gentlemen, is Berlin. I know we were there a few days ago but we have to keep the pressure on them. There are a few diversionary changes tonight which should help you get through to the target without fighters all over your backs."

Clarke and Tucker looked at one another. This was only their second raid and now they were off to the 'Big City'. The squadron had missed out on that last Berlin job but the buzz was that it had been an expensive flop.

The Squadron Navigation Officer was talking.

"The route tonight will be different to usual – we hope to trick them this time! The bomber force will head out towards Heligoland before turning southeast and then finally northeast towards the target. Navigators you will need to pay particular attention to your timings for the turns. There will be a number of diversions planned to try and fool Jerry and to give you all a trouble-free run" he smiled. "You will return using a southerly route so this is going to be a very long trip."

He was followed by the Squadron Flight Engineer who reminded them about the vital importance of fuel management.

"You will be getting pretty low by the time you get back" he emphasised. "Don't risk trying to get back to base if your reserves are marginal- look for the nearest bit of concrete!"

The Met man was a jolly, rather rotund man with a cheery red face.

"Hallo chaps" he began "Good news and bad news. The good news is that there will be a strong wind blowing you to Berlin. The bad news is that it will be trying to keep you there" he chuckled.

The briefing came to an end but as Tucker and his crew walked out, Tanner pushed past them and was sick in the flower bed just by the door.

"Ah Bill, I ain't feeling too good, mate. Do you think you could get someone else tonight?"

"Not a bloody chance kid. Go and get your head down for a couple of hours and don't forget you need to eat, so meet us in the canteen at five o'clock, OK?"

Tanner didn't reply but walked off towards the billet dragging hard on his cigarette.

* * *

It was bitterly cold as the crews walked to the Crew Room to get ready.

"You OK with the route Nobby and all those bloody timings? Wish we could have gone on a shorter trip. Still it will be good to get this one out of the way."

"Yes, think I've got it all sorted Bill. Out to sea, turn left, turn right, turn left, turn right and there we are!"

"Piece of piss then" Tucker smiled at him as the truck drew up to get them out to the aircraft.

The ground crew were scrapping the ice off the wing of P-Peter as they arrived and one of them came over as they jumped down from the truck.

"Evening Sarg. Everything is alright and once we have got the wings swept she's ready. Good luck."

"Thanks" Tucker replied and joined the others having a pee before getting aboard. He noticed Tanner was bending over and heard him retching again.

"You OK Jim?" he asked.

"No, I bloody ain't. I should be in the sick bay not flying over fucking Germany."

"Well tough. You're going and that's that. Try drinking less. Now get aboard and check the guns are OK."

Tucker had reached the conclusion that he didn't like Tanner all that much. He got on well with the rest but there was something odd about Tanner. Untrustworthy almost, not really a characteristic you want in your gunners.

With everyone on board the crew went through their checks and eventually got the signal to taxi out to the runway along with the other nine aircraft.

"Right. Everyone ready to go?" Tucker asked and all reported in except Tanner.

"You OK, Jim?" resulted in a muffled "Yeh."

They were at the end of the runway and the flares alongside stretched out in front of them.

"OK everyone. Green light, we're on our way." And with that Barton and he eased the throttles forward, left slight ahead of right to counter the swing of the aircraft as it gathered speed.

P-Peter was slow to accelerate down runway two-six and with her being so full of fuel and bombs it seemed to take forever before she was ready to fly and Tucker could ease her off the concrete.

They climbed steadily turning gently to the left until they were heading for Skegness.

"On to zero-seven-five Bill. And climb to 15000 feet. We will join the main stream in about two hours with this tail wind."

"OK Nobby. Jim, Taffy fire your guns now to see that everything is working. Dave can you see anything below?"

"Yep. We have just crossed the coast. Can see really clearly for once. Even see the aircraft in front of us."

"Good. Keep a sharp lookout everyone. Charlie engines OK?"

"Yep. Running like silk."

It seemed a long time before Clarke said that they were coming up to their rendezvous point.

Tucker felt tense. The consequences of over five hundred Lancasters coming together to form the main stream if someone's timing was out did not bear thinking about.

"OK there now" Clarke was saying "Come on to one-two-zero. That should allow for this westerly wind. About two hours to the next turn."

"One-two-zero. Anybody see anything?" Tucker asked.

"Looks like coastline ahead. And I can see an aircraft right below us. Not that far away Bill. Maybe less than five hundred feet" Brookes said.

"OK keep an eye on him. If he stays with us we need to make sure he's not in the way of the bombs."

They droned on into the night and it seemed so quiet that Tucker even began to wonder if they were going the right way.

"That aircraft still below us, Dave?" he asked.

"Yes, still there. I can just see the glow of his exhaust stubs."

"Nobby, we still on course? It just seems really quiet out here."

"It looks OK. The wind is just as forecast for a change. We are not far from our next turning point. I can try an astrofix if you like. It's nice and smooth and the sky is clear."

"Yes, do that. I just can't believe that there seems to be nothing happening around us."

After a while Clarke said that it looked like they were in the right place and it was coming up to the time for the next course change. "Zero-six-zero Bill for seventeen minutes then we turn to the target."

"It's getting cloudy Bill. I can't see much below us although that other Lanc is still there. I can pick him out quite clearly against the clouds."

"Turn coming up now" Clarke called. "Zero-nine-zero, thirty minutes to target."

"Zero-nine-zero. Looks like we will get there this time everyone" Tucker said. "Gunners keep your eyes peeled. Taffy you OK back there?"

"Yes, Billy boy I'm OK."

"Jim you alright?"

There was no answer and Tucker asked him again but there was no reply.

"Phil go and check and see if Jim is OK, will you?"

Smith quickly came back "He's lying in the cot. Says he doesn't feel well."

"Tell him to fucking well get back in his turret or else. What does the bastard think this is – some bloody joy ride?" Tucker was furious and the tension of the flight just made him even angrier.

At this moment Brookes called out "I can see a lot of flashes up front Bill. I think that must be our target."

"Thanks Dave. OK everyone let's get ready for the bomb run. Nobby how long to the target?"

"About ten minutes."

"All I can see is cloud Bill. Looks like the pathfinders are using sky markers." Brookes was saying.

"OK we'll bomb on those. I can see a glow slightly over to the right. There are markers going down there so let's use those. Christ, look at the flak we have to go through before we get there?"

Tucker had heard the stories about the flak barrage but to see it like this was terrifying.

P-Peter was beginning to buck up and down as they got to the barrage. The flak was really close now and shrapnel was rattling against the fuselage.

"Keep it coming" Brookes was saying. "Come right, right, steady, steady, bombs gone. Hold it steady for the photo although I can't see the point."

The sound was now deafening but at least the cloud kept the searchlights from them.

"Flash gone"

"Right let's get out of here" Tucker said as he turned P-Peter for home. "Course, Nobby?"

"Two-four-zero"

Just at that moment there was a flash over to their left and Tucker looked over to see an aircraft going down in flames. And almost as soon as it had gone, another one about two miles in front also caught fire.

"Right gunners. It looks like Jerry has been lying in wait. They have worked out the diversions so now they are ready for us."

"Corkscrew port" Docker cried and Tucker threw the aircraft into a steep turn. He heard the guns firing and felt the aircraft shudder as it was hit. He pulled them round to resume their course and called to make sure everyone was OK. They all replied, even Tanner, although his voice was more like a whimper.

"How long before we turn, Nobby?"

"About another hour. This takes us well south of the Ruhr. But like the man said we've got a bit of a head wind now."

Tucker felt drained already and they still had a long way to go to get back home and plenty of opportunities to run into Jerry.

"How are we for fuel Charlie?"

"Yep, OK so far. Unless something happens, we should manage alright even with this head wind."

Tucker could see nothing else around him. The sky seemed empty but he knew it wasn't. Could be a Jerry fighter creeping up below them just this very minute.

"Everything OK below Taffy. No one there?"

"Not a thing boyo. Blackest night I've ever seen. Mind you cloud is breaking up now."

It felt like they were only just crawling towards home when Clarke gave another course alteration.

"Another hour and we should be out of Germany" he said "About two hours to the coast."

"Christ" Tucker exclaimed "We seem to have been going for bloody hours already. Have we really got enough fuel Charlie?"

"That's what the numbers say, Bill. Mind we won't have much in reserve."

"Gunners report" Tucker said tersely. Docker reported immediately but Tanner just gave a groan which at least meant he was in his turret. The enveloping darkness seemed to almost suffocate him and, if he was honest, he felt very frightened. It seemed an age before Clarke said that they should be coming up to the coast and soon after Brookes reported that he could see the sea.

"Right I'm dropping down to see if we can get out of this wind. Dave tell us when you see Blighty. Gunners make sure no one is tailing us."

"Turn three-three-zero Bill. That should take us almost straight to East Kirkby. Should be there in about forty-five minutes."

"We should manage with the fuel, Bill" Barton added.

The East Kirkby beacon came into view about when Clarke said it would. Tucker turned into the circuit to land and as the wheels touched the ground, he breathed a sigh of relief. They had finished their first complete trip but as they gathered outside the aircraft Tucker was determined to tackle Jim Tanner and in front of the others he asked him what the hell he meant by leaving his post.

"Didn't feel too good did I and there was nuffing going on in any case. Thought I'd just have a kip."

"You bloody fool" Tucker replied. "Don't you realise you, yes you, could have got us all killed. What the bloody hell do you think you are sitting in the turret for?"

"Do we want him with us or not?" he said turning to the others.

Clarke was the first to speak. "I say we give him another chance but anymore of that nonsense then that's it. We are meant to be this together Jim and if one of us screws up it could be the end for us all."

"Well, I think I agree" Brookes said hesitatingly. "Just one more chance seems reasonable."

"I agree too. But I tell you this boyo, you do that again and it won't be bloody Jerry you need to worry about, it will be me" and Docker came over and shook his fist in Tanner's face.

"You know what you lot? I don't give a fuck. I don't want to fly again in any case so you can all bugger off and stuff it up your arses." and with that Tanner walked away from the aircraft.

"They'll bust you down to LAC, you stupid little bugger." Tanner shouted after him.

"Don't bloody care. At least I'll be alive at the end of the war."

The truck came up to collect them and they all got in with Tanner sitting aside from the rest dragging on his cigarette. At the debriefing there was an embarrassed pause before Tucker told the Intelligence Officer about the raid and that things had gone pretty well.

"Number one is the worse" the officer was saying. "Get a couple more under your belt and it seem much easier. Well done."

"Thank you, sir." He wasn't going to say anything about Tanner just now and thought it would be better if he left things for another day.

CHAPTER 9

Friday 11th February 1944

Lyons Corner House was crowded by the time Anne got there and she was pleased that she had booked a table. She was also relieved that she had arrived before Clarke especially after the debacle of their last meeting. "Anne Johnson" she announced at the counter. "I have booked a table for two for one o'clock."

"Er, yes Miss Johnson. You are on the table in the corner. Would that be satisfactory?"

"Yes, fine thank you." The corner was particularly convenient because Clarke had arranged to bring Scrap and she reckoned that he could be easily secreted between the table and the wall. Anne was going back home to Worcester the next day so she would only have to smuggle Scrap once into the hospital before she took him home to her parents.

Clarke arrived at a quarter past one. Anne noticed that he looked much more tired than at their last meeting and also that Scrap was at his heel as they came over to the table.

"Hallo Anne. Sorry I'm a bit late but the bus seemed to take forever. Oh, here's Scrap. I think he was as pleased to get out of the camp as I was. Here you go boy. Your new owner."

Anne kissed Clarke's cheek and took Scrap's lead and made him come around to the side of the table nearest the wall.

"Are you alright, John? You look weary."

"Not too bad really. We had three trips back to back to Berlin and then we have been training pretty hard as well. It's been rather tough Anne, to tell you the truth. But then you will know that from Matt. Any news incidentally?"

"No nothing. His mother hasn't heard anything either. She sounded very down when we spoke on the phone a few days ago. The worse thing John, is not knowing what is going on. Is he a POW, is he lying dead somewhere? I suppose it is bad for everyone, and I don't have any right to be considered special. This sort of thing is happening all over isn't it? Sorry, time for me to stop" and she wiped a tear away from her eye. "Three trips to Berlin. That must have been hard?"

"Well not helped by one of our gunners deciding that he would just have a sleep on our first outing because there wasn't much happening! I thought the other gunner was going to brain him at one point" he smiled. "Anyway, he did a bunk when we got back and no one has seen or heard of him since. Dread to think what will happen to him when they catch him. Wasn't a very nice young man in any case."

"Would you like to order?" Anne asked and waved to one of the waitresses. "The steak pie is usually very good here."

"Did you come here with Matt?"

"No I don't think we did come here actually, but it is close to the hospital and some of us come here now and again to get a change from the hospital food. What will happen to that gunner when they get him? Matt's friend had trouble too and he managed for a while and then cracked up; he was the Flight Engineer. He was threatened with being labelled LMF. But, you know, he was a very brave man and he managed to carry on and then he got killed." The memory of those last few weeks came flooding back to her and she had to catch her breath. "So, will this chap be made LMF too do you think?"

LMF – Lack of Moral Fibre

"Don't know Anne. I doubt it because he only did one trip. In any case it sounds very different to Matt's friend. This chap was just a bit of a lout and I suspect they will just throw him in prison and chuck away the key! Desertion in the face of the enemy used to be punishable by death but probably not him. I bet he will be really good at peeling spuds by the end of the war!"

Anne found herself laughing something she hadn't done since they last met.

"And what about you at the end of the war, John? Will you go back to the university?"

"Probably, although you know I quite enjoy this navigation lark. There is something really satisfying about finding the target – it's an even better feeling finding your way back home though" he smiled again. "Mind you I am glad that I don't have a window to look out of. It is jolly scary when folk are trying to kill you. Bill Tucker is a good pilot, though. He doesn't lose his cool although he gets a bit cross with me sometimes if I can't give him a course quickly enough!" They chatted for a while over the meal and each had a cup of tea before Clarke noticed the time. "I better get going. Wonderful lunch Anne, thank you. Time seems to fly. It is good to have someone else to talk to and it would be good if we could do it again. I hope everything works out with Scrap. He's a lovely dog. Doesn't seem to bat an eyelid and really seemed to enjoy the bus ride."

"It means a lot to me to have him, John. A kind of link with Matt I suppose although Stephen, the flight engineer I mentioned, was the one who took most care of him. Many thanks for bringing him. Oh, and thank Barker too will you?"

They left the restaurant with Scrap in tow, tail wagging. After Clarke had left, Anne walked to the park close to the hospital. It was somewhere that she and Matt had been to several times before, sometimes with Scrap. It was cold but the sun was shining and walking through the park with Scrap scampering around felt almost normal. 'If only....' she thought. 'If only Matt was here it would be almost perfect.'

She had brought a large shopping bag with her and as she approached the hospital she bundled Scrap into it and put a towel over him. Keeping her head down she walked quickly through into the Nurses' Home and up the stairs to her room. She shut the door and took the towel away and sat down on her bed looking at Scrap as he sat in front of her his trusting, deep brown eyes looking up at her. She started to cry and held his head in her hands until the crying stopped and she felt better. "Home tomorrow" she said quietly "You'll enjoy that too."

CHAPTER 10

Tuesday 15th February 1944

Clarke lay in his bed thinking about Anne and the lunch they had enjoyed. Apart from the delight of spending time with someone who wasn't smelly and dressed in air force blue, he really liked her company. He felt a bit uneasy with Matt still being in the background but it was just a friendship and unlikely to develop further. It must be hard for Anne not knowing what had happened to Matt and they had obviously been very much in love.

No operations over the last couple of weeks, and hence no losses, had allowed the squadron to recover its strength and their hut was full again which at least made it moderately warm. Clarke got up and went over to shake Tucker out of his sleep. They had become good friends after arriving in East Kirkby and had got into the habit of going off for a cup of tea before the others surfaced.

It was still very cold as they walked over to the canteen and Clarke peeled off to the Flight Office to check the Ops Board. He couldn't believe that they could go much longer without action and sure enough P-Peter was there on the board. He went over to the canteen and sat down next to Tucker.

"We're on. Knew it couldn't last! Briefing fifteen hundred."

"Well we will do an air test – what do you reckon, usual time? At least we went easy on the beer last night. That new gunner, Alan, is OK isn't he?"

"Yes, nice kid. He's only eighteen, joined up straight from school. He's from Devon. Dad wanted him to stay behind to help with the farm. One thing is certain he should be a pretty good shot all the practice he must have had shooting rabbits!"

"We better go and stir up the others – do you want to do that. I have to go and see Simmons apparently. That little bastard Tanner has been found at last and I have to give a statement or some such. We could drop him right in it by saying he deserted his post but I don't feel like doing that. He's in enough trouble as it is. So long as there is no question of him coming back I think I'll just leave that bit out."

"Agree Bill. In World War 1 he would have been shot for what he did I suppose? See you later."

Briefing followed the usual pattern and Wing Commander Squires opened proceedings by saying that the target was again Berlin.

"We have let them have two weeks of peace and quiet. Time to shake them up again. This will be one of the biggest raids on Berlin. Conditions look quite good so you should be able to do some real damage tonight. Good luck."

He was followed by the other specialists and the navigator pointed out the route which, this time, would be to the north over Denmark and returning westwards in almost a straight line. Once the briefing was over Tucker and his crew walked over to the canteen for the standard bacon and eggs, after which, they moved off to the crew room and then out to the aircraft. It was very cold as they climbed up the steps and into the fuselage and no one spoke as they made their way to their posts. Tucker

Author's note – it was the largest Berlin raid with 875 aircraft)

checked and signed Form 700 and then he and Barton did the checks prior to engine-start.

Clarke felt uneasy. Maybe it was just that they had not been flying on operations for a while, maybe it was just the anxiety of being sure that he had the route correct.

Tucker's voice came over the headset asking if everyone was ready and then Clarke felt the starboard inner engine begin to turn followed by the three others.

"Everything OK, Charlie?" Tucker asked and Barton put his thumb up.

"Alright everyone here we go. Trip number four is underway!"

The Lancaster rumbled its way down the runway gradually gathering speed. Clarke hung on to his charts and navigation paraphernalia as the aircraft swayed and bounced until the wheels lifted off and everything settled down. They climbed steadily towards the coast which Brookes could see clearly through the plexiglass window in the bombaimer's post.

"Coast coming up Nobby. Skegness, I reckon."

"Hope so Dave. That's what it says here. Bill come on to zero-six-five. Just over the coast now."

Tucker adjusted the aircraft heading slightly and they continued to climb towards the point where the various bomber streams would come together out over the North Sea. It was a clear night for once and as Tucker looked around he could just make out some of the other aircraft. They flew on for about two hours before Clarke said they were approaching the assembly point.

"Eyes skinned everybody." Tucker said. "Hopefully they are all as good as us at navigation!" Clarke smiled because he had certainly done alright up until now.

"Zero-nine-five Bill. We should be at 15,000 feet now but we need to climb to 20,000. Thirty-five minutes to the next course change"

"OK Nobby on our way up now."

They were now over Denmark and the hope was that the diversionary aircraft were dragging the German fighters south and away from the main bomber stream. Tucker had just settled on the new course when there was a flash of red and orange away over on the left side.

"There are fighters around you gunners. Alan, Taffy everything OK?"

They both answered quickly – thank God we got rid of the other useless lump, Tucker thought to himself.

Just at that moment there was a huge explosion below and in front of P-Peter the force of which lifted the aircraft three or four hundred feet forcing Tucker to quickly bring everything under control to prevent then colliding with other aircraft in the formation.

"What was that?" Clarke called from the darkness of the navigation station.

"Someone just under us blew up" Tucker said. "Must be fighters all over the place. I have seen several others going down. How long before we turn?"

"Two minutes. New course is one-three-zero."

"Corkscrew starboard" called Docker and as Tucker threw the aircraft into a diving turn he heard the guns firing.

"Got him" he heard Alan Trelick call out "Bloody got him"

Tucker looked over to the left and saw the fighter diving with flames coming out of one engine.

"Well done Alan. But you just keep looking now."

All seemed to go quiet for a while until Clarke called another course change which put Berlin right in front of them.

"Forty-five minutes to target"

"Thanks Nobby. I think we are going to get a hot reception this time. After all it's not just us that have had two weeks off. Their pilots have had their feet up as well!"

After about twenty minutes Brookes said he thought he could see a glow in the sky ahead but also that it looked like there was some cloud developing below. Slowly but surely they crept towards Berlin and about ten minutes away Tucker saw that there was an apparent wall of flak.

"Christ everyone this flak looks pretty bad tonight but here we go. Dave you ready?"

"As I'll ever be. Looks like quite a lot of cloud cover but I can see the target indicators clearly enough. Need to come to the right Bill."

They seemed to be almost through the flak when there was a loud bang from the front of the aircraft. Tucker realised they had been hit and he called Brookes.

"Dave you alright?"

There was no answer and he got Clarke to go and check on him.

There was a hole in the side of the aircraft's nose and Clarke could see that it looked as if Brookes had been hit in his side.

"Dave you OK? Can you hear me? The bombs – how long before we drop?"

Brookes nodded "About two minutes. Give me a hand over to the bombsight will you? Whatever hit me shoved me over a bit."

Clarke carefully eased Brookes over so he could use the sight.

"Sorry Bill normal service and all that. Come a bit further right. Right, now steady coming up to the target. Steady. Bombs away" he called quietly. He seemed to be having trouble breathing and Clarke wondered if the flak had hit his chest. "Wait, photo coming up now. OK all done."

His head slumped forward as Tucker banked the aircraft away and Clarke tried to turn him over so he could see what was happening.

"Bill, Dave looks pretty bad but I need to get back to give you the course out of here. Perhaps Phil could get down here for a while?"

"Yes do that. Phil do what you can."

Clarke ran back past Tucker and gave a thumbs down before he got back to his post.

"Bill you need to steer two-seven-zero and just keep going until we get home. I'm going back to see if I can do anything for Dave."

"OK Nobby. Do your best."

P-Peter was being thrown all over the place by the blasts from the flak and occasionally other aircraft exploding added to the turmoil.

"It looks like the fighters are with us this time" Tucker was saying. "Gunners keep sharp. Hopefully we can get out of here soon."

Just then Trelick shouted that a fighter was coming straight at them beam on.

"Which side" shouted Tucker.

"Port" and Tucker heard the guns firing again as out of the corner of his eye he saw the enemy aircraft cross over the top of them.

"Jesus, what the hell is going on. We haven't seen this before" and just at that moment they flew out into the darkness, leaving the inferno of Berlin behind them. Tucker was sweating and he noticed his hands shaking on the controls.

"Everyone alright?" he asked. "Charlie how are things? Any problems?"

"No, everything sounds OK. We might be losing some fuel from the left wing tank but we are alright at the moment."

Clarke got back to Brookes and saw that Smith was still bending over him.

"How is he Phil?"

"I think he's still alive but he's not moving much."

"Can we get him out of here between us do you think? If we could get him back to the cot we could have a good look."

Together they lifted him as gently as possible through the cockpit and over the main spar to the cot. Clarke got a light out and had a closer look at the injuries. Brookes had some blood coming from the corner of his mouth but the main wound seemed to be on the right side of his chest. His breathing was very laboured and his heart beat weak.

"Let's give him some morphine" Clarke said. "And we must make sure his oxygen is OK. He needs surgery really. Suspect he's got something called an haemothorax."

Smith looked at Clarke. "You a doctor Nobby? I don't understand what you're saying."

"Basically, he has probably had it, Phil. Blood in his chest. We'll do what we can."

Just then Tucker threw the aircraft down to the left and they could hear the gunners letting fly again.

"That won't help much" he said quietly to Smith. "Why don't you stay with him while I try and figure out where we are."

Clarke went back to the navigation station just as Tucker frantically tried to shake off another fighter. He was thrown against the side of the fuselage and then on to the floor as the aircraft climbed. He got his headset back on and heard Tucker asking Docker where he should go next.

"Think they've gone just now. Al can you see anything?"

"No, looks clear. There has just been a couple of bright flashes like something blowing up over to the right."

"Nobby are you alright? How about Dave?"

"Well let's say I'm in better shape than Dave. What course are we steering."

"Christ knows. I've been chucking her around so much the direction indicator doesn't seem to be working just now."

"OK from my compass looks like we are heading three-three-zero so not the way we want to go. Come back on to two-seven-zero for now and let me see if I can figure out where we are. Charlie can you go down to the nose and just see if you can make anything out. Be careful though – there is a hole in the nose and I am not sure what other damage there maybe."

Charlie crawled along the fuselage and quickly confirmed that there was unbroken cloud below them and that there were, indeed, some big holes in the aircraft's nose.

"OK just carry on this course Bill. H2S is still working but it is difficult to work out what it's showing. Theoretically we will be in GEE range in about an hour. I'll try and get an astrofix in a minute. Just going back to see about Dave."

Clarke worked his way down the aircraft and over the spar. Smith was still there just looking at Brookes.

"Any change?"

"No Nobby. He's just lying really still now."

Nobby bent over bomb aimer and shone his torch. He felt for a pulse in Brookes' neck but there was nothing. "He's gone I'm afraid" he said quietly. "Best get back to the radios"

Clarke and Smith scrambled forward and Clarke went up into the cockpit and did a thumbs down to Tucker.

The astrofix showed that they were about thirty miles north of Hanover so not far from the planned return course and half an hour later Clarke got a GEE fix.

"About eighty minutes to Blighty, Bill"

Tucker was feeling the strain. His arms ached from manoeuvring the aircraft and his eyes felt they were on stalks. Just then the sky light up with searchlights and suddenly flak was curving up towards them.

"Jesus, where did this lot come from?" He dived the aircraft and managed to avoid being fixed by a searchlight but he

GEE – A system of radio beams which allowed the aircraft to fix its position noticed another aircraft over to the right had been coned and was quickly destroyed by flak. They were back in the darkness before anyone spoke.

"Probably just on the Dutch/ German border. They didn't seem very pleased to see us."

Charlie Barton had gone forward again and this time he said that he could see the sea and not long after reported the coast which they crossed just over Great Yarmouth. The East Kirkby beacon showed up clearly in the crisp early morning light and they were soon turning on to finals to land.

Tucker taxied over to their spot and he and Barton shut down the engines. Tucker sat for a moment in silence before going back to see Brookes. The medics were already on board but he was clearly dead. They all jumped down and waited quietly while the body was removed and then they went to look at the nose. It was peppered with flak with some big holes on the side just where Brookes would have been.

"You know Bill, Dave did bloody well. He was really bashed up but he stuck at it. He made me help him forward so he could see the bombsight properly."

"Yeh, he did great. You know I feel sick Nobby. Let's go and talk to the intelligence guy and grab a cup of tea. I'm done for."

The debriefing went fairly quickly and but Tucker had made it clear that Brookes had made sure that the bombs had been dropped even though he had been severely injured. When they had finished, the six weary men made their way to the canteen for breakfast and then back to their beds for a rest.

CHAPTER 11

Saturday 19th March 1944

Clarke and Anne had not been in touch since their lunch together almost a month ago when they met at the Red Lion along with a group of nurses on the Friday night. Anne had been on night duty and obviously Clarke had been flying a lot and he was proud of the fact that they had now completed nine trips. Anne saw the familiar signs of fatigue beginning to show, however, and he had clearly been upset by Brookes' death. But now he had a few days off and with a newly acquired car, he had suggested they meet up the next day to go for a walk and lunch.

It was a lovely morning and as Anne waited outside the hospital the sun, at last, appeared to have some strength and she could feel its warmth on her face. The sky was a clear pastel blue and there was a gentle breeze all of which promised a lovely Spring day.

Clarke eventually got to the hospital at about ten o'clock, his old MG trailing a stream of blue smoke as he pulled up in front of the hospital.

"Hallo Anne. What a fine day" he called. "Sorry a bit late but things turned ugly after you all had left! Where shall we go – any ideas? I was wondering about the Lincolnshire Wolds? They are meant to be very pleasant. I think if we get to Louth we should be able to find our way from there."

It took them about forty-five minutes to get into Louth and Clarke parked the car next to St James church, whose tall spire seemed to stretch up into the blue sky above.

"I think this should be alright" he said. "We need to find the road to Donington."

"Well you're the navigator" Anne laughed as they walked away from the car.

"Down here. I think we go through Hubbard's Hills. There should be a path through here somewhere."

They walked in silence along a path which led to a ridge leaving a hill on their right and a slope down to a river on their left. Eventually they came to the road Clarke was looking for, which they followed until they reached Hallington. They turned right and climbed up the hill which led them onto the Wold and they stopped at the top looking west. It was a beautiful sight with wisps of mist in the shallow valleys on either side but there was a lot of activity in the fields all around them and several of the Land Girls waved at them as they walked past.

"What a lovely morning" Clarke said. "Feels almost like Spring doesn't it? I think these are the only hills around here. We might even be able to see the tower of Lincoln cathedral once we walk on a bit further and when this mist clears. Let's press on; it's quite a long way but a wonderful day for a walk?"

"I agree" Anne replied. "What's the name of those birds we can hear singing?

"Chaffinches. They always sound so pleased when they think that the Winter is over even though it may not be!"

"What's the other one – tic,tic?"

"That's a robin. Birds not your thing then?"

"Not really" Anne replied "Stephen, Matt's flight engineer, was keen on bird watching. Funny you know, Matt hadn't realised that until Stephen got killed and he found the bird book amongst his other bits and pieces. Amazing what we don't know about people isn't it? Anyway, when did you first get interested in birds?" She smiled at him "Feathered ones!"

"When I was a kid actually" Clarke replied "My father was a keen birdwatcher and I suppose it just developed from that. Dad took some beautiful photos of birds. He used to go up to Scotland quite a bit. Perhaps you would be interested to see some of them. I brought a couple of his albums with me when I moved up here."

"Sounds a bit corny John. Come and see my bird photos!"

To her surprise she noticed that Clarke blushed deeply and she took his hand.

"Sorry John, just joking. I would love to see them sometime, really."

The road ran along a ridge with valleys on either side and gradually the sun's heat was strong enough to burn off the mist leaving the valleys clear to see.

They walked along for a while in silence before John asked about how long she had been a nurse.

"Oh, I went straight from school when I was eighteen. Went in as a student nurse and then gradually worked my way up. Been a theatre sister for about three years now."

"Why nursing though?"

"Well my father is a GP and I suppose I just grew up with medicine all around me. I knew I could never be a doctor so I thought nursing would be the next best. Love it really, John. Wouldn't do anything else. What about you. Why aren't you a doctor? Surely if you had the brains to get to university you could have done medicine?"

"I don't think I ever thought about it, you know? My parents are ordinary folk, my dad is a teacher and my mum's just a mum who brought up me and Richard, my brother. No one had ever been to university and I don't imagine they thought that I was bright enough to break the mould. But I did well in my exams and the school suggested that I consider going to read Physiology. No one ever mentioned Medicine!"

"How do you feel now? Do you think you would rather have done Medicine after all?"

"Well it's funny you mention it. When poor old Dave Brookes bought it, I did wish that I could have done a bit more than just stuffing him full of morphine. I like doing what I do, you know, but maybe when I get back to university I might think of doing Medicine. Need to get through this lot first though" he smiled.

"And what about Richard?"

"Ah well. He was the adventurous one and went into the army before the war as a career soldier and is a captain now. In fact, he nearly got caught at Dunkirk. He was a great brother I can tell you. He's a couple of years older than me but kind of looked after me at school. Kept the bullies away. He, dad and I would always go out walking at the weekends whenever we could hence my knowledge of birds! Haven't seen much of him over the last few years but we had some good times as we grew up."

Neither of them had realised how far they had walked but as they breasted a hill they could just make out Lincoln cathedral right in the distance.

"There I told you so – pretty amazing we can see it from here – it must be about twenty-five miles away." As the road began to descend, they realised that they were looking down into a river valley.

"That will be the River Bain. That road you can see will lead us to Donington and lunch." Clarke said. "Have to say this walking has given me a bit of an appetite."

They turned down the road and shortly came to the Black Horse Inn. It was quiet when they went in with just a few of the locals supping their beer. Clarke ordered some drinks with bread and cheese for lunch and they went out into the garden at the back of the pub. The sun felt quite warm as they sat there drinking but the peace was broken every now and again by a low flying bomber.

"Probably out of Ludford" Clarke said. "Impossible to get any real peace and quiet around here. How's Scrap doing by the way?"

"Oh, he's getting on fine. Mummy likes walking him and sometimes he goes with my father on his rounds. My brother was home a few weeks ago and said he would take him back with him, but mummy put her foot down and said that Scrap had had enough to put up with over the past few years. She seems to have got very fond of him and him of her! Do you want another drink or shall we make our way back?"

They retraced their steps towards Louth. It was a truly lovely day and as they walked along, the birds singing in the hedgerows were almost deafening. Clarke held his arm out to stop Anne.

"Look there" he whispered. "There, just tucked into that bush."

Anne peered into the bush and then suddenly saw a tiny bird.

"It's Troglodytes – a wren" Clarke said before she could ask. "One of our tiniest birds. Cheeky too."

They carried on walking. Anne was beginning to feel weary but the beautiful countryside that spread out around them made her feel that she just wanted to keep walking. Clarke was good company and she was impressed with his knowledge of the countryside and it gave her a very different view of things.

"Any news about Matt?" he asked.

"No nothing. I think his mother will get the "missing believed killed in action" telegram any time soon. It's been two and a half months you know? I feel that I should go up to see her but it's quite a difficult train journey and they live in the back of beyond."

"I could take you, couldn't I? Obviously stay in the background. Must be a pub around I could go to for the night."

"John, that is very sweet of you – depends how things work out. I might take you up on it. I haven't given up hope that Matt is out there somewhere you know."

"Well the offer's there so long as I can get some time off" he said as they got back into Louth. "We better get our skates on. I'm meant to be in by six o'clock."

"You're not flying though?" Anne asked anxiously.

"Classified information" Clarke replied smiling. "No, we are on standby just now. Ready for any eventuality!"

As they got to the car Anne linked her arm through his.

"Thanks for today, John. It has been lovely. It is so good to get away from the hospital but just to be with you has been wonderful. Thanks again." She put her arm round him and gave him a hug and then got into the car. "Home James" she laughed.

CHAPTER 12

Friday 24th March 1944

They had missed the previous night's Frankfurt raid because P-Peter had developed a serious fault in one of the engines, but by all account it had been pretty successful and all the aircraft from East Kirkby had returned safely. However, Clarke was surprised to see that everyone, even those from last night, was listed to fly this on this raid with briefing, as usual, at fifteen hundred hours.

The mess was crowded with crew getting their breakfasts when he got there and he went over to tell the crew of P-Peter the news.

"Well at least we had a good night's kip" Ray Beavers replied. "Some of the others look pretty ragged." Beavers was the bombaimer replacement for Brookes. He was a jolly, ginger-haired man with sharp blue eyes who had been working in insurance before joining up. He was twenty-five years old and had lived close to Southampton on the south coast.

"OK lads" Tucker said "Usual routine. Air test, lunch, sleep, briefing. Charlie do we know how they are getting on with that engine? I would reckon that it should be finished now – they were nearly done last night but let's wander down there and have a look."

It was tough for the ground crew. They were often working outside or at least in a cold hangar for many hours, racing against time to complete their work of getting the aircraft ready for another raid.

"Nearly there then?" Barton asked the sergeant.

"Yep, pretty well. Just need to top up the oil and she's ready. You on for tonight then?"

"Looks that way. We need to take her up sometime this morning if poss."

"Give me an hour and she's yours" he said wiping his hands clean. "Try to bring her back in one piece won't you."

"Do our best" Barton replied and they got on their bikes to go back to the Mess.

The air test went well and after lunch Tucker and the others headed back to their hut for a sleep. Briefing indicated that they were off to Berlin using a northern route to approach and a southern one to escape. The main problem, insisted the met. man would be the very strong northerly winds which might make accurate navigation difficult. Clarke's confidence had grown as the tour had gone on, but he found that it was often the unreliability of the wind forecast that made his life very difficult at times. He checked and double-checked all his calculations and indicated to Tucker that he was as happy as he could be. After kitting up they made their way to the trucks waiting to take the ten crews to their aircraft.

It was a clear, starry night but the wind was quite strong even on the ground and it was very cold. The crew climbed up into the aircraft each working their way along to their stations and after a wait of about half an hour Tucker told them they were ready to leave.

Due to the wind direction they were using runway zero-two and P-Peter slowly picked up speed as the four propellers began to bite on the cold night air but the heavily laden bomber seemed to take an age before the wheels eventually lifted off and they climbed away to start trip number ten. As they flew over Skegness Beavers called out that he could see the coast clearly.

"Turn on to zero-seven-five Bill" Clarke said "We need to climb to 15,000 feet." He thought about the wonderful day he and Anne had spent walking through the beautiful countryside only a few days ago. Now he was here.

"Two hours thirty to the turning point."

The aircraft droned on through the night and although it was possible to determine the effect the wind was having on their course from their GEE apparatus Clarke began to realise that the signal was being blocked by the Germans. They were now effectively blind until they reached the coast of Denmark another hour away.

"Bill I can't get a fix anymore – they are jamming us. I've adjusted for the wind but that seemed to have changed quite a bit when I last checked. I'll try an astro in half an hour."

"OK Nobby. Let me know how that looks. It's still very clear up here. I can just about pick out two or three other aircraft around."

Clarke repeated the astrofix a couple of times before he could get a reliable reading. It did not look good and, at first, he could not believe the result.

"Bill, it looks like we could be sixty or seventy miles south of track. This bloody wind must be much stronger than predicted."

"What do you want me to do? We still have some aircraft around us. They seem to be going this way too. A change of course might be risky at this stage."

"I think we need to come left ten degrees so at least we don't go any further south. We could be close to Kiel at this rate."

"OK. Zero-six-five then. All of you keep a sharp eye out for other aircraft. We could be setting out across the bomber stream."

An hour later Beavers shouted that he could make out the coast ahead and Clarke started to pick it up on H2S. At first, he was puzzled by what he could see and his memory flashed back to their first training cross country night flight after they had just joined the squadron. He was looking for the island of Sylt with its very characteristic shape. It should have been south of them but in fact it was to the north.

"Jesus, Bill we nearly *are* at Keil! Just hold this heading for another eighteen minutes then we will do our turn but I think we are going to get a pretty hot reception very soon."

He had just finished when a battery opened up below them. The flak curled slowly up towards them before passing by harmlessly. Tucker felt a trickle of sweat go down his back. To be so far off their course this early on did not bode well. Apart from the danger of flying over heavily defended areas the timing for the whole route could be way out.

"Can anyone see any other aircraft out there or are we on our own?"

Trelick was the first to reply. His sharp eyes had picked out another Lancaster over to the right and below them but nothing else.

"OK Bill, coming up to our turning point. Remember there may be aircraft coming in from our left. Turn now – new heading one two five. We have a pretty strong tail wind now. Could be quick down this bit before we head to the target."

Clarke could see the coast clearly now on H2S and he began to feel a bit more confident about exactly where they were. But he was concerned by the apparent strength of the wind which by one of his calculations might have been over a hundred miles per hour. The north German coast appeared on his screen – remarkably it looked like they were close to Rostock, so, where they should have been originally although not by this route. Now they were going to be far too early.

"Come onto one-six-zero Bill. We are about ten minutes ahead of schedule. Maybe we should orbit?"

"Not a bloody chance Nobby. We get where we think we should be and just drop the bloody eggs. I'm not buggering about up here with hundreds of aircraft around."

"OK Bill I understand. In any case you should be able to see something up front any time soon. You keep a look out too Ray. About thirty minutes to target."

Soon after Beavers called to say that he could see some searchlights ahead reflecting off the clouds.

"That must be Berlin then" Tucker said "But I don't see any markers and not much in the way of flak either. Are we sure this is right?"

"Can you see anything below, Ray?" Clarke asked anxiously "We should be coming in over the north of the city but we are pretty early."

"No, can't see a bloody thing. Lots of cloud below us. Oh, a sky marker has just gone down over to the right but I can't see any signs of action."

"Ray let's just go for where that marker is. We can't piss about here forever"

"OK Bill. Come right, right, hold. Keep on that course, we are coming up to the marker. Steady, steady, bombs away"

There was a pause before he said the photoflash was done and Bill asked for the way home.

"Course three-zero-zero which will adjust for this wind Bill. It seems very strong."

Just at that moment there was an explosion to their left which rocked P-Peter. It was followed by a further one, minutes later.

"Two aircraft have just blown up. No flak so there must be fighters here. Christ there goes another one. They've been waiting for us here the bastards which is why we didn't see anything on the way in here."

"Corkscrew port" Docker called out and Tucker threw the aircraft into a steep dive. Just as he was getting the aircraft level Docker shouted again. Tucker could feel his arms aching as he reacted to the call and once again desperate fear began to creep into his mind.

"I'm going to get us out of this. This is a bloody ambush" he said and with that he dived the aircraft so that the engines were screaming and P-Peter began to shake.

"We're down to 10,000 feet already, Bill" Barton said quietly. "I'm going to throttle back before the engines fall off." He looked sideways at Tucker who appeared to staring straight ahead.

"Bill, we must pull her up now" Barton shouted. "For Christ's sake Bill what are you trying to do?"

Tucker at last seemed to react in response to the sharpness in Barton's voice and started to pull back on the control column so that P-Peter began to level out. He was sweating hard now and his hands tightly gripped the controls.

"We needed to get out of there" he said, his voice almost a whisper. He wasn't sure he could carry on, manage to get them back home even. It would take hours to get to the coast and if they were attacked again he doubted he could cope.

"Bill are you OK?"

"I think so, Charlie" he replied quietly "I think so."

Just at that moment he saw another aircraft going down in flames away to their left. He'd lost track of how many he had seen but it just seemed to be one after the other.

"Nobby any idea where we are?"

"We should be north of Magdeburg but with this wind we could be south for all I know. Shaking off those fighters has made it hard to tell. We are still steering three-zero-zero aren't we?"

Tucker checked quickly. With all the manoeuvring the aircraft was way off course.

"Course two-seven-zero just now" Tucker said "I'm coming back onto three-zero-zero."

Clarke suddenly felt a great dread. The truth was they could be anywhere. What did they tell him at Navigation School? You must believe in your calculations whatever else is happening – believe in the calculations. What they hadn't said was what to do when the wind direction and speed weren't known and the aircraft was being thrown around trying to escape enemy fighters.

"Bill, really not sure where we are. Can you climb over this cloud so I can get a sight?"

Tucker did not reply for a while.

"Bill?"

"No we're staying put. Those bloody fighters will pick us off against the cloud. Just do your best. Charlie how's the fuel?"

"Well OK for now. We have about five hours worth I would reckon."

"Right we'll stay down here. Nobby you will just have to do what you can."

Clarke shrugged his shoulders in resignation. If he could not get a star sight their present position would be at best an educated guess, at worse a shot in the dark. He tried to reason out where they might be – now about an hour and a half from Berlin- and he drew an arc with a diameter of about two hundred and seventy miles which put them anywhere between Munster to the north, or with this wind, Dortmund or even further south into the Ruhr. That little wriggle when Tucker was trying to throw off the fighters followed by steering due west for a while, favoured them being a good deal further south than he estimated

"What are you steering now Bill?"

"Three-zero-zero is what it says. Where does that put us?"

Before Clarke could reply P-Peter was suddenly caught in the glare of what seemed to Tucker to be twenty or more searchlights followed almost immediately by flak pouring up towards them. Tucker turned the aircraft to the right and instinctively dived and almost before he realised it, they were already down to 5000 feet. As he levelled out there was a loud explosion from behind him and he realised they had been hit. There was an acrid smell of cordite and Smith looked over his shoulder to see flames just the other side of the main spar.

"Fire" he shouted and ran back grabbing an extinguisher on the way. Trelick had jumped down from the upper turret and was also trying to smother the blaze with a blanket from the nearby cot. He glanced up as Smith ran towards him and between them they got the fire under control and eventually it went out leaving the fuselage full of smoke.

"Fire's out Bill" Smith said once he got back to his post. There was no reply. "Bill?"

"Yes. Good. Much damage?"

"Bit scorched but otherwise OK."

"Bill, I think that reception shows that we are probably nearer the Ruhr. It would make sense with this wind. Come back on to three-zero-zero. That should take us to somewhere on the Channel coast and then hopefully I can work out where we are by using H2S. Ray can you see anything from up front?"

"Not really. It's pitch black out there but we are below the clouds. I'll keep looking."

"Everyone alright" Bill asked. It was the first time he had spoken to the crew since they had left Berlin. Everyone replied and Taffy at the rear commented he felt happier now that he was not getting smoked out. "Beginning to feel like a bloody kipper" he quipped.

About an hour later Beavers called out that he thought he could see some water ahead of them but this coincided with more searchlights and then flak.

"Christ, Nobby where are we now?" Tucker asked.

"Could be Antwerp or thereabouts. They don't see very pleased to see us?"

The aircraft was rocking around as the flak got closer and closer and eventually Tucker said he could see water ahead and that he was going to dive the aircraft towards it.

"If I get really low it will make it harder for them."

Once again P-Peter was screaming her way towards the ground and Barton looked anxiously across towards Tucker to see his face grimaced with the effort of keeping the aircraft steady.

"Bloody hell Bill we are pretty low now" shouted Beavers who was now manning the forward gun and letting fly at searchlights or anything else he could see.

The Scheldt estuary opened up in front of them and Tucker took them even lower so they were soon tearing over a mass of shipping before heading out to sea. Tucker was sweating hard as they cleared the end of the estuary.

"Where to now Nobby?"

Clarke's navigation table looked like a war zone itself and some of the charts and his rulers and calculators had fallen on the floor and some small pieces of flak were still smouldering on the table surface. Clarke looked around the corner to see Smith slumped in his seat with a deep gash on his head.

"Need a minute Bill. And Phil's hurt – looks unconscious." He edged over to Smith and found that he had a pulse and after a shake he saw his eyes flicker open.

"You OK?" to which Smith gave a thumbs up sign. He was bleeding quite badly from the head wound and Clarke spoke into the intercom to get Trelick to have a look at him whilst he worked out how to get them home. It looked like they were still being pushed south in spite of their heading but that would take them towards Kent. They could put down at Manston. With this strong northerly wind, they would be unlikely to have sufficient fuel to get back home.

"Bill. I think the best bet is Manston. We should be there in half an hour but the runway is two-eight and with the wind in this direction that could be tricky."

"How much fuel, Charlie?"

"About an hour."

"Right, well let's try Manston. Is Phil up to talking to them Nobby?"

"No. I'll see what I can do." Clarke checked the frequencies from Smith's notes and then tried to raise Manston on the radio. To his relief they answered almost immediately and confirmed that they were using runway two-eight. The wind was northerly but had dropped to about twenty knots.

"Well done Nobby. Now let's see if we can find the bloody airfield. I'm going to climb to 2000 feet – that should help."

As they climbed Beavers could gradually see more and he soon spotted the coastline ahead.

"Hopefully I can see England" he called out. Clarke had been busily trying to work out which bit of coast they were approaching when Beavers shouted out that he could see a beacon over to the right.

Clarke went into the cockpit and identified the beacon as Manston's and got them clearance to land.

"This could be difficult lads" Tucker called. "Everyone to their crash positions."

Tucker had the runway clearly in sight as they crossed the coast and flew over Ramsgate.

"Nearly there" Tucker said. He was having to crab his way on to the runway to make allowances for the wind and straightened P-Peter up just as they touched down.

"Well done Bill" Barton said giving a thumbs up. "That was a bloody experience and a half" he continued as they went through the shutdown drill.

Clarke got up as soon as they landed to look at Smith. He had lost consciousness again and looked very pale but his pulse was still strong. The medics got him out and on to a stretcher and as they wheeled him away, he woke up and gave a feeble wave.

The rest of the crew jumped down just as a truck arrived to take them over to the mess. Clarke could see that Tucker looked completely done for and he moved over to help him into the back of the truck.

"You OK Bill?" he asked quietly

"Not too bad. I got pretty scared up there this time."

"Not bloody surprised. I think we all did. Still at least Phil will be OK. Just a bump on the head!"

They arrived at the Sergeant's Mess but Tucker said he needed to let East Kirkby know where they were and he and Clarke stayed with the truck and carried on to the Operations Room.

The sergeant in the Ops room looked up as they came in.

"Hallo, you lot from East Kirkby then?"

"Yeh, that's right. I need to let them know where we are. Can I use the phone here?"

"Sure go ahead. The numbers are all listed. You two look all in. Want a cuppa?"

"Thanks" Clarke said quietly. "That would be very good. Pretty quiet round here isn't it?"

"You should see it during the day, mate. Blood planes everywhere. 'Ere you are. I've put some sugar in."

Tucker had managed to get through to East Kirkby and whoever he was talking to sounded as if they were shouting into the telephone.

"We got blown off course sir, and we were running low on fuel. Also, we had a casualty on board – head injury. Manston seemed the best bet."

There was more talk from the telephone which Tucker held away from his ear and rolled his eyes to heaven.

"Well we need to refuel and the crew need a breather, sir. The fuel bowser won't be ready until the morning." Further talking was followed by silence.

Tucker put the telephone down and looked at Clarke.

"Only one guess who that was. He wanted us to refill and fly up now. I said it wasn't possible and then he hung up."

"Here get this tea down your neck and let's go and get some shut eye. Many thanks sarg."

The two walked out and once outside Tucker said, almost to himself, "I don't think I can stand much more of this."

"You'll be OK after forty winks" Clarke said encouragingly "You've had a really bad night and we were all scared. But you got us back didn't you? Wasn't helped by the bloody wind – nothing like they said. Wonder what happened to the others?"

"It's not that so much, Nobby. At times up there tonight I just felt almost paralysed with fear. It was as if it would have been easier just to fly us into the ground and end it all. And then to have that stupid prick Simmons shouting like a bloody maniac....". His voice tailed off to a whisper. "Not sure I can carry on Nobby, really not. I'm afraid I could do something stupid that would kill us all."

"I think what you need is some sleep. Come on this is the billet – let's get our heads down for a while. Maybe a spot of breakfast in the morning and then back to Happy Harry."

* * *

The next morning, they gathered quietly in the NAAFI and ate their breakfast in silence. Eventually Clarke felt he needed to say something and asked if they had managed to sleep.

Barton was the first to speak. "Thought we were dead men last night." he said slowly, his eyes flickering towards Tucker. "Thought we was goners."

"Well, we weren't were we?" Clarke replied. "We're all here, except Phil of course, and he just got a bump on the head – couple of stitches and an aspirin and he'll be as right as rain. Bill did a bloody good job getting us back here."

"What was all that diving the bloody aircraft about then?" Barton asked angrily. "Looked to me like you was throwing in the towel."

With that he got up and pushed passed the others and went out of the door. Clarke looked over towards Tucker who had gone pale and looked as if he was about to be sick.

"Come on Bill let's see if we can get the bowser organised. Probably need to be on our way pretty soon."

As they closed the door behind them Tucker said "He's right you know. I could have got you all killed. I've never felt like that before."

"Come on Bill. You're the best hope we have of surviving this bloody war. You're a good pilot. That landing last night was fantastic taking everything into account. OK, so last night you got a bit spooked – who doesn't. There's certainly no need to give up on us all."

Clarke was beginning to feel a little angry with Tucker. It had been bad but they had made it back and he dreaded the thought of them getting some green pilot with no experience of raids under his belt.

When Clarke and Tucker got down to the aircraft they found the ground crew checking her over and that she had already been refuelled.

They went back to the NAAFI now filled with men and cigarette smoke and eventually found the others.

"Come on then," Bill said "Aircraft is ready and waiting and so will Flight Lieutenant Simmons!"

There were no further comments and the six men, leaving Smith with the medics, picked up their flying kit and jumped into the back of a waiting truck. Clarke had already filed a flight plan so they were ready to go as soon as everyone had checked their stations. Beavers came back to man the radio – luckily he had trained as a radio operator before he became a bombaimer.

The Lancaster rolled down the runway and without its cargo of bombs lifted off easily. It seemed strange to be flying in daylight and Tucker felt better as the vista of the land around them came into view as they climbed steadily to 10,000 feet. They headed north over the Thames estuary, leaving Colchester on their right and they once they had crossed the Wash they picked up East Kirkby's beacon flashing at them and about forty minutes after leaving Manston, Tucker made a perfect landing back on runway zero-two.

Barton looked across and gave a thumbs up. "Well done Bill, sorry about my outburst. You did well last night to get us home."

The truck took them to the debriefing room where they were met by Simmons. He looked even more tired and dishevelled that usual.

"Well what the bloody hell happened to you lot this time?

Tucker explained that the wind had been much stronger than forecast and they had been blown way off course. They had been hit by flak and their wireless operator had had a serious head injury.

"So, what do you expect me to do about that" Simmons snarled back. "Where is Smith now. I suppose you left him down in Kent? Bloody useless lot. You probably didn't even hit the target. Well you are on again tonight so you need to make a better job of it this time."

Clarke looked across to see Tucker visibly shaken by the prospect of another trip so soon.

"We had quite a bad time of it" Clarke said. "Is there any chance we could leave it tonight, sir?"

"Of course there bloody isn't. Good mind to have you put

on a charge Clarke for refusing an order. What are you bloody suggesting? You can sit this one out just because you had to work hard last night." He was shouting now and others in the debriefing room were looking round. "I suggest you all go and get some sleep and get to the briefing this afternoon on time. Any more talk like that and you are all finished, washed up. Now get out of my sight."

Tucker turned to his crew and pointed at the door and they wearily walked out.

"Christ, that bloke is crazy" Barton muttered "Needs bloody locking up."

"Doesn't look too good to me" Clarke said quietly "Apparently half our lot didn't get back yesterday. I think it's probably getting to him as well – he probably wasn't a bastard originally!"

"They just don't give us chance do they Nobby?" Tucker said quietly as the others moved ahead. "They really don't seem to care about any of us. I'm not sure I can manage tonight. What if I do something stupid again. Get you all killed."

"Well you won't will you? Come on Bill get your head down for a few hours and then you will feel better."

They trudged their way to their hut only to find a military policeman clearing out the lockers of those that were not coming back. He lifted his head as they came in. "Sorry. Just need to collect these things. Won't be long."

Tucker turned on his heel and walked out before anyone could say anything. Clarke felt too tired to go after him and he flopped down on to his bed still in his flying kit. He had just closed his eyes when he heard a shot and jumped off his bed and ran outside. About a hundred yards away he saw Tucker's body and as he ran over he knew he was going to find him dead. The shot had been to the side of his head and the service revolver was still in Tucker's hand with blood and brains spreading out from the back of his head. The four others came running over and gathered round the body and Al Trelick, the youngest of the crew, looked very pale and turned away to be sick on the grass.

"That bastard Simmons is responsible for this" Barton was shouting. "He drove him to it no bloody doubt about it. Good mind to go and give him a thumping!"

"Won't help" Clarke whispered. "I'll go to the flight office and let them know. Poor old Bill. He told me last night he didn't think he could cope any more. Thought he had let us all down."

Deep down he was seething with anger. What sort of bloody system drives good men like Tucker to do this, he thought.

By this time a small group had gathered around the body and one of the WAAFs had brought a blanket to cover Tucker and the MP who had been in the hut came over and told them all to go away whilst he sorted things out.

Clarke strode off to the office where, predictably, he found Simmons working his way through a pile of papers.

"What do you want? I thought I told you to get some sleep."

"Thought you would want to know that Sergeant Tucker has just blown his brains out. Probably thanks to you" Clarke added. He thought that Simmons would explode with anger but instead he put his head in his hands and for a moment Clarke thought he was crying. There was silence for a few minutes before Simmons looked up.

"Thank you for letting me know Clarke," he said softly. "I'm sorry to hear that. Another letter to write eh? You and the rest will probably be sorry to hear that I will be your pilot for the next few trips. The trip for today has just been scrubbed and you chaps better get some rest especially after this. We will meet tomorrow at zero eight hundred hours, understood?" And with that he returned to his papers.

CHAPTER 13

Monday 27th March 1944

It had been a long day in the operating theatre and as Anne walked out on her way to the sisters' canteen she bumped in Jess.

"Hallo Anne. Haven't seen you for a few days. How are things. Have you heard anything about Matt?"

"No Jess I haven't but then I have been working pretty well flat out recently. We were on take for the weekend you know."

"How about going to the pub for a drink? You look as if you could do with one."

"Good idea. Let me go and change out of this lot – see you down at the porters' lodge in about five minutes."

Anne ran upstairs and nearly knocked over one of the matrons.

"An emergency is it Sister Johnson?"

"No matron, sorry. Just keen to get out."

This met with a tutting but no further comment and Anne got into her room and turned on the light to find a letter put on her bed. Her heart missed a beat when she recognised that the writing on the envelope was that of Matt's mother.

Dear Anne,

Sorry to have to tell you that I have just heard from the Air Ministry that the remains of Matt's plane have been found with two bodies in it one of which would seem to be Matt's. So that's the end of it Anne. At least we know but I can't stop crying and I am so sorry to have to tell you all this by letter. Unfortunately Matt won't be sent back to us as he was buried by the Germans with full military honours next to the rest of his crew who now lie in a cemetery near to Magdeburg.

Perhaps you could come up and see us when you have a moment.

Love

Flo

Anne read the letter again before collapsing in tears on her bed. The hope that had kept her going had been torn out of her by the letter. He hadn't escaped or been captured and imprisoned – he was dead all the time and what they had together was destroyed. She had forgotten all about Jess until there was a tap on her door and she came into the room.

"It's Matt isn't it?" she asked.

Anne nodded and showed her the letter.

"I'm very sorry, Anne. Is there anything I can do? I could go and get something from the canteen."

"No thanks Jess. Let's go to the pub. I need to get out of this place and probably get drunk."

Jess looked quizzically at her friend "Are you sure?"

"No bloody point hanging around here is there? Let's go." And with that she put on her coat walked out of the door.

They went down the stairs in silence and Anne hardly acknowledged the wave from the porter as they went through the lodge. It was cold outside the hospital but the night was clear and Anne glanced up at the stars and started to cry again. She remembered Matt's letter – *I shall be up there somewhere.* Jess put her arms round her and they stood on the pavement huddled together until the crying stopped.

"Anne shall we just go back? I can get something for us to eat."

Anne shook her head and, wiping her eyes, said they should carry on to the pub. When they got there it was very crowded and smoky and Jess sat Anne down in a corner and worked her way through to the bar.

"Hallo Jess" the barman said "What's it to be?"

"Two gin and oranges and whatever you have on the go, to eat."

"Cottage pie is pretty good, so they say."

"Right two of those as soon as you can. We are over there."

She managed to get back to Anne who was looking slightly better and with a wry smile downed her drink in one.

"I'll get some more" she said and before Jess could stop her she was on her way to the bar.

When Anne came back Jess was chatting to another nurse and at first did not notice that she was carrying four glasses of gin and orange.

"Blimey Anne. Are you having a party" the other nurse asked.

"No – mind your own business. I intend to get drunk. The fucking Germans have killed my Matt, the most important person in my life. I think I deserve to get legless, don't you?"

"Oh God, I'm sorry Anne" the nurse replied and walked away.

"Steady on Anne. She was only asking. Anyway, let's toast Matt and the others. They've all gone now haven't they?"

"Yes, seven perfectly good blokes blown away for what? Because of some little German shit who thinks he's God. Christ, Jess what a bloody mess this all is. And you've lost two – poor old Stephen so brave just to keep going."

She had been talking quite loudly and was crying again now and people were beginning to look over to where they were sitting, so Jess was relieved when the food arrived.

"Come on Anne let's tuck in."

Anne looked up sullenly, her reddened eyes full of tears and dug her fork into the pie. She picked away at her food for a while and then banged her fork down.

"Let's have another bloody drink. I'm not that hungry."

"OK Anne. Let me finish this and I'll go and get us something" but before she could do anything Anne had stood up, determined to make her way to the bar. She walked a few paces and then collapsed on the floor amongst a crowd of servicemen one of whom bent down to pick her up.

"Come on lass" he said quietly "You don't look too good."

"Of course I don't. My fiancé has been killed and isn't coming back can't you understand? Doesn't anyone understand?"

She was shouting now and it took Jess quite some effort to guide Anne towards the door and out into the cold darkness where she vomited into the gutter and then sat down. She was sobbing again and Jess put her arm round her shoulders.

"Come on Anne. Let me help you back to the hospital. Maybe one of the docs could give you something to help you sleep. I'll go and see matron in the morning and explain. You should get off for a few days you know?"

Anne nodded in acquiescence and they made their way slowly down the road and back into the hospital. One of the porters came out when he saw them and offered to help but Anne waved him away with a "No, thanks".

Once they got to Anne's room Jess helped her on to the bed and covered her up, sitting with her for a while until she was asleep.

CHAPTER 14

Thursday 30th March 1944

It seemed almost impossible to think that Tucker had killed himself only a few days ago. Since then the crew had flown a couple of times with Simmons who, Clarke noticed with interest, once in the air, seemed to become a completely different character. He had got up early and walked over to the flight office. It was a fine, late March morning, cold but with white clouds scattering the pale blue sky. He was pretty sure they would be flying that night although it was very close to the period when the light from the moon would inconveniently show their whereabouts to the fighters. And then they were due some leave!

As Clarke walked into the office Simmons shouted through the open door.

"We're on tonight before you look Clarke. Get the others together for ten hundred hours so we can do an air test."

Clarke acknowledged the order and was just turning to go when Simmons shouted again. "For some reason best known to themselves they are offering you a commission – God knows why they do that for you Auxiliary types. You need to report to the Old Man at zero nine hundred hours – don't be late."

Clarke walked out and went over to the others still in the hut.

Thursday 30th March 1944

"On tonight. Air test ten hundred." The others looked up at the slight edge in his voice. Since Tucker's death Clarke had rather taken over as leader of the crew and they looked to him for help and support. Of course, he was older than all of them but nevertheless the relationship had changed and if he was honest with himself, he really quite enjoyed it.

He had some breakfast and then reported to Wing Commander Squires.

"Come in Clarke" he said briskly. "Sit down please. Clarke we are very happy with how you have been doing lately and Flight Lieutenant Simmons speaks highly of you."

Clarke stared incredulously at the thought of Simmons having anything but disdain for him.

Squires continued "We would like to offer you a commission – of course this would mean leaving the squadron but it would be worth your while in the long run. You're a university chap, aren't you?"

"Yes, sir. Sir, would I be able to think about this for a bit? I would be reluctant to leave the squadron and particularly the crew just now. We have completed ten trips, so maybe when we have finished."

"You know, I like your attitude Clarke. Very commendable. I have the discretion to make you up to Acting Pilot Officer for now – you can stay with us. How would that do?"

"Thank you, sir but I would like to stay as an NCO for now."

"Alright Clarke. Have it your own way but please think about the commission."

Clarke stood up and saluted before walking out of the office and back to the others who were still arriving at the canteen. Beavers walked over to him as he came in. They had become closer following Tucker's death which had understandably altered the dynamics of the group. Beavers was older too and had had a life outside the RAF so in many ways they had more in common.

"So, how's Happy Harry this morning?"

"Well since you ask Ray he seems in remarkably good form. Apparently, he had even recommended me for a commission!"

"Blimey. When do you leave?"

"No, I turned it down."

"What! You must be bloody mad. Commission would get you out of this lot, at least for a while. You might even live long enough to see the end of the war."

"Well I decided to say no. I mean I can't leave you lot to find your way home, can I?"

"I'll tell you something straight Nobby, if they ever give me an offer like that I'm bloody well out of here and you all will have to look after yourselves."

As they lined up for their breakfast Beavers regaled the story of how Clarke had turned down a certain ticket out of the squadron. Only Docker didn't seem to share Beavers view that he needed mentally certifying.

"Well good for you Nobby" he said in his Welsh singsong voice. "Good for you, for sticking with us. Would be easy enough to clear off out of here. Thanks, Nobby I'm glad you aren't going."

"Well I'm pleased to stay but thanks for saying that Taffy. In any case just imagine what bunch I could end up with after I got my stripe!"

They finished breakfast and walk over to the Crew Room to get ready for the air test. Simmons was already there getting into his gear and he walked over purposively to Clarke.

"Hear you turned it down?"

"Yes sir. I would like to stay with P-Peter for now but thank you for the recommendation."

"Oh, don't mention it. I only hope you don't live to regret not going," and to Clarke's surprise he patted him on the shoulder. "Let's get this out of the way as soon as we can."

The flight went well as usual and the crew gathered at three o'clock for the briefing which was led by Squires. The target was to be Nuremberg but he seemed to have something on his mind which made him uneasy as he spoke to the crews and, unusually, he gave some meteorological information himself. There was to be good cloud cover on the way over to the target, important because there would be nearly a full moon, and, as another bonus, the target would be cloud free.

"The C-in-C has called for a 'maximum effort' and the raid will remind the Germans that we mean business" Squires was saying, Clarke thought, rather unconvincingly. "Nuremberg is important for a number of reasons but especially as a transport hub and you will see the aiming point is close to the railway station."

The Navigation Officer indicated that they would form up over the North Sea before turning southeast towards Charleroi. But he drew gasps from the crews when he told them that from there, they were to fly in a straight line right through the heart of Germany until they turned down towards the target.

The Met man confirmed Squires's view that although there would be a bright moon, they would be shielded by cloud cover virtually all the way there. He then reminded them that the wind would probably be quite strong from the northwest.

After the briefing Simmons drew the men around him.

"OK chaps like it or not this could be a rough do – I feel it in my bones. So, let's get the kite and us up to scratch so we don't leave anything to chance. Clarke are you happy about the course and this wind issue they were talking about?"

"Yes, sir. It sounds a bit odd sending us in a straight line there doesn't it?"

"Like I said this all sounds tricky. Let's just deal with it. Who knows it might be scrubbed like last night."

Clarke was surprised about the change that had occurred in Simmons. He was a very different personality to the bastard that usually occupied the Flight Office.

They went through their routine checks and Clarke paid particular attention to the wind information he had received at briefing. As usual the trouble was that the wind changed strength and direction as they went along and his experience was that the information that they were given was almost invariably wrong.

Simmons called to make sure everyone was ready and then he and Barton got the engines started leaving P-Peter noisy and vibrating. They taxied out to the end of runway three-zero to wait for the green light. Simmons called that they were on their way and as the throttles were opened P-Peter started to roll down the runway shaking the objects on Clarke's desk so much that he had to cover them with his hands to keep them from dropping on the floor. Once the tail came up the whole aircraft snaked slightly from one side to another and as Clarke peered forward through the cockpit he could see the lights along the side of the runway steadily diminishing in number as they raced along. It almost looked as if they weren't going to make it and a lesser pilot might have panicked but Simmons smoothly pulled the Lancaster into the sky and as they climbed, the aircraft started a slow turn to the left.

"OK navigator where to first" Simmons crisp voice came over the intercom

"Steer one-two-zero, sir"

"One-two-zero but cut out the sir. I am your Skip now. Understood everyone?" Rear gunner can you see anything at all?"

"No sir, Skip. Black as the ace of spades out there."

"Time to the assembly point navigator?"

"About fifty minutes, Skip. Ray if you can see the ground let me know when we cross Southwold."

"Will do Nobby."

As they flew south, the sky got clearer and Beavers said that he could make out the coastline in front of them. They climbed steadily to their allocated altitude and as they approached the assembly point other aircraft came into view turning, as if on railway tracks, towards Belgium. Crossing the Channel it became obvious, to Simmons at least, that there had been a monumental foul up. The sky was cloudless and in the bright moonlight the aircraft around them were clearly visible. As they crossed the coast Simmons said "OK everyone, it is as clear as a bell up here so basically we are sitting ducks. Navigator how long to the turning point?"

"About thirty minutes Skip. But I am picking up that the wind has come around to the west and is quite strong. We need to adjust our heading or we will end up north of where we need to be."

"Skip, turn now. New heading zero-nine-zero. About ninety-five minutes to the next turning point unless the wind strength changes."

Simmons looked about and felt horrified at what he saw. Other aircraft could easily be picked out all around them and now, in addition, some freak meteorological quirk meant that the aircraft were all showing distinct contrails. It was almost as if they were shouting their presence to the Luftwaffe.

"Right navigator we are getting out of here. I am going to try going lower to see if we can stop these contrails. Otherwise it will be a turkey shoot."

Clarke had just acknowledged Simmons when the cockpit was lit up by an exploding aircraft and P-Peter rocked violently in the blast before Simmons had her under control.

"OK everyone there are fighters around" but almost before he had finished there was another explosion.

Clarke suddenly felt very scared. He could see the moon shining into the cockpit so he could only imagine how clearly the aircraft must appear to the fighters. He tried to concentrate on his maps and dials to take his mind off what was going on outside. Simmons calm voice came on.

"Any idea where we are Navigator? By my reckoning it is about an hour since we crossed the coast."

"My calculation is that we should be just south of the Ruhr, Skip." Clarke had trouble keeping his voice from trembling – he had never felt so frightened.

"OK. Bombaimer can you see anything apart from bombers being shot down?"

How does he keep himself so calm, Clarke wondered?

"There looks like quite a big river down there which we are flying over now."

"Rhine" Clarke replied. "Should be about an hour to our turning point."

"Yes, should be nice and quiet when we get there" Simmons replied evenly.

"Skip, lots of kites going down behind us."

"Thanks rear gunner. Just keep your eyes peeled for the fighter that wants us to join them."

"Yes Skip. Christ, corkscrew starboard."

Simmons stood P-Peter on its right wingtip and the dive took Clarke's stomach away and then he was pressed into his seat as they climbed back up again. Both gunners let fly but there was no cheer of triumph. But almost immediately Docker called for another corkscrew and this time it was more violent than the first and everything rolled off Clarke's desk and along the fuselage. Just as they came on to an even keel there was another explosion which shook the aircraft.

Clarke was not sure how much more of this he could stand – it was like flying into a hell and they still had some time before the target as well as the long trip back. He felt vomit come up into his mouth and he swallowed hard before managing to retrieve his bits and pieces just as Simmons reported that there were a lot of searchlights and flak up ahead.

"Everyone OK so far? Looks like it might be a bit rough in about quarter of an hour. Gunners keep a good look out now. No sleeping on the job!"

"Gawd Skip, chance would be a fine thing."

"Just checking Taffy."

After what seemed an eternity Clarke calculated that they were approaching the point at which they would turn south towards Nuremberg.

"About twenty-five minutes to the target Skip/"

"OK Navigator. It still looks as if the bloody fighters are everywhere so keep sharp everyone."

Gradually they got closer to the line of flak and Simmons had to dive a couple of times to avoid the searchlights which were pointing like multiple bright fingers into the sky. At last they were through and soon after, Beavers reported that there appeared to be cloud up ahead and that he was losing sight of the ground. So, they had come all this way and now the target was covered in cloud. There were some sky markers around but it was impossible to know which they should aim for.

"What do your numbers say Navigator?"

"By my reckoning we are about five minutes from the target."

"OK bombaimer you see that green marker over to the right. Let's go for that – it would fit best with the Navigator's plot."

He manoeuvred the aircraft towards the marker and Beavers led them in.

"Bombs gone, flash done"

Simmons banked the aircraft steeply away and into the cloud and dark.

"Course Navigator? Let's just get out of here as quickly as we can."

It was the first time Clarke had noticed any urgency in Simmons' voice.

"Two-seven-zero should work so long as we are over Nuremberg. This wind is quite strong."

About an hour after leaving the target Beavers reported that the cloud had disappeared and even though the moon had set, there was the awful realisation that even more bombers had been shot down, many still burning on the ground in front of them.

"Right, I am going down low. The bloody Krauts must think we've come out just to give them some gunnery practice. We must stand out like a black cat in a snow storm."

Never heard that one before Clarke smiled to himself. He felt slightly better and the griping pains in his guts had eased off. At least they were on their way home.

"Skip just going to take a star sight. At least one of the benefits of the clear sky."

"Good, Navigator let me know as soon as you can. I want to get us as low as possible without bumping into anything."

Once Clarke had worked out the numbers he was shocked to realise how far north they seemed to be and he went back to do a second sight.

"Skip, I've done a second sight because I didn't believe the first. It makes us about fifty miles north of where we should be and quite close to Mainz."

"Christ that's all we need. Give me a course from here then."

"Two-six-zero for an hour should make it safe. Well safer. And it's not exactly flat round here though."

"OK I'm coming down to 2000 feet. Bombaimer keep your eyes open and shout if you see anything hard up front that we might bump in to. Course in an hour Navigator?"

"Three-one-five"

They sped along across the countryside and eventually Beavers reported that he could see the coast ahead. Apart from some sporadic flak they had been unscathed and once over the sea Simmons asked for the course back to East Kirkby and home. They were still alive.

As usual, Clarke was struck by the extraordinary silence once the engines had been shut down. He looked across at Smith who appeared just to be staring ahead.

"You OK Phil?"

Looking as if he was just coming out of a daze Smith nodded his head and wearily gave a thumbs up. Clarke started to clear up his charts and all the bits and pieces which had been scattered over the floor. He was surprised that Simmons had not moved and he walked forward to touch his arm.

"You OK sir?"

"Yes, thank you, Clarke. That was a bit of a run wasn't it? God knows what the losses will be tonight. Come on everyone let's go and meet the clever people."

The crew gradually got themselves together and jumped down from the back of the aircraft. Most of them lit up taking a deep drag as if their lives depended on it. The truck came along to take them for debriefing and they threw themselves in the back.

"Well done chaps" Simmons said. "That was a pretty shaky do. Let's meet down the Red Lion tonight. You are all due some leave, aren't you?"

"Yes, I think so" Clarke replied but he was almost too tired to answer "A bit of a bash would be good, sir."

They threaded their way into the debrief room but one look at the Returns Board told them all they needed to know.

"We saw burning aircraft littering the ground from France to the target. The sky was clear going there and there was thick cloud over the target. It was a fiasco"

Simmons was speaking quietly but the anger in his voice was clear. The Intelligence Officer kept writing and did not lift his eyes from his paper.

"How many missing from here?"

"Um, so far there are three."

"What do you mean – so far?"

"Some haven't called in yet. They may have landed elsewhere."

Simmons suddenly stood up. Come on chaps let's go and get some breakfast. There won't be a queue!"

"Bet you wished you'd taken that commission now?" Simmons said as they walked over to the canteen.

"Not really, sir, but it looked a pretty bad night."

"Bad. It was a bloody disaster."

The crew ate largely in silence too tired and too troubled to speak. Eventually Simmons left, reminding them that they would meet later in the pub. After he had left, Charlie Barton was the first to speak.

"Bloody hell, talk about Jekyll and Hyde. He was a different bloke, like we're all chums together. Seemed a bloody good pilot too – never looked like he was going throw the towel in, not like poor old Tucker."

"Well flying is the thing he likes. Not built for pen-pushing I suppose."

"Yeh, but Nobby, to change so much?"

"Well it happens."

"Not sure he will come to the pub" Beavers added, "And once we are not his crew anymore it will be back to the old days you see if it isn't. A bastard is always a bastard in my books. In any case I'm off to get some sleep."

Clarke walked away from the group. He badly needed to get out of the camp and away from everyone else. He had never felt such fear as he had last night. It was as if the world had gone mad sending them up there in the first place – he was sure that without Simmons they would all be dead. For the first time in his life he had literally felt that every moment was his last. He had even wet himself at one point. He walked past the guardroom and onto the road. There were some woods nearby and he strode towards them keen to get there before anyone saw him and offered to join him. He desperately needed to be alone.

The sky showed clearly through the winter-bare branches of the trees and the wind stirred some of the nearby evergreens. The only other sound he could hear now were the chaffinches proclaiming the coming of Spring and the occasional aircraft running up its engines and even that got less, the further he walked into the wood and away from the airfield. Eventually he came to a fallen tree trunk and he sat down heavily. The ringing in his ears from the hours in the aircraft was beginning to lessen and up until then he had just not realised how tired he was but now he felt completely exhausted. Thank God they had some leave. He was sure that he would not have been able to go up again tonight if they were ordered. Maybe he should have taken up the offer of a commission after all. He would be packing his bags now.

He put his head in his hands and to his surprise he started to cry. He still could not come to terms with what had happened and how someone had so clearly screwed up. Everyone knew the phases of the bloody moon for God's sake. The Arabs had worked that out centuries ago. He was getting angry, something which rarely happened. The frustrating thing was that there was no one who he could get angry with and, in any case, who was responsible? The RAF brass, Simmons, the crew, Hitler? Even Simmons had probably got over his rage and had reverted to type. No. Hitler was the one. It was all his fault they were here in any case. He had killed all those chaps last night. Suddenly he felt real fury at Germans in general. I'll kill as many of the bastards as possible, he thought.

Clarke sat for a while until he realised he was getting cold and he started to walk back. He had never felt like this before. In fact, he had never felt animosity in general to Germans in the past and the fact he did now, troubled him. He needed a break. Perhaps he would try and see if Anne was around. He hadn't spoken to her for a while and it would be good just to hear her voice. Perhaps she had had some news about Matt – probably bad he thought to himself as he crossed the road and back into the camp.

Author's note: this was one of the most disastrous raids of the war – 95 bombers were listed destroyed on the raid – 13.1 % of the original force. A further 13 were lost on diversionary raids and secret missions. The total loss of aircrew was 723, 545 of whom were killed.

CHAPTER 15

Saturday 1st April 1944

Clarke woke up with a distinctly sore head, collected at the Red Lion the night before. Against the odds Simmons had turned up and, along with some of the surviving crews, they had made quite a night of it. He had not managed to contact Anne the previous day when he got back from his walk because she was still working, and then as soon as he had gone to his bed, he fell asleep only to be woken by the others when they were on their way down to the pub in the evening.

He glanced at his watch and saw that it was nine o'clock and the rest of the hut was empty. He got up, washed and shaved before he remembered they were on leave and that he needed to get out of the place before some bright spark suggested he might like to do another trip that night as an "odd bod". He got his kit together and throwing everything into the back of his car, drove out of the camp and on his way to where, he wasn't sure. He had decided to call at the hospital first to see if Anne was around and then probably head off to his parents for a few days hiking through the countryside around their home. The morning was bright with a blue sky and fluffy white clouds and there felt, at last, to be some heat in the sun.

The lanes were remarkably empty as he drove along and as he got further and further from the airfield, he began to feel a weight being lifted from his shoulders and it seemed in no time at all that he was outside the hospital. He asked at the Porters' lodge whether Anne was around and when he was told that she was not, he remembered about her friend Jess and asked if she was free. After a while the porter came out to say that Jess was on her way down.

"Hallo. It's Nobby isn't it? Anne has spoken about you. I think she calls you John?"

"Jess, thanks for coming down. I'm just starting some leave and I thought I would see if Anne was here. Obviously, she's not."

"No, she went back to her parents this morning. She heard a few days ago that Matt's body had been found and so she took some compassionate leave – only got it after a struggle with matron too."

Clarke's head dropped when he heard. Having escaped from all that had happened in the last twenty-four hours, the fact that Matt was dead brought everything flooding back to him.

"You OK Nobby?" Jess asked "You look terrible. Do you want to come in for a cup of tea?"

"Sorry Jess. We have had a pretty bad time of it and now this. How did Anne take it?"

"Well, as you might expect I suppose. They should have been married for a couple of months by now you know? On the other hand, knowing is probably better than not. She was very upset by wondering what had happened to him. At least she knows now. I think she was going to go up and see Matt's parents sometime. Perhaps that will bring things to a close, although I don't know – she and Matt were very close and so much in love. Such a shame. What are you doing now, for your leave I mean?"

"Oh, catch up with my parents then maybe spend a couple of days walking somewhere – get out in the open."

"Anne said you were very good at birds"

"Oh, she did, did she? Well certainly the feathered ones. Thanks for letting me know about things Jess. Can you tell her I called? When does she get back from leave?"

"Next Wednesday, I think."

"Tell her I will try and call her on Wednesday night. Maybe we can all go out for a drink?"

"OK I'll let her know. Maybe see you next week" and with that Jess turned and walked back into the hospital.

Clarke got back in the car. He suddenly felt very tired and he sat for a while gathering his thoughts before starting the car. He momentarily wondered about going back to ask Jess where Anne's parents lived – he thought that it was somewhere in Worcester – but then rejected the idea. She may not want to see him in any case and it could be embarrassing for her in front of her parents. No, he better head off to his parents in Berkshire – bloody long drive at the best of times and with that he put the MG into gear and set off.

It was late by the time he arrived at his parent's house just outside Newbury. He put his arms around his mother as she kissed him but as he went over to shake his father's hand he was shocked by his appearance. He had become stooped, looked unwell and had certainly seemed to have aged since they had last met three months ago.

"John you look very weary and I am sure that you have lost weight."

"It's alright, mother. It was a long drive and they are working us hard. Shall be as right as ninepence after a nice cup of tea and a good night's sleep. You look well though. Any news from Richard?" When Clarke last heard he was in North Africa.

"Not for a while, dear. We are not sure even where he is although we think he maybe in Italy now." She added some sugar to the tea and handed him the cup. "Have you been flying very much, dear?"

"Yes, quite a bit really. They are a good group of chaps and we all get on pretty well." He avoided saying anything about Tucker having killed himself or the terrors of the last trip. He noticed his father had gone to sleep in his chair and nodded towards him. His mother signalled for them to leave the room and she only spoke once they were settled in the kitchen.

"He's not well John and has been off work for a month now. The doctor thinks it's cancer although he's not sure where. He reckons father has only a few months to live. That's terrible dear, isn't it? I haven't written to tell you because you have enough to worry about. I did write to Richard last week but there is nothing any of us can do."

"Has he seen a specialist, mother? I could probably arrange for someone in Manchester to see him."

"He went up to Oxford to see someone the doctor recommended but they only gave the same opinion."

Clarke felt a dreadful sadness. His father was a primary school teacher, and not a very well paid one at that, and yet he had seen both him and Richard through university. He had been a good father doing whatever he could for the family usually at some sacrifice to himself. Now here he was just fifty-five years old and dying. Christ what a world. There was even death at home.

"Mother I think I will turn in. I feel whacked."

"But you haven't had anything to eat yet dear. Let me make you a sandwich at least."

"No, I'll take my cuppa up to bed and I am sure I will feel fine by the morning." He went back into the lounge to where his father was sleeping and bent over and kissed his forehead. He had to get to his room before he broke down and he quickly went up the stairs and quietly shut his door. He slumped down on the bed and put his head in his hands and let the tears run down onto his hands. After a while he felt a bit better and even though his tea was cold he gulped it down, undressed and got into bed. His mother had put a hot water bottle in and he pulled the covers up and tried to warm up. Sleep did not come immediately as all the things that had happened in the last few weeks swirled around in his mind. Tucker's death, that terrible flight with Simmons, Matt's body being found and now his father's fatal illness. He was almost too exhausted to think straight but gradually sleep crept over him.

CHAPTER 16

Sunday 2nd April 1944

It was nearly eleven o'clock by the time Clarke woke up and he lay in his bed for a while, just trying to gather his thoughts. His father's illness was the most upsetting thing, probably because it had come as something of a shock – he had been fine when Clarke had last seen him. Then there was Anne. How to deal with that? He had become very fond of her even though they had hardly had a chance to be together and even if they had, there was always the uncertainty about Matt in the background. Well that had changed now that Matt's body had been found although to what extent that would have any influence on their relationship remained to be seen. Then there was the wretched war. Simmons was just filling in after Tucker's death and sooner or later they would get a new pilot, probably someone just out of flying school, wet behind the ears and not quite sure where the bloody levers were!

It would be funny if it wasn't so serious. Clarke got out of bed and went down the hall to the bathroom. It was quite a while since he had had a nice hot bath and it was a luxurious feeling as he lowered himself into the water. His mother had heard him moving about and brought him a steaming cup of tea.

"Father wondered if you would like to go to the pub for a drink before lunch?" she asked.

"Tell him I will be down soon. Love to have a beer with him."

His father was waiting in the hall when Clarke came down feeling refreshed after his bath.

"Shall we take the car father, or will we walk?"

"It's only the Stag we are going to lad. Walk will do us good" and with that he moved towards the front door. His mother had come out of the kitchen and she smiled and waved at Clarke as he went out "Lunch at one o'clock, dear. Don't forget."

Clarke smiled too. Lunch had been at one o'clock as long as he could remember.

Clarke and his father walked slowly down the road.

"Mother told you the problem?"

"Yes father. I'm sorry to hear about things. You saw a specialist I hear?"

"Bloody waste of time. Think the GP knew more than he did."

The pub was quite crowded and Clarke settled his father in one of the benches outside.

"Father let me go and get the beers. The usual I suppose? Why don't you sit here? It's quite warm in the sun."

Clarke went into the Stag and his uniform had an immediate effect and a path opened up between the crowd jostling around the bar.

"What would you like young man?" the barman asked. "Hey, you're Tommy Clarke's boy, aren't you?"

"Yes, that's right. Just home for a spot of leave. We'll have a pint of bitter and a mild and bitter with a small whisky please."

Clarke took the drinks out and sat by his father.

"Do you want to see someone else? There are a few chaps in Manchester I could recommend who know a thing or two."

"Thanks John but I don't think so. The doc said it was my prostate and it's spread everywhere. Pretty sore when I walk about, I must say, but he gave me some painkillers. I'll be alright for a while. Bit worried about your mother that's the only thing. I haven't told her what's going on you know? Only make things worse. What with you and Richard fighting for King and country as well. They say the war maybe all over soon now. Talk of an invasion or something – that could fix it?"

"Well don't worry about us father, I'm alright and I'm sure Richard is too."

"You look pretty worn out lad. Is it bad? Don't know how you do it night after night. The reports on the radio always sound grim. *Last night our bombers undertook a successful raid somewhere in Krautland but several of our aircraft failed to return.* Bloody Nazis, I hate them. All the trouble they've caused."

"Well it certainly has its moments, father. But we are all in the same boat. Look how terrible it was for Richard when he had to battle his way back from Dunkirk in 1940. And for you at Passchendaele in '17 for that matter?"

His father smiled wanly and Clarke noticed for the first time the yellowish tinge of his skin and that he had clearly lost a lot of weight very quickly.

"Do you want another one father or shall we get back? You know what mother is like if we get back late for lunch."

"No, I think one is enough. Let's walk back. I'm a bit slower going back." He levered himself up from the seat and leant on his stick for a while apparently trying to get his breath.

"You OK father?"

"Yes, fine just need to take things more slowly these days, old lad. Bit different from those days when the three of us used to walk for miles bird watching" he smiled. "Tell me, have you got another lady friend after that last one. What was her name again, Sylvia wasn't it? Didn't like her much."

"No, not really. There is a nurse who I have met a couple of times. Her fiancé's aircraft was shot down before Christmas and he was missing for a while and now they have found his body. I haven't seen her for a while but she was very upset by the whole thing."

"Well my advice is that you should get yourself a good woman. If you were really lucky you could get someone like your mother" and he winked at Clarke as they went through the door.

"Home mother" he called out "And we are hungry, isn't that right John?"

Clarke and his father sat down around the table whilst his mother brought in lunch.

"Bit of pork, John. The local farmer has been very good to us. Some fresh veg as well. What's your food like? I hope they feed you well but looking at you it doesn't look like they are doing a very good job. Good mind to write to your commanding officer."

She laughed but Clarke reckoned there would be every chance that she wouldn't think twice about carrying out her threat!

"Grub's not too bad mother but sometimes we don't get much time to eat it!" Truth was most of them couldn't force the food down because they were so fearful about what was in front of them nearly every night. He looked across the table and noticed that his father had only eaten a few mouthfuls and that he was picking at the food on his plate.

"You OK father? Pork's lovely isn't it? Mother is such a great cook."

"Yes, it's fine. I just don't feel too hungry all of a sudden. I'll have another glass of wine though."

"You be steady with your drinking dear especially at lunchtime. You know it only gives you a headache. I'm not sure that stuff you brewed up last year is really all that good for you." She turned and grimaced at Clarke.

The meal ended in silence and Clarke's father moved away from the table, settled down in his favourite old chair and in moments was asleep.

Clarke and his mother cleared the table and started the washing up,

"What are you going to do whilst you are here, dear?"

"I thought I would do some walking. I need to get out in the fresh air and away from aeroplanes and the RAF" he laughed. "Also need to do some thinking. I have met this lovely nurse although it is not straightforward – her fiancé was killed just before Christmas."

"Oh dear, oh dear" his mother sighed. "Poor thing. Where does she live?"

"She works in Lincoln but her parents are in Worcester – she's there now in fact. In any case I suspect she doesn't want to get into another relationship so soon. But I could wait, I really wouldn't mind waiting, mother. She is pretty smashing!"

"Well dear these things have a habit of working themselves out that's what I always say. When will you leave to go walking? It would be nice if you could stay tonight."

"Yes, I will mother. I think it is quite difficult to find anywhere to go at the moment. When I was driving down there seemed to be loads of restricted areas and anywhere on the coast will be completely out of bounds from what I hear."

"Well I'm sure you will find somewhere and your uniform will open some doors?" she smiled. "We are very proud of you, you know dear. But we worry so about both you and Richard" and suddenly her head dropped and she started to cry. "Sorry dear, it just seems that everything is so difficult at the moment and what with your father as well." She was sobbing now and Clarke put his arms round her.

"Come on old thing" he said quietly. "Richard and I will be OK and father seems comfortable just now. You know, I am going to try and speak to someone I know in Manchester to see if they have any ideas. While there's life there's hope isn't there?"

His mother moved away and wiped her eyes. Clarke felt very mournful – he had never known his mother cry, at least not in front of anyone else and it made him realise what a dreadful burden she was under.

"Mother, I have changed my mind. I think I will just stay around here. I can go for walks during the day but I want to be with you and father as much as possible."

"Thank you dear, you have no idea what that means to both of us," and with that she lifted her head and kissed him on the cheek.

John went up to his room and sat down on his bed. For the first time in his life he felt completely lost. It was a struggle enough to keep going what with the flying and the war, but now he saw that his parents' lives were on the verge of falling apart. It was almost too much to bear. He swung his legs up on the bed and curled up and before he knew it, he was asleep.

It was almost dark when he awoke to hear his mother calling up to see if he would like some tea. He felt a bit better for his sleep and, after coming downstairs, he discovered one his father's maps which he used to plan tomorrow's walk, trying to decide a good area and one likely to be free of the military.

Their village of Leckhampstead was well placed in the Berkshire downs and Clarke reckoned that he would set out the next day to walk over the hills to Lambourne. He decided that he would stay with his parents until returning to East Kirkby on Thursday and he would telephone Anne on Wednesday. If he couldn't speak to her then, he would call into the hospital on his way back to try and see her. The present situation at home had convinced him that he needed to get on with his own life, in spite of the war. Leave it too long and you could lose everything –

look at his father and mother, look at the chaps in the squadron. Here one minute gone the next. No, he had to get going.

* * *

For all his resolve to get out of the house and go walking, both Monday and Tuesday turned out to be dreadful days, with strong winds and rain on Monday which turned to snow and sleet on Tuesday. In a way Clarke was not too bothered – it gave him time to talk to his mother and to help his father struggle down to the Stag for their daily beer. Worrying about his parents helped him forget about the squadron for a while and being there gave his mother some much needed support and him an opportunity to fix some of the repairs around the house which had been rather neglected. Although his father had always been a practical man, his illness had obviously prevented him from doing very much for quite a while and only went to confirm that he had, in fact, been feeling ill for many months.

Wednesday, however, dawned clear and bright and, with a sprinkling of snow on the Downs, it looked very beautiful outside. Clarke got on his hiking boots and some warm clothing and, with a flask of tea and sandwiches from his mother packed into his knapsack, he set out.

He walked south along the main road about a mile before turning right down Manor Lane and eventually on to Hangman Stone Lane, a route he had often been along with his father when he and Richard were teenagers. It was a bit of a ritual, but after Sunday lunch the three of them went out, no matter the weather, leaving mother behind to do the clearing up. His father had always been a keen bird watcher and had taught both of his boys a lot, not only about ornithology but also how to read the countryside. He smiled as he thought how impressed Anne had been about his knowledge on birds. *Knew it would come in useful sometime, he thought.* As he passed some woods on his left the sounds of the chaffinches reminded him that Spring had arrived and their song followed him through the still, cold air as the road climbed Buckham Hill. He paused at the top to take in the breathtaking view of the Lambourne Downs, wearing a covering of snow, in front of him and, high above, a red kite wheeling around in the still cold air. He started off down the hill before picking up the path which climbed steadily up onto the Downs and, reaching the top, turned around to look back from where he had come. It was a gin-clear day and he could see the village of Peasemore over to the east and follow the course of the Lambourne River down to Newbury in the south east and the Chilterns in the distance. The view was beautiful but it was the silence which really astonished him. At last he was away from everyone and everything, and the war could have been on another planet for all he was concerned. He turned and continued to walk the remaining few miles into Lambourne for a beer and a well-earned sandwich.

It was six o'clock by the time Clarke got home. He felt tired but exhilarated by his walk of almost twenty miles. The scenery had been spectacular and he had managed, all be it briefly, to escape in his mind from all the problems that surrounded him.

"We were going to have supper about seven" his mother said as he got in. "There's plenty of hot water if you want a bath."

"Righto mother just going to make a quick phone call," and with this he went to the hall. He got through to the hospital almost immediately and one of the porters said he would try the telephone on Anne's corridor.

A voice answered and Clarke asked for Anne but was told that although she was in the hospital, she had just started her night duty shift. Clarke considered pulling the same stunt as last time and pretend to be a doctor but then thought better of it and asked if a note could be left to say he had rung and that he would try and catch up with her the next day. He was disappointed but went upstairs to have his bath cheered by the thought that perhaps he would have better luck next time. He would need to leave his parents early so he could get to Lincoln before she started work and, in any case, he could always ring during the day.

Supper was a rather quiet affair. His father didn't look at all well and once again picked around at his food and his mother was clearly upset at the thought of Clarke leaving.

"When will you be flying again John?".

"On operations do you mean, father? Might be a week or so I would think because there's too much moonlight for raids just now. But we don't get much spare time because they send us out practicing all the time

Clarke's mother looked relieved. "Could you not stay with us a bit longer then, dear?"

"No mother I'm afraid not. We have work to do pretty well all the time, you know. It's not just flying every night."

"Well you make sure that you look after yourself and get enough to eat. I'm going to pack you up some food."

Clarke smiled – his mother had always worried about him and Richard getting enough food where ever they were. He thought that it was a good job he did not work close to home because he would be quite sure that she would be up at the guardhouse every week with a food parcel of some sort.

They finished supper and Clarke's father sat in his usual chair whilst Clarke helped his mother clear the table. He was about to start the washing up when his mother told him to go and sit with his father.

"It's been good seeing you John. I know it has meant a lot to your mother. It's hard for her with both you and Richard away – well, me too. It's not good for you chaps is it? There is stuff in the papers today about that Nuremberg raid. Were you on that one? Apparently quite a few planes brought down?"

"You shouldn't believe everything you read in the papers, father, you know that."

"Still lad, all the same it sounds pretty dangerous to me."

"I think I would rather do that, than what you did. Standing in front of thirty children everyday sounds risky to me."

They both laughed and then Clarke's father leant over towards him.

"John, I don't have much longer you know. Maybe a month or so at best that's what the specialist said. Of course, I haven't told your mother. If there is any way you can get through to Richard, I would feel happier but God knows where he is. And if you can get back here before I'm a goner that would be nice too. Maybe a last pint at the Stag eh? I'm going to go off to bed now. Mother said you were leaving early in the morning so probably won't see you tomorrow – well possibly never again" he added with a wry smile.

Clarke stood up and put his arms round his father trying not to show how upset he felt. They shook hands and after his father was gone, he sat down and put his head in his hands and sobbed.

CHAPTER 17

Thursday 6ᵗʰ April 1944

Clarke was out of bed by six o'clock and gathered his few belongings together before going down stairs to where his mother was preparing some breakfast.

"You need something inside you before you drive all that way, dear. Managed to scrounge some bacon from the butcher and the hens are laying well just now."

"Thanks mother. It is a pretty long trip – the roads seem so busy at the moment."

He ate in silence whilst his mother made herself busy with brewing tea and preparing some toast.

"I don't know why you took up flying, John. Scares me to death it does, thinking of you up there."

"Oh, it's not too bad mother. You shouldn't worry so. Hopefully I can get some more leave soon and I will come down and see you both again. Maybe bring a girlfriend next time?"

"Well it would be lovely to see you on your own or with someone, you know that."

"Must get going mother. It's been a lovely few days. I will write to you when I get back and you let me know how father gets along."

He walked out to the car and put his things on the passenger seat, together with the inevitable sandwiches from his mother.

It was a beautiful morning with blue sky and the sun just beginning to peek over the hills. The early morning light on the freshly budding trees look exquisite and Clarke wished he could just go off walking again and forget the war.

The engine started first time and as he looked up to wave to his mother, he noticed that his father had come to the bedroom window to see him off. He slipped the car into gear and drove slowly down the road away from the house until past a rather sleepy Peasemore village, after which he pulled the car over to the side of the lane. He suddenly felt very sad and his father appearing at the window as he was leaving touched him deeply and, in his heart, he knew that he would probably never see him alive again. He sat for a few minutes trying to get his thoughts together before driving off. The road lay across to East Ilsley and then he turned north towards Oxford and eventually, Lincoln. For once the roads seemed quiet and uncluttered with the usual military traffic and, after all the sadness at home, he felt strangely exhilarated as he drove along, his mood helped by the possibility of speaking to or, still better, seeing Anne. He had got to just outside Leicester by midday and he found a suitable looking pub for a beer and lunch. He had already eaten his mother's sandwiches and was feeling hungry again and besides he reckoned that this might be a good time to try ringing Anne.

The pint of beer went down well, the sun was now really quite warm and he was pleased to be able to sit outside to have his meal, a meat pie, which proved delicious. He went back into the pub to get a second pint and asked the barman the whereabouts of the phone.

"We don't have one of them in the bar. But you come around here young man and use ours. Be our pleasure."

Clarke thanked the man and asked the operator to get the hospital number. He felt both excited and anxious as the number rang to be answered by one of the porters.

"Yes, she is in sir. I'll try the corridor number to see if anyone can find her. Wait a minute."

Clarke suddenly felt quite nervous about speaking to Anne. Maybe she wouldn't want to talk to him after all. Then the phone was picked up.

"Hallo" Anne said. Who is this?"

"Anne it's me, John, Nobby Clarke. I was sorry to hear about Matt. Jess told me last week when I popped in to see if you were around."

"Thanks John. In a way it's best to know, I think. Where are you in any case?"

"I'm on my way back from my parents. They live just outside Newbury. I have had a few days off and it was good to see them again. I wondered if there was any chance we could meet if you feel up to it? I am still on leave so we could meet tomorrow"

"John, everything feels pretty raw just now. I know it's been nearly four months since Matt was lost but I was just hanging on to the hope that he was still alive and now that hope has gone."

"Yes, I realise must be very hard but maybe we could meet for lunch? I think it will be the last time that I will be able to get away for a few weeks. It would be so good to get together."

"Well I am working nights for the next fortnight so lunch would be possible. I agree it would be nice to meet but I need to warn you that I am not great company at the moment."

"I understand, Anne, really. To be honest I'm not feeling that jolly either. Our last trip was a nightmare and when I went home I found that my father is dying of cancer."

"Oh John, I'm sorry to hear that. Well perhaps we could try and cheer each other up a bit. Yes, let's meet for lunch tomorrow then. Would about half past twelve be OK? When will you get back tonight?"

"Should be back by six o'clock I reckon if the roads stay OK. See you tomorrow. If there is a problem when I get back to the camp, I will let you know. Bye for now."

Clarke felt quite flustered when he had finished speaking and he decided to have a further pint by way of celebration. She hadn't told him to go to hell and they had a lunch date for tomorrow. Altogether a good result.

The rest of the drive was uneventful if tedious and he arrived back at East Kirkby by about eight o'clock. Everyone was back except Bob Docker who had apparently missed his train from Cardiff. No one seemed to know who the new pilot was which probably meant he was an officer and not billeted with the sergeants.

"Let's get down to the Red Lion and see what the buzz is" Phil Smith suggested and all agreed that would be a good plan. It was never wise to hang around when you were on leave in case the CO came looking for volunteers.

The pub was crowded when they got down there and it took a while to get a beer. As usual the din made hearing any serious conversation impossible and the fug in the bar made seeing who was there pretty difficult too.

Eventually Clarke managed to find Fred Elliott, who had been on his navigators' course, and who had not been away on leave.

"How's it going Fred?"

"Bloody awful Nobby. How long have you lot been off then?"

"Just a week. We left after Nuremberg."

"Christ what a mess that was. It sounds like at least a hundred bombers were lost one way or another. Mind we haven't done anything this week. Licking our wounds a bit. You met your new jockey yet? Looks about eighteen but rumour has it that he's already got a DFC."

"God, he could be one of those gung-ho merchants. Where did he come from?"

"Well Nobby it seems that he started flying Hurricanes towards the end of the Battle of Britain."

"Hope he doesn't start throwing the Lanc around like it was a fighter!" Clarke smiled. "I'm off to my scratcher. Spent all day driving up from my parents and feel I need to get my head down. See you later."

CHAPTER 18

Friday 7th April 1944

Clarke was in no hurry to get out of bed and he reckoned it would be sometime before he would have the luxury of another lie-in. Eventually he got up and went down to the Flight Office to check the notice board. He was surprised to see a notice for '*The crew of P-Peter to meet Flying Officer Paul Cowan this evening in the Red Lion at 1700 hours.*' He crept out of the office before he could be nabbed by Simmons for some duty or other and went over to the canteen to find the others.

"Have you seen the noticeboard? Our new driver wants to meet us."

"Well I hope he's bloody buying the drinks" scowled Barton. "I'd just as rather still be on leave. Any case have you seen him yet Nobby? Looks really young."

"What like me you mean?" Nobby replied.

"No, Christ you're bloody ancient" Barton smiled.

"Well in any case I am out of here on a lunch date although I guess I will be back by five!"

"Who's this then Nobby. When did you have time to pull a bird?"

"She's not a bird – she's a lady."

"Yeh that's what they all say" Beavers joined in. "I thought I was going to get lucky on leave but she said she couldn't because of her old man. Bloody fine excuse that was. And it cost me a couple of glasses of wine too!"

"Last of the big spenders, that's you Ray. Maybe three glasses would have done it" and they all laughed.

"Seriously though do we know anything about Cowan?" Clarke asked. "I got talking to a guy I knew in the pub last night who said that he had been a fighter pilot."

"Yes, I heard that too," Beavers said. "It sounds like he was flying just at the end of 1940 and then was posted to North Africa and then Italy so he has been around a bit. And since he has survived this far maybe he's good or lucky or, hopefully, both."

Clarke went back to the hut to smarten himself up before meeting Anne. As he left the base several aeroplanes were taking off and landing and he was especially pleased not to be involved. The drive into town was easy and it was a beautiful day with fluffy white clouds and a clear blue sky.

He arrived at Lyons corner house a bit before the time they'd agreed to meet. He felt like a kid on his first date as he went into the restaurant and found a free table.

"My friend will be joining me soon," he said to the waitress. "I would like a glass of white wine if that's possible."

She brought him the wine and he sat sipping it although he would probably have rather gulped it down. He saw Anne coming down the street. She was wearing a coat against the slightly chill April wind but he was pleased to see that she had let her hair down. He stood up as she came into the restaurant and he kissed her on both cheeks as she sat down.

"How are you Anne? It must all be rather difficult?"

"Oh, not too bad. I am going up to Matt's parents this weekend. They are having a memorial service for him at their local church." She looked sadly at Clarke. "Maybe this will help to put an end to things although I will always love him you know?" As she turned her face to look out of the window, Clarke saw her tears running down her face and he reached across the table to take her hand.

"Would you like to go somewhere else Anne? We could just walk if you like."

"No, no I'll be fine, thank you. I'm quite hungry, actually. Haven't really eaten properly for a while. Let's stay."

They ordered the dish of the day, chicken pie, had some more wine and talked about the trip to her parents.

"Scrap is doing well. Seems to have been delighted to take up residence," she smiled wanly. "You said that you were at your parents. They must have been relieved to see you? Sorry to hear about your father though. Had you any idea?"

"No, complete surprise. Of course, mother would never have told me in any case – she said she thought I had enough on my plate. Talking of which you seemed to have cleared yours."

"Yes, it was lovely. Good to have the chance to talk too. What have you got to do when you get back from leave?"

"Well the first thing is this evening when we meet our new pilot."

Anne tensed slightly. "What happened to your first one then?"

"Oh, he was transferred. He didn't quite fit in" Clarke lied to avoid discussing what really happened to Tucker. "The new chap has been flying quite a bit. Was a fighter pilot at some stage apparently, so at least he should know what he is doing."

They finished their meal, Clarke settled the bill and they left the restaurant and went for a walk in the nearby park. It was a lovely afternoon and the sunshine was quite warm.

"Can we do this again?" Clarke asked. "It would be nice if we could."

"Of course, John. It has been a real help to be able to talk about things and I would love to meet up. I think I shall feel a bit better after the weekend."

"Shall I call you sometime next week then? Are you still on nights?"

"Until Friday week. But I will be working over the next weekend. Try ringing me after about seven o'clock if you can."

"Do you want a ride back to the hospital Anne?"

"No thanks John. I'll walk if you don't mind. You take care and I look forward to hearing from you."

She kissed him on his cheek and walked away without turning back and Clarke made his way back to the car. He was happy that Anne had seemed keen to see him again. Of course, it was going to be a difficult time but he felt elated at the thought that they would meet again. He drove the car quickly back to the camp and obviously looked very pleased with himself when he got into the billet.

"Blimey Nobby, looks like you had a good lunch. What's her name then? What did you have for pudding?"

"Actually, bread and butter pudding. And she's called Anne."

"I've never heard it called bread and butter pudding before have you Charlie?"

"No Phil. Called a lot of things but not that." They all laughed and got ready to go down to the Red Lion.

Flying Officer Cowan was propping up the bar when they arrived and there were six pints already set up for them. Cowan was just under six feet in height, well built with a generous moustache and grey-green, genial eyes. He had striking ginger hair and a ruddy complexion and, greeting them with a cheery smile, Clarke warmed to him immediately. Everyone introduced themselves and then Cowan asked them what they had been up to over the time they had been at East Kirkby before he explained what he had been doing before he got there.

He had joined the RAF as a sergeant- pilot and he confirmed that he had started flying Hurricanes right at the end of the Battle of Britain in October 1940. He had two kills then and at the end of the year had been transferred to the Middle East and he had been there until after El Alamein. He requested transfer to Bomber command and had flown Hampdens and Whitleys until the middle of 1943 when he had been offered a commission. And now here he was at East Kirkby.

"Blimey sir" Barton ventured "Makes what we've done look pretty pathetic – eleven trips is all we've done so far."

"Well I've been at it a bit longer. And you have seen some of the toughest fighting after all. Let's have another round. Oh, and incidentally call me Paul at least when we are meeting like this. I still don't really feel like an officer."

Eventually the evening drew to a close and the crew made their way back to the camp and Cowan and Clarke walked together.

"You seem a bit out of place here, old boy, if you don't mind me saying?" Cowan said. "What did you do before joining up?"

"I was a physiologist actually. Manchester University."

"Ah that explains it. I had a place in London to read Engineering but decided to do my bit first. How's it been? Really, I mean. What happened to your pilot?"

"Blew his brains out. Couldn't cope I think. Good chap, good pilot actually. We've had some adventures but then so have many others. Our last trip, Nuremberg, was a complete, bloody, shambles. Simmons was our pilot. To be honest without him I don't think we would be here. But then you must have seen some things yourself?"

"Yes, one or two. The Hampdens were pretty slow and not very effective and I was glad to be finished with them. The Lanc's a great aircraft you know. When you compare it with the others there's no match. Looking forward to flying with you all in fact."

Clarke looked at this large, jolly man. Here was a completely different attitude. How could anyone actually look forward to what they did night after night?

"See you in the morning Nobby. We need to take the old kite up tomorrow sometime. Would you be good enough to get the ground crew sorted out? Shall we say about ten o'clock?" With that he walked off to the officers' mess and Clarke made his way to the billet.

When he got in the others were chatting about their new pilot.

"Well Nobby how do you rate carrot-top then?"

"Seems OK to me. At least he's not some jerk just out of flying school. I reckon he will be alright but I think very different to poor old Tucker. He won't be turning back because one of the engines is on the blink, I can tell you. Oh, and he wants to take us all flying tomorrow so better be around by eight o'clock."

CHAPTER 19

Sunday 9th April 1944

The crew had flown with Cowan on several training flights after they had first met up in the pub. Clarke was struck how different he was to Tucker. He was obviously very experienced but he also had a presence about him which instilled confidence. He was very disciplined in the air and insisted that they call him Skip, whilst he would speak to them by naming them according to their role in the aircraft. He forbade any unnecessary chatter and expected complete concentration when they were flying. Clarke liked him and reasoned that there would be half a chance that they would survive with Cowan as their pilot.

The war was changing too. The rumour was that more raids were now going to be in France and Belgium in preparation for the Allies invasion sometime in the summer and, as if to emphasise the fact, there had been a raid on Toulouse just a few nights ago. Of course, there had been talk of invasion for a couple of years but this sounded different and definitely more hopeful.

Clarke walked over to the Flight Office after breakfast to find that they were on the Operations board for that night. As he was reading the notice Flight Lieutenant Simmons came rushing out of his room and nearly collided with him.

"Ah Clarke. How are things going with your new pilot? Got you someone really experienced, didn't we? Think yourself lucky. Must dash, see you for the briefing."

He was gone before Clarke could say anything but he certainly looked less drawn than he had been after their dreadful trip to Nuremberg. May be things were beginning to get easier for everyone after all.

Briefing was scheduled for four o'clock that afternoon which made it likely this trip would not involve them flogging across Europe to Germany. And this was made even more probable because the ground crew were not filling the tanks to the brim with fuel.

On the dot of four o'clock Wing Commander Squires entered the briefing room together with his other officers.

"Sit" he said. "Tonight, we are off to France again. A small force but with a vital task of destroying the railway yards at a place called Villeneuve-St-Georges. As you will have gathered our targets are changing from towns and cities in Germany to tactically important areas closer to home. Accuracy is vital, not only so we destroy the target but to limit damage to French and Belgium homes and people. As our Met expert will tell us, it looks to be a clear night so that should help you but, of course, also the German fighters. Just to remind you that these French jobs only count for half a trip."

There were groans around the room along with some unhappy chatter. Most thought it was very unfair these raids didn't count fully – they were still bloody dangerous after all.

The Navigation Officer was next and described their route north and east of Paris approaching the target from the north east. "And for God's sake don't drop any bombs on Paris. If you do, don't bother to come home" he smiled.

The Bombing Officer talked about the Pathfinder marking and that they should not start their bomb run until told to do so by the Master Bomber. After everyone had had their say the crews dispersed for their traditional meal before heading out to the aircraft. Take off was scheduled for nineteen hundred hours and with a four-hour flight they should be tucked up in bed by about two o'clock. Seemed quite civilised really, Clarke thought.

The truck dropped them at their new aircraft T-Tommy. New did not quite describe her but she was not in bad shape given this would be her thirtieth trip.

Once everyone was on board and in place Cowan called around to check that everything was in order before firing up the engines and beginning to taxi down to the hold at the end of the runway. There were only four aircraft flying from East Kirkby so it did not take long to get in line and once the green flare was fired, he opened the throttles and T-Tommy started down runway zero-eight into the gentle easterly wind. Being relatively lightly loaded she lifted off easily and they climbed away from the gathering gloom and up into the light of the setting sun.

"Everything working navigator?" Cowan's clipped voice asked.

"Yes Skip, toys are all OK. Once we get to 5000 feet we need to turn on to one-five-five."

"Turning new course one-five-five and climbing to 20,000 feet"

"Twenty-seven minutes before we overfly Clacton. Bombaimer can you let me know as we cross the coast?"

"Will do. It is a very clear night"

After a while Beavers called "That's Clacton now."

"Thanks. Eighteen minutes to French coast. Should fly over Calais. H2S working well Skip."

"OK everyone. Eyes out of the aircraft. There have been reports of fighters trying to catch bomber streams out over the Channel."

"French coast coming up Navigator."

"Maintain height and heading Skip. Forty-five minutes before we turn to target."

As they crossed the coast, strings of flak looped up towards them from the German batteries but they seemed quite random and with nothing like the ferocity of those they had experienced in Germany.

"Bombaimer, we are coming up to the Marne and you may be able to see Paris on the right. I have got the river on H2S very clearly. Turning point for the target coming up Skip."

"OK Navigator, I think I can see the Seine but it is a little misty now."

"Skip two minutes to turn on to two-two-zero. OK turn on my command. Now! Three minutes to target."

"Master bomber has cleared us to bomb on the markers. You have the aircraft bombaimer."

"Skip come left, left steady now, steady. Bombs gone, flash complete."

"I am continuing on this course Navigator. Tell me when you want me to turn for home."

The lack of flak and searchlights was almost unnerving and Clarke kept waiting for things to liven up.

"Watch out for fighters, gunners. This is too quiet for comfort" Cowan said "They must be out there somewhere. How much further for the turn Navigator?"

"Three minutes, then turn on to three-four-zero. We should cross the French coast just north of Dieppe."

T-Tommy had just made the turn when they struck.

"Corkscrew port, Skip." The aircraft was thrown over as Cowan responded to Docker's shout and it shook as the guns were fired.

"Missed the bastard. He's coming back again Skip abeam from the right." Cowan banked the aircraft to the right and dived whilst both Docker and Trelick let fly.

"We've got him" Trelick shouted "There he goes. A real flamer. Good bloody riddance"

"Good shooting lads. That's one up to us! I'm going to come back onto three-four-zero Navigator would that be about right?"

Clarke was trying to recover his bits and pieces and didn't answer straightaway.

"You OK Navigator?"

"Yes, fine Skip. Just a bit of a mishmash back here. Three-four-zero is the course."

Eventually Beavers announced that he could see the French coast and, shortly afterwards, Hastings.

"Come ten degrees east to three-five-zero Skip. On our way to East Kirkby now. Forty- five minutes to home."

Cowan brought T-Tommy in for a perfect landing and taxied to their stand and the waiting ground crew. Clarke couldn't believe it when he looked at his watch to see that it was only half past eleven. Be in bed by one o'clock and a good night's sleep.

The crew jumped down and made their way to the waiting truck when Cowan called out.

"Bloody hell. Look at the wing. That fighter hit us after all. The outer third has been shredded. Good job you nailed him when you did Trelick."

The truck took them to the debriefing where Simmons was just finishing with his own crew.

"Cake walk eh lads? Still make the most of it. We are on again tomorrow so look sharp here and then get some sleep. Any trouble with this lot Cowan?"

"No sir. Everyone did very well. We even bagged a fighter. Suppose you didn't you get one yourselves by any chance, sir?"

Simmons scowled and walked away leaving the crew of T-Tommy secretly smiling. They made their way back to their billet and Clarke had trouble believing that he had been flying at all, such was the contrast with their earlier efforts. Still tomorrow was another day and bed and sleep beckoned.

CHAPTER 20

Saturday 22nd April 1944

The night after their trip to Villeneuve their target was the railway sidings at Tour followed by a visit to Aachen just inside Germany. Both were relatively easy runs and there was a real danger that everyone was beginning to think that the danger was all over. Jerry hardly ever appeared and the defences around the targets were fairly desultory. Even the trip to Cologne on the 20th April proved straightforward.

When Clarke checked the ops board however, he was not too surprised to see that they were on for that night. Another milk run he thought and he went to tell the others.

"Bloody hell" Docker exclaimed. "It's Saturday. I was hoping we could have the night off and pull some birds."

"Well it looks like tonight's not the night. Never mind Taff we should get a break soon."

"Alright for you Nobby. You've got a bird, haven't you? It's the rest of us that are struggling, like. Haven't had a shag for weeks now. Not even when we were on leave. Forget how to bloody do it soon"

They were still discussing the potential benefits of a night off when Cowan came up to them.

"Well off we go again. Let's get the air test done as soon as possible You've seen the time for briefing. Looks like we might be going a bit further tonight. See you around ten o'clock in the crew room. Don't be late"

As Cowan moved away the rest looked at one another.

"He seems a bit sharp this morning, doesn't he?"

"Well maybe he knows something we don't Al," Clarke replied. "I mean we have had it pretty cushy lately and we all know that can't last for ever unless Hitler throws in the towel."

"No bloody hope of that" Beavers grumbled. "Maybe he couldn't get a bird either" and they all laughed.

The air test went without problems and they were all gathered for the briefing at four o'clock when Squires arrived.

"Well chaps. We have had it fairly easy for the last fortnight but the Boss has decided it is about time we reminded the Germans that the war isn't over. The target for tonight is Dusseldorf and we haven't been there for a while so navigators dust down your charts." There was nervous laughter around the room. Dusseldorf had been badly damaged before in previous raids but it was strongly defended. This would definitely not be a cakewalk! The Ruhr was not called "Happy Valley" for nothing.

The briefing followed its usual course and the crews filed out of the room when it was over. Some of the old hands were looking anxious.

"It can't be as bad as Nuremberg can it?"

"Well it's not as far to begin with, Ray. But on the other hand, I don't think that they will be particularly pleased to see us. And they have had it easy as well for a few weeks."

"At least we know what to expect Nobby don't we?"

"That's right Al. Some of the other crews have only flown to France and back – haven't seen any real flak. Could be a rude awakening."

They left the canteen and walked back to their billet for a sleep. Take off was at eight o'clock so they had a couple of hours to get their heads down. Clarke found himself dreaming about

Anne and when he woke, he realised he hadn't managed to speak to her since their lunch together. They had been too busy but he would try after tonight – it would be good to meet her again and maybe she was feeling a little better after she had seen Matt's parents.

Cowan was already in the crew room when they arrived.

"OK chaps, so as Wing Commander Squires was saying this will not necessarily be an easy trip. Let's get everything as well prepared as we can, and that includes the coffee Alan."

Trelick smiled. Being the youngest he was the scapegoat for just about everything that happened or should happen. They filed out to the waiting trucks. Ten aircraft were going tonight so there was quite a crowd. Theirs came eventually and once the usual formalities were concluded they climbed aboard T-Tommy and completed the checks.

They were number four in line and as Cowan lined up on the runway he noticed the usual gathering by the control van. Green flash and off they went.

The aircraft was much more heavily loaded and it seemed an age before the tail lifted and T-Tommy took to the air. The sun was just setting as they climbed away and they remained in the light whilst the ground below them steadily darkened.

"Turn onto one-one-five and climb to cross Great Yarmouth at 10,000 feet."

"One-one-five, thanks Navigator."

"Bombaimer about half an hour to Great Yarmouth. Let us know when you see the coast. I am following on H2S."

"Will do. It is quite clear just now."

About twenty minutes after crossing the Wash, Beavers called out that the coast was coming up.

"Maintain course, climb to 20,000 feet. We alter course to the target in ninety minutes." They had been told at the briefing that their course would suggest their target was Nuremberg again but over Neuss they would turn towards Dusseldorf and approach from the southwest, hopefully fooling the German defences. The theory, at least, sounded convincing.

They were about thirty minutes from the turning point when the aircraft was rocked by a nearby explosion, followed quickly by another.

"Eyes peeled gunners. Fighters are with us."

"Rear gunner, here. Looks like someone is under attack behind and to our left. Christ corkscrew starboard."

Cowan stood the aircraft on its wing and dived but he heard shells hitting the fuselage and then realise they were just about to fly under a nearby Lancaster. Trelick was screaming as they just missed the other aircraft.

"Is everyone OK?" Cowan's voice was calm but Trelick could still be heard.

"Upper, put a sock in it. Concentrate or we'll all be killed. Now Navigator what's the course?"

"Continue one-one-five. About five minutes to the turn. New course zero-four-five. Bombaimer you should see the Rhine soon on the left."

"Better than that, I can see where the bombs are going. Looks quite a party."

Cowan could also see the target and, uncomfortably close and getting nearer, the lines of flak.

"OK everyone. Target is coming up. It will be a bit sticky as we go through this flak. Navigator you sure this is it?"

"Looks OK to me. GEE agrees"

"OK bombaimer all yours. There are markers dead ahead. Looks like we are spot on."

The flak was very dense and as they went through there was a load bang from the rear of the aircraft and Cowan had trouble keeping the aircraft straight.

"Rear turret's gone."

"Keep quiet Trelick. Nearly there."

"No it's bloody gone" Trelick sounded almost hysterical. "It's gone."

"Left, left," Beavers steady voice "Steady, steady. Bombs gone. Hold. Photo flash."

Cowan turned the aircraft steeply to the left and out of the way.

"Now what's happened, Trelick?" There was no reply.

"Rear gunner?"

"Radio op go and see what the hell is going on. And gunners keep looking."

Cowan realised they had suffered some considerable damage. The aircraft was much slower in the turns and he wasn't surprised when Smith reported in.

"Rear turret's gone Skip. Just a big hole at the back. No sign of Taffy, sir."

There was silence for a moment and then Cowan asked Smith to look at Trelick.

"Trelick's bought it too Skip. Looks like he has been hit in his head by a bit of flak."

"Navigator give me a course for home and then go and help Smith will you. Engineer is everything working up this end. We haven't collected any other damage?" Barton nodded that all was well. "I'm happy we can just carry on as planned."

Clarke's navigation table was complete chaos. He tuned in GEE and worked out a course for the coast.

"Two-eight-five, about ninety minutes to our coast."

Clarke got up and went back to where Smith was waiting under the upper turret. Trelick was hanging in his straps and half his head had gone. Together they managed to ease the body down onto the floor of the fuselage. The turret itself was blown apart and the guns were pointing at odd angles. Clarke patted Smith on the shoulder and helped him back over the main spar.

He was suddenly gripped by the fear of imminent death and struggled to keep himself under control.

"Trelick's had it too and the turret's wrecked."

"Right" Cowan's seemingly unflappable voice replied. "Well let's hope we get some luck and no bloody fighters want to come and say hallo. Get me a position Navigator. Once you're happy where we are, I'm taking us down to the deck."

Clarke could hardly control his trembling hands as he tried to get some order on his table. He checked GEE again – at least it was still working but even as he was writing down the bearings he vomited uncontrollably.

"What's up Navigator. I need our position."

Clarke wiped the vomit off the table and began calculating where they were.

"Steer two-nine-zero, it's about thirty-five minutes to the coast."

"Anything high we might bump in to that I need to know about?"

" Should be OK down to a thousand feet Skip."

With this Cowan dived the aircraft into the darkness below them. "Open the throttles, Engineer. We are in a hurry. Keep an eye on the fuel."

"Fuel's OK Skip. We are doing about 250 mph now."

"Bombaimer keep a bloody sharp lookout – pylons are of special interest."

T-Tommy was racing along through the dark, and the aircraft was shaking at this speed so close to the ground. Clarke felt almost resigned to instant death and he struggled to keep thinking about their position. GEE did not work at this height so he resorted to old fashioned compass and watch.

"Should be north of Antwerp now. At this speed we should be over the Sheldt estuary any moment now"

"Thanks Navigator. I am going to go really low. There will be a lot of flak round here."

No sooner had Cowan spoken than flak appeared all around them and several pieces came through the fuselage some landing on Clarke's table. Clarke went forward to see what was going on. It looked like they were flying into hell itself and with the engines screaming the noise was deafening. Then suddenly as if by a miracle they were out over the sea. Cowan kept them low and Clarke became transfixed looking the sea below them. He went back to his post and saw that Smith was staring straight in front and didn't acknowledge him as he sat down.

"You alright" he said shaking Smith who seemed to wake up and raised a hand.

"About twenty minutes to our coast Skip."

"Thanks. Let's ease back on the engines. Don't want them to blow up do we?" Cowan put the aircraft into a gentle climb so they could more easily identify where they were crossing the coast. "Keep a sharp lookout bombaimer. God knows where the navigator has got us to."

Clarke smiled more in admiration than anything else. *Some pilot we've got ourselves here, he thought.*

"Coast ahead. I think I can recognise the lighthouse at Southwold."

"Well done navigator. Spot on. Radio ops send a message to base. Tell them we have damage and dead. Course to home?"

"Three-one-zero. About twenty minutes to base." Clarke looked at Smith and realised he hadn't moved and certainly hadn't spoken to East Kirkby. "Phil. Come on" he said shaking him. Smith looked back, his eyes staring. "You need to call base, now."

"Got a problem Skip. Radio operator is US just now. I will try and make the call."

"OK navigator. Get on with it."

Clarke managed to get the set to work and eventually got through to East Kirkby and gave them the message.

"Everything seems to be working but I am not sure we still have a tail wheel. We won't find out until we land so take up crash positions once we get in the circuit." Cowan's voice showed no sign of concern. It was almost uncanny how he could be so unaffected by the carnage that was all around him.

"They are saying we can join the circuit. We are number one to land. Blood and fire wagons are ready Skip."

"Thanks. OK engineer let's get everything set up. Downwind now."

The aircraft turned on to base leg and then settled on to their final approach. Flaps and undercarriage were down and Cowan brought the battered Lancaster in for a perfect touchdown. They taxied to the stand followed by the ambulance and once the engines were shut down the five weary men made their way to the rear door and Clarke helped Smith out. The medics ran forward but Clarke put his hand up.

"No need to rush" he said "One man is missing and the other has been dead for a while."

The destruction at the rear of the aircraft was appalling to see. The rear turret had been blown completely off the fuselage taking Taffy with it and just leaving tangled metal. The fuselage was riddled with holes, some of them large enough for a man's fist.

The men just looked but no one said anything. The last few hours had taken them closer to death than any of them would want again and even Cowan looked shaken by the aircraft's appearance. Smith stood next to Clarke and was staring at the ground.

"Come on lads lets go and tell teacher what we have been up to" Cowan said quietly. "Bloody shame about Taffy and Al. I reckon they won't send us again tonight so down the pub and let's drink to them."

Clarke took Smith's arm and led him towards the waiting truck. "Paul, I think I will take Phil to the sickbay. He isn't looking too good."

Cowan paused and looked at Smith and shook his head "OK, but after the debrief – get that done then go" he said sharply.

After the debrief there was talk of going to the mess for a drink but Clarke knew that he could not manage that and that anything he ate or drank would almost certainly end up on the floor. So, when Barton and Beavers peeled off for a beer Clarke led Smith back to the sickbay and handed him over to one of the nurses.

"He had a bad time and needs a bit of help, thanks" and as he turned away Clarke himself felt almost too tired to walk back to the billet. Once he got in, he dropped onto his bed and tried to sleep but instead lay staring at the ceiling and thinking over the last few dreadful hours. Eventually he drifted off, waking every now to recall the terrible noise of that last flak attack as they went out over the sea, before dozing off again.

CHAPTER 21

Sunday 23rd April 1944

It was about six o'clock when Clarke awoke from his troubled sleep. At first, he felt disbelief at what had happened the previous night and horror at the thought of the two who had been killed and the several empty beds that were a testimony to what had happened, not only to them, but to other crews too. Barton and Beavers were still fast asleep and he noticed that Smith had come back from the sickbay. He thought that he was asleep too until he looked more closely and realised that his eyes were open and that he was still in his flying kit, curled up under a blanket.

Clarke sat down on the edge of the bed.

"You OK Phil? When did you get back? I thought that they would have kept you in the sickbay. How about going for a nice cup of tea?"

Smith shook his head and pulled the covers over his head.

"Come on. You need to get up. There will be no flying today so there's time to get ourselves back together. And Skip has promised a drink down the pub" Clarke said encouragingly. He felt anxious and concerned that here was, maybe, someone else willing to blow their brains out. "Come on old chap. Cup of tea will fix things. Maybe we should go back to see the doc as well. What do you say?"

As there was no response he left Smith where he was, got dressed and then headed over to the canteen. There were only a few men there and as he could not face eating, he just grabbed a cup of tea and sat with one of the other crews.

"What a bloody mess that was Nobby? Hear you lost Taffy and your mid upper. There's a rumour that Simmons got the chop as well. And we all thought it was going to be easy from now on?"

Clarke was still struggling to come to terms with what happened to his crew last night let alone anyone else. Still, Simmons had been quite a force, pain in the arse sometimes but generally pretty good, and his loss would be sorely felt whatever people thought about him. He had certainly kept them alive on that Nuremberg trip. He finished his tea and went to the Ops Room. Sure enough Simmons was not there and there was a notice instructing all aircrew to assemble at ten o'clock in the Briefing Room. The squadron had been stood down for seventy-two hours. He walked back to the billet where the others, apart from Smith, were beginning to stir.

"Stood down everyone. Good news eh? We have to go to the Briefing Room for ten o'clock."

Barton's rheumy eyes peered at Clarke.

"Tell them to fuck off for all I care. Two good blokes just blown away. They can have their fucking war and stuff it up their collective arses."

Beavers looked as if he was going to agree and then just sat on his bed and buried his head in his hands and for a moment Clarke thought he was crying.

"Well, at least we have a bit of a break. Looks like we weren't the only ones last night."

"You know Nobby that doesn't bloody help much does it? Certainly doesn't help Al and Taffy. I bet bloody Simmons is still sitting in his bloody office."

"Actually, he went missing last night."

Barton muttered something and walked out of the billet. Clarke followed him.

"You know Charlie this isn't going to help anyone is it? Last night was a mess and I guess there will be other fuck ups in the future but we still have a job to do."

"Christ you should have taken that commission, Nobby. You sound like a sodding officer already, you do."

"I'm just trying to be reasonable. We need to stick together and get through this. Your outburst will hardly help poor old Phil will it? I wouldn't be surprised if he ends up in the sickbay after all this in any case."

"Look I'm sorry Nobby, didn't mean to sound off like that but I was really shaken up by that Nuremberg outing and now this last night. It has really put the shits up me no mistake."

"I don't think it has done any of us much good to be honest. God only knows how Cowan managed to get us back last night. I think he must have ice rather than blood in his veins. Come on let's see what the boss has got for us before we all chuck in the towel. I think I might go down and see what the old crate looks like. Sort of face our demons. You coming?"

Barton nodded and they set off on bikes down to the hangar. It was a fine morning and the sun was warm on their faces as they cycled along. Almost everywhere they looked ground crew were swarming over the aircraft catching up with maintenance, changing engines or repairing damage. It was an endless task. They arrived at the hangar and went in to its gloomy interior and were looking at T-Tommy being steadily dismantled when Flight Sergeant Myers walked up to them.

"Morning chaps. Sorry about your gunners. Bit of a mess I'm afraid. You was lucky though. Chunk of flak missed the fuel lines in the starboard wing by a whisker and another bit shredded the aileron. We are going have to take out the outer starboard engine in any case. Your pilot did a bloody good job getting you back you know. Cowan isn't it – he's a good bloke he is. You better hang on to him."

Clarke and Barton walked to the back of the aircraft to look at where the rear turret had been. In the light of day there were obvious bits of Taffy where the turret had been attached.

"We'll get this cleaned up soon, don't worry" Myers said quietly. "Sorry we haven't really had time yet."

Clarke and Barton nodded and headed back for the briefing neither of them speaking until they were well away from the hangar.

"Well he wouldn't have known anything about it Charlie. Neither would Al come to that. Maybe that's something of a relief."

"S'pose so. Bloody waste of two good guys though isn't it? Let's go and see what they have to tell us."

The briefing room was already over half full when they arrived and they found the others together with Cowan in one corner but Clarke was worried to see that Smith was not amongst them. The chattering ceased as they all stood when the Commanding Officer, Group Captain Brookes and his other officers came in to the room.

"Sit" Brookes said sharply. His face looked drawn as if he had also been up all night.

"I have called you here this morning to explain what is going on. As you know we had a bad time last night with two aircraft missing and another badly shot up with crew killed. I'm afraid it looks as if Flight Lieutenant Simmons's aircraft was one of those lost but at this stage we have no idea what happened. I have been speaking to Group and they have agreed for us to stand you down so we can lick our wounds so to speak." The murmur of approval died away as he continued. "I don't need to remind you that this is not leave as such and no one must leave the station without permission from your flight commanders. Which brings me to the replacement for B Flight – Flying Officer Granger will take over from immediate effect. Finally, I just want to make the point that although the nature of the war seems to be changing it is not in any way nearly over and it is every bit as dangerous as it was. Please don't forget that. If there are no questions – dismiss." The crews stood as the entourage walked out and T-Tommy's crew gathered around Cowan as they left the room.

"Well we have a couple of days to enjoy" Cowan said as they walked into the Spring sunshine. "Definitely down to the Red Lion tonight. Any other ideas?"

"How about a game of soccer?" Barton asked. "We could get the others together – probably enough of us left to manage a couple of teams. Mind you Nobby's a bit past it – he could play in goal."

The others laughed but they agreed it would help to take their minds off things for a while.

"Where's Phil" Clarke asked.

"Left him in the hut. Said he didn't want to come out."

"I'll go and see him" Clarke replied anxiously. "He probably needs to see the doc."

"You chaps arrange the match. It's a really good idea Charlie" Cowan said. "I'll go with Nobby to see if we can straighten Phil out."

As they walked away from the others Clarke turned to Cowan.

"Thanks for coming Paul. You seemed a bit sharp towards Phil last night, mind I think we were all on edge."

"Nobby, I suppose many of us have an in-built irritation with blokes who don't seem to cut the mustard. But Phil is OK – he probably needs a bit of a rest. I have always thought being the radio operator isn't much of a job. Most of us are too busy doing things in the aircraft to be scared. Come on let's check him out."

When they got to the hut they found Smith still in his bed although he did seem to be asleep this time. Clarke went over to shake him and he stirred only to turn over.

"Come on Phil. You need to get out of your scratcher. We don't have anything to do for a couple of days."

"Sorry Nobby, Skip. I can't bear it anymore. Last night, last night …."

"Come on old chap. We got back didn't we?"

"Skip, just down to you I reckon. Thought we was goners. And Taff and Al – they were my mates."

"Phil, let's get the doc to look you over. This sort of thing can happen when you get shit scared. He'll know all about it, give you something to help."

"Is that an order Skip?"

"Well, yes, it is. I'll come down to the sickbay with you. Nobby you head off and see how the match is coming on. I'll take care of Phil here."

And with that Smith got dressed and with Cowan at his elbow walked off to see Wing Commander Spear the MO. Clarke sat for a moment thinking about the last twenty-four hours during which he and the crew had faced almost certain death. He was not sure how much more he could stand, let alone Smith. Last night's deaths had brought to four the crew deaths in the last three months – three killed and one suicide out of seven did not sound very good odds. He felt a sickness deep in the pit of his stomach, something he had never experienced before. He shook his head and, leaving the hut, went looking for the footballers but then changed his mind determined to try to speak to Anne. He felt he needed to speak to a human being outside the station to prevent him being dragged down into a pit of despair.

He called the hospital from the Mess and got through to the Porters' lodge. They said that they were sorry but they couldn't find her although they would leave a message that he'd called.

Clarke slammed the receiver down and walked out to find the others. The match had been arranged for two o'clock but Clarke could not face lunch or in fact the company of others. He just had to get out of the station and on his own for a while – he was sure they would find someone to take his place for the match.

He got in his car and headed out of the gate and towards Louth where he and Anne had walked a few weeks back. It was a lovely day with a few frothy white clouds against an amazingly deep blue sky and he began to feel easier as he drove along. He went through Raithby where the road climbed up on to the Wolds and stopped at the top. It was a crystal-clear day and he sat down on the ground to take in the view. He listened to the twittering of the skylarks flying high above and gradually he began to feel better and the claustrophobia he had felt in the camp, eased. He breathed in the fresh air trying to force the smell of the aircraft and of death out of his lungs. He stayed for a while until the sun had disappeared behind clouds leaving him feeling cold. As he drove back, he thought of his father and then of Anne and the need to get in touch with her and seeing a telephone box he stopped and dialled the hospital. To his surprise he got through and within a couple of minutes she came to the phone.

"John, how are you? Sorry I missed your call?"

"Not too good Anne to be honest. Can we meet sometime? We're stood down for a while. Maybe lunch somewhere?"

"I'm working days just now. How about meeting for a drink one evening? Maybe grab something to eat in a pub?"

"Yes lovely. How about tomorrow, Monday?"

"Seven o'clock by the hospital then?"

"Done. See you there."

Clarke felt as if a great cloud had been lifted from his mind and on the drive back to the camp, he felt heartened by the thought of seeing her. When he got back it seemed that the football match had gone well and everyone was looking forward to the evening session in the pub. Clarke managed to get Cowan on his own to find out what had happened to Smith.

"Usual bloody medics" he said laughing. "*We'll keep him in overnight and give him some pills. Be right as rain by the morning!* Anyway, where did you get to? Bloody A Flight beat us – you could have made a big difference you know."

"I don't think so Paul. I was hopeless at sport at school and hated football most of all. It always seemed to be raining when we played. No, I needed to get out of this place to be honest. Just get away for a couple of hours."

"Don't blame you, old chap, but you are coming to the Lion aren't you? Need some intellectual input!"

"I'm not sure I will be able to provide too much of that. In any case you can never hear yourself speak in there, let alone think! But yes, I will be there fear not!"

The session at the Red Lion went much as Clarke had anticipated and once the singing started, he decided to slip out and go for a walk. Leaving the smoke-filled pub, the cold, fresh night air almost took his breath away. As he moved away from the pub and into complete darkness the stars above him seemed to glow and his navigator's eye easily picked out the constellations. He had always found the stars remarkably comforting, perhaps because of their reliability and permanence. And the fact that they would still be there swinging their way across the sky long after he was gone and forgotten, put things in to a kind of perspective. He was reluctant to go back to the camp and he stepped along the road and past the entrance to the base and out into the countryside. He just felt a need to get away and he walked for several miles through the darkness before turning back. There was a gentle breeze which hummed through the new Spring leaves in the trees and, in the distance, Clarke heard an owl hooting. He felt more settled in his mind as he walked back towards the station. He was still alive, they had a good pilot and he was going to meet Anne tomorrow. Maybe things were not so bad after all. Sad about those chaps though but their deaths were, at least, quick. Shame about old Simmons too. Happy Harry may have been a pain in the arse but he was a good pilot and he definitely saved their lives on that Nuremberg outing.

When he got back, he found the others had transferred to the sergeant's mess with Cowan in tow and he decided that he definitely felt more like going in for a glass or two with them than settling down to sleep.

CHAPTER 22

Thursday 27ᵗʰ April 1944

It had been very good meeting up with Anne again on the Monday. They had gone to a pub close by the hospital and although it was crowded, had managed to find a quiet corner. Anne had been to see Matt's parents the previous weekend and although it had been a tearful time, Anne had felt it had brought some closure for everyone. Clarke talked about his father's illness but said little about most of the recent flying events. He walked her back to the hospital and was pleased when Anne kissed him gently on the lips as they said goodbye. As the slack period for operations was coming up because of the full moon, they planned that they would get together again as soon as they could and it was with a lightened heart that Clarke raced the MG back to the camp.

He was up early and made his way down to the Flight Office. The new Flight Commander was hard at work but looked up as he went passed the door.

"Morning Clarke. Looks like they have got some business for us tonight."

"Isn't it a bit 'moony' for that, sir?" Clarke replied grimly remembering their last escapade in bright moonlight.

"I don't make the rules old boy. We will have to see what the CO has to say this afternoon."

Clarke liked Bob Granger. He was quite tall and had sandy coloured hair and a rather fine handlebar moustache over a wide generous mouth. He had a pleasant, easy-going manner and was a very different character to his predecessor. He had been a geography teacher in civvy street and had joined the RAF and started flying in early 1943. Promotion had been rapid and he already had a DSO.

He walked back to the hut to find the others in general disarray. They had several new bods, two of whom were replacements for Taffy and Al. Jerry Bennett was the mid-upper gunner, an Australian sheep farmer with hands like paddles. His last crew had gone missing whilst he was off sick and he had already done fifteen trips. Gus White, Chalky to his friends, was also quite experienced. He was a Londoner, a true Cockney with wit to match and was going to prove quite a comedian. Phil Smith had remained in the sickbay in spite of the doctor's optimism and their 'odd bod' radio operator was an American called Hank James.

"We're on for tonight everyone" Clarke called out. "Briefing is at seventeen hundred hours."

As Clarke filed into the briefing room with the others, he was struck by the fact that only he and Charlie Barton remained of the original crew. Phil clearly was not going to come back anytime soon, if ever, to their crew. They sat themselves down in the corner at the back of the room and sat waiting whilst Chalky White regaled them with tales of his latest conquest.

All stood as Wing Commander Squires and the other officers came into the room.

"Sit, men. Hope you have had a good few days off but now it is back to work. The target for tonight is Friedrichshafen. It is a long way I'm afraid but the raid is of vital importance and must be accurate. The factories there produce engines and gearboxes for tanks. Now the moon will be bright so you should be able to see things clearly and, in addition, the target is on the edge of Lake Constance so should show up easily on H2S."

The memories of Nuremberg flooded back and Clarke felt his scalp beginning to prickle with anxiety. Surely, they can't be sending us out again with the moon like this?

Squires continued "A number of significant diversions are in place and your route will be through France and then a short leg north of Switzerland. No ducking out for a bar of chocolate or to get your mum a cuckoo clock!"

Polite laughter concealed the concern which all the crews felt. Briefing followed the usual pattern but some time was spent on the role of the Pathfinder Mosquitoes and the target marking that they would be using.

Outside Cowan gathered the crew together.

"OK chaps this is going to be a long outing. Take off is twenty hundred hours so I suggest you get a bite to eat and get a couple of hours rest. Nobby can we sit down and just check the route and winds?" When the others had gone he turned to Clarke "This could be really tricky you know Nobby? Bloody long way, bright moonlight, small target. Sounds familiar doesn't it?"

"Sounds like Nuremberg to me Paul. Gives me the shivers just thinking about it."

They were third off down the runway, this time in F-Freddie since T-Tommy was still being put back together. The Lancaster, heavily loaded with fuel and bombs, clawed its way into the sky and at about 5000 feet Cowan turned the aircraft towards the south.

"Everyone OK? Course navigator."

"One-five-zero. Climb to 10,000 feet. We should leave England via Harwich. Should be there in just under half an hour. Bombaimer let me know when we cross."

"Will do. Very clear tonight, which doesn't give me a very good feeling!"

"Engineer everything OK? And guns keep your bloody eyes peeled."

They flew over Harwich and crossed the French coast between Calais and Dunkirk before climbing to 20,000 feet. It was so clear that Cowan could easily see the other aircraft around them and he felt very apprehensive about the possibility of fighters.

"Eyes peeled everyone. It's like daylight out there."

Clarke shivered at the thought of another disastrous run but as they got deeper and deeper into France without any reports of fighters, he began to feel more confident and they reached their turning point about three hours after takeoff without meeting any resistance.

"Turn on to zero-nine-zero. About two hundred miles to run."

"Thanks navigator. Fuel OK Engineer?"

Barton replied all was well and they continued unmolested as they approached Switzerland.

"The Alps look incredible" Beavers called. "You can see them glinting in the moonlight."

Clarke got up and went forward to look out of the windscreen. It was an amazing sight but it also seemed incredible that they had got this far without being attacked.

"Large lake coming up on the right Navigator"

"Thanks. That will be Lake Constance. Need to be careful not to upset the Swiss. Skip wait for my call to turn to the target in a couple of minutes. OK, turn now onto one-two-zero. We should have the lake to our right."

"I can see that navigator. Also, can see some activity up front. Bombaimer are you ready?"

"Corkscrew starboard"

The aircraft banked and dived towards the lake and Cowan heard the guns."

"Bloody fighter Skip."

"Let's get back on the bomb run. Bombaimer have you got the target markers. They seem very closely grouped."

"Got them Skip. Bit of flak up front but looks like they weren't expecting us this time. I have got them lined up Skip. Left, steady, steady. Bombs gone, flash gone. Aircraft going down over to the right Skip."

"I see him. Watch out for fighters they must have been waiting for us. Course home navigator?"

"Three-one-zero should do. Hopefully it will be as quiet going back as coming."

"Don't bank on it. They know we are here now and that bloody moon is no help to us. Engineer how are we for fuel?"

"OK Skip about five hours left."

"Distance navigator?"

"By dead reckoning about six hundred and fifty miles to run – so about four hours if all goes well. I should pick up GEE in a couple of hours."

"Let me know. Everyone alright? Tail, mid-upper still awake?"

They replied simultaneously and the crew settled down for the long haul back home. Every now and then a searchlight flicked on but nothing else troubled them and after a while Clarke said that GEE had confirmed their position and that the Belgium coast was about thirty minutes away. They crossed just south of Ostend and then back over Harwich and home and a perfect landing.

"Well done boys that went OK didn't it?" Cowan said once the engines were shut down and silence had descended on the aircraft. "Everyone out and let's go and tell them what we did?"

During the debrief the IO told them that it sounded as if the raid had been completely successful and certainly, for a change, the squadron had no losses. Even though things had gone smoothly, Clarke felt exhausted so excused himself from the drinking, dropped down on to his bed still in his flying gear and fell asleep almost immediately.

CHAPTER 23

Monday 1ˢᵗ May 1944

After the raid on Friedrichshafen they had had two further outings but these were only to France, a factory and then an ammunition dump. It was becoming clear to them all, that things were changing and that the endless flights into the heart of Germany were becoming less and less of a feature.

Clarke had been mulling over whether to take the commission that he had been offered earlier, and after he talked it through with Cowan it seemed an increasingly attractive idea. After all only Charlie Barton remained of the original crew and whereas he had felt a sense of loyalty when Simmons had first recommended him, that seemed less important now. There would be the usual red tape but Granger had said that he would put him back up to Group Captain Brookes for the commission. It would probably take weeks in any case.

In any case, he was really excited that he was going to see Anne at lunchtime. When they had met the previous week, he thought she seemed happier to be with him and he could still remember the kiss that she gave him when they parted. The plan was for him to pick her up from the hospital and for them to drive out towards Louth again. It had been agreeably quiet when they went there to go walking several weeks ago, and Clarke had noticed a rather good-looking pub that had looked very welcoming.

It was a lovely morning and even though Cowan had wanted them to do an air test there was going to be plenty of time to pick up Anne leaving the rest of the day to them. The test completed, he climbed into his car feeling happier than he had done for some time. The French raids were not nearly as stressful and although things could always go wrong, at least you did not feel as if you had been through a mangle. And, in fact, the new crew all got on really well and more importantly everyone seemed to know what they were doing.

As he drove down the lanes the sun shone through the tree branches which, slowly but surely were beginning to carry the fresh green leaves of Spring and, here and there, the white May blossom was bursting into view. Overall, he reckoned he was feeling pretty good. When he got to the hospital Anne was waiting. She looked lovely with her long hair brushed out and wearing a white silk top and long emerald green skirt. She waved as he came up to the front door and walked to his side of the car as he drew up.

"Hallo" Clarke said as he got out of the car and he kissed her cheek. "Are you ready to go? I thought we would go back to Louth. There was a pub there, the Whyte Swan, I noticed when we were there last." He went around and opened the passenger door for her and then got back in and started the car. They said very little on the way to Louth, both lost in their thoughts and enjoying the ride through the beautiful countryside. The winter had been bad for them both, Anne losing Matt and Clarke struggling to keep going through trip after trip, the loss of most of the crew and now his father's impending death. Somehow this ride took them both away from all of that and in their own ways it felt like a fresh beginning.

The pub was busy when they got there but Clarke managed to get a table for them overlooking the gardens at the back.

"This is nice. Clever of you to remember it. Any more news about your father? It must be difficult."

"Well it is but there is nothing I can do about it. I wondered about getting him a second opinion but to be honest I'm not sure there is any point and it would be difficult for him to travel, and painful too. I'm more worried about how my mother is going to cope with him especially if he gets bed bound. In any case less about me, how are you doing?"

"I think I am beginning to come to terms with things, John. Moving on was what Matt would have wanted but it's not easy not to think about him. And I don't think I could bear the thought of losing some else that I loved."

"I understand, you know Anne. But war produces some strange effects and time can seem to become compressed. When I think about what has happened to us as a crew since we started operations it's difficult to believe that only four months have passed. And who would have thought that only a few months after we met here, we are sitting having lunch together? It's almost beyond belief. In any case shall we order?" Clarke reached for the menu and as he passed it over to her their hands touched and he suddenly felt very much as if he wanted to lean over and kiss her.

Whilst they were waiting for their meal Clarke plucked up courage to tell her how he felt about her. It seemed pointless to delay saying how he felt – he could be dead tomorrow. To his surprise and relief, she reached over the table and took his hands in hers.

"John, you don't think less of me for saying that I could become very fond of you? I mean so soon after Matt."

"Well, I would quite understand if you didn't want to have much to do with me just now but I would be happy to wait for you, you know until it felt easier for you. After all that has happened to you and, I suppose, what could happen to me. Although I feel I will get through, you know. We have a great pilot, a good crew and for the most part just now we are mainly doing trips to France and Belgium. And I am going to be put up for a commission so that's not too bad either is it?" And he laughed, feeling more cheerful than he had done for weeks.

The meal went well and they sat for a while afterwards drinking wine and chatting.

"Do you want to get back or shall we go for a drive?"

"No rush, John. A drive would be lovely. Where to, do you think?"

"Shall we go back up on the Wolds, it should look wonderful today?"

The road led out of Louth winding its way through some small hills and then climbed up towards the Wolds. They turned left along a road which led south and stopped at one of the highest spots around. It was still a lovely day with a gentle breeze and the sky blue with some large lumps of cumulus bubbling up in the afternoon warmth. It was very still and quiet once the car stopped and Clarke turned towards Anne and putting his arms around her kissed her gently. They held one another for a while and then Clarke realised that she was crying and lifted her head up towards him and wiped her tears away.

"Sorry, John" she smiled at him. "This feels wrong but I know it isn't and I know that it would be what Matt would have wanted. This has been one of the best days for a very long time" and she turned and kissed him again.

They sat in the car for a while before Clarke suggested they got out for a walk.

"Don't have quite the right shoes on John. High heels won't do really will they?"

They laughed as Clarke got out of the car and came around to Anne's side.

"Well let's just stand then. At least I can hold you more closely."

Anne opened her door and Clarke helped her out and they stood together with their arms round one another. The smell of her perfume reminded of the first time they had met and as he felt her breasts firm against him, he started to harden. It had been a long time since he had felt like this and he could have stayed there all afternoon.

"Let's go back John. This has been lovely and I hope we can do it again soon. Maybe I'll wear the right shoes next time!"

The drive back seemed to be over quickly and almost before they knew it, they were back at the hospital.

"When can I ring you?"

"Anytime John. I am working days for now. Can we meet one evening? I would like that very much."

"I'll see when I can get off. You know what it is like?" something he immediately regretted saying. "Sorry Anne, I didn't mean that, stupid of me."

"Don't worry. I *do* know what it's like after all, don't I?" She leant over and kissed him and before he knew it she was gone, with no backward glance.

CHAPTER 24

Wednesday 3rd May 1944

When Clarke got back after his afternoon with Anne, he found quite a party underway at the Red Lion. Cowan had just been made up to Flight Lieutenant and Chalky White had turned nineteen.

"Drinks on me Nobby. Usual pint?"

"Well if you insist Paul. How long has this been going on? Quite a while by the looks."

A pint was thrust into his hand "Cheers Paul, congratulations."

"Well, we have something else to celebrate too."

"Why has someone got their girl up the duff?"

"No, Chalky. Our very excellent Navigator has just been made a pilot officer?"

"Really, Paul. How do you know?"

"On the bloody noticeboard, old boy. Well done."

Clarke could not quite believe it, especially as no one had actually said anything to him.

"Well it's the first I've heard of it. I'll buy the next round then. And Chalky, happy birthday!"

Charlie Barton pushed his way through and grabbed Clarke by the hand.

"Well done Nobby. Glad you took my advice at last. When do you leave?"

"Haven't the foggiest idea. Better go and check with the boss tomorrow."

"Where have you been in any case? I bet it's with that bloody lovely nurse isn't it? You quiet buggers are the worse. Getting a leg over without us even knowing."

Clarke thought Barton was just about to announce this to the rest of the pub when he turned to him and quietly said "I'm very happy for you Nobby. Good for you. Well deserved" And patted him on the shoulder.

Cowan wandered over and signalled they should step outside.

"Quite a stew in there isn't it? Bit of fresh air is what I need. Nobby, sorry springing that promotion thing on you. It just seemed a good time what with everything else. Actually, it's not on the noticeboard, Bob Granger told me this afternoon. You'll need to go and see Brookes in the morning – that *is* on the board" he smiled. "I hope you will be happy to stick with us for a while? It will take some time for the promotion to come through but you're a bloody good navigator and I would be especially pleased if you don't get sent off too quickly."

"Thanks Paul. Well, while we on mutual admiration I think you are a bloody good pilot so I'm happy to stay!"

The next day Clarke presented himself to Group Captain Brookes.

"Well done Clarke. I am promoting you to Acting Pilot Officer. I have applied for you to go on the usual Officer Course but I'm afraid that may take a while to come through – might be a couple of months as things are. You OK with that? You will be allocated a room in the Officers' quarters when one becomes available. Once again congratulations. Dismiss."

Clarke walked out in a bit of a daze and hardly heard the Adjutant remind him to remove his Sergeant's stripes and put a stripe on his sleeve. He walked across to the Flight Office to find Granger hard at work with piles of paper on his desk.

"Well done Clarke. Much deserved. I hear that you're buying drinks tonight – Officers' Mess of course" he laughed.

The Wednesday morning was a bit of a blur for Clarke at least until breakfast. He realised that he must have had rather a lot to drink the night before because although celebrations started in the Officers' Mess, they ended with his sergeant friends with, it is true to say, Cowan in tow.

"Gee man you limeys certainly know how to drink. How you feeling Nobby?"

"Somewhere between shite and death, thanks Hank. In fact, death would be a happy relief!"

"We're on the board for tonight if that makes you feel any better?"

"Christ that's all I need. Hope it's a nice quick one and not off to Krautland."

"Skip says we need to do an air test this morning, usual, 'bout ten o'clock. Said maybe you would fix it up now you're an officer!"

Clarke shook his head and gradually got himself together. He had rather hoped that he was going to take Anne out tonight but that would have to wait for now. He got some coffee and a bite to eat and then set about arranging the test, relieved that gradually his hangover was beginning to clear. Everything went well and when they had finished Cowan had them go for lunch and a rest and beckoned Clarke to walk over to the Officers' mess.

"Rumour has it, tonight's trip is to France. Should be a piece of cake as far as anyone can tell. Fancy a beer?"

"To be honest Paul, not just now. I'm still recovering from last night. How did you manage to put all that booze away last night and not feel like crap?"

"Ah it's all down to training, old boy. Essential part of the officers' course you see if it isn't."

"Well just a half then. How did you find out about tonight?"

"Bob Granger but don't ask me where he got the gen from" he winked. "The old man I suppose. He did say that the plans sounded a bit complicated which may not be such good news. He also said we might be stood down again for a short while. Now what would *you* do with a bit of leave then? Anyway cheers – your round when we get back."

"Well at the risk of sounding boring I would probably need to go south and see my parents. My father is dying of cancer."

"Oh Christ sorry to hear about that old boy. Let us know if there is anything I can do – people to speak to, that sort of thing."

"Thanks Paul. I suppose I'd better get my head down for an hour or two. See you later."

Briefing was at five o'clock and the room was full which indicated that the raid was a big one. Clarke thought that was a bit odd, because often the French ones involved relatively few aircraft. The place was thick with smoke as Brookes walked in with his officers and all stood to attention.

"Afternoon everyone. We have been ordered to undertake a very important raid tonight. As you know plans are well underway for an allied invasion in the not too distant future. Tonight we are going to attack an army camp in France thought to contain a Panzer division together with their tanks and support vehicles. If we can cause sufficient damage, we will significantly reduce any resistance our troops may face when they go ashore. The problem is that we have to be accurate to prevent injury to French civilians. The target is called Mailly-le-Camp. Navigation Officer"

"Yes chaps. This is a small target about seventy-five miles east of Paris. You will leave the English coast over Beachy Head and cross the French coast north of Dieppe to rendezvous to the north west of the target and hold there until told to bomb by the Master Bomber, the Master of Ceremonies. Timing and accuracy are everything and you must wait until the MC is satisfied that the markers are accurately in place. Now there should be clear moonlight which will help with accuracy."

This produced a groan from the crews – this was exactly the same problem during the Nuremberg raid and several hands went up.

"Several important differences chaps. The route to the target is much shorter and there will be a number of diversions undertaken so it is unlikely that Jerry will realise where we are going until we are there. You will also be chucking out chaff to fool their radar"

Next the Bombing Officer described bomb loads and the importance of the position and type of marker to be used and the timing of the attack. "Not a moment too soon or too late" he emphasised. "Timing is particularly important because 1 Group will be bombing after you."

Then Brookes summed up. "I cannot stress how important this raid will be to the invasion plans. Good luck chaps."

Cowan and his crew stepped out into the bright light of early evening.

"Well that all sounds very clear, I don't think. You got all the navigation stuff Nobby? And Hank you sure about the radio calls. Sounds as if we need to be good boys and not go and play until we are told to."

After the briefing the crews went to have something to eat and an hour's rest before getting kitted up. Cowan's crew walked out to wait for the truck to take them to dispersal and Jerry Bennett was telling them a string of jokes in his Cockney accent.

"Here Skip did you hear the one about the sergeant who went to the CO and asked if he could go home for the weekend because his wife was going to have a baby. When he got back the

---

Chaff (Window) – metallic strips thrown out of the aircraft in bundles to interfere with the enemy radar

CO asked him whether he had a boy or girl. "Gawd blimey sir, it takes longer than a weekend!"

They were laughing as they got on to the truck and a few minutes later they reached F-Freddie and clambered in. Clarke thought that they all seemed remarkably relaxed and he hoped that that was not going to make them easy targets, but once they were all settled Cowan made it very clear that this could be just as dangerous as any other trip.

Engines were started and Cowan called to check that they were all ready and they taxied out to the end of the runway. Cowan opened the throttles and the aircraft started to roll forward gradually gathering speed until it took off into the dark. They climbed steadily and Cowan banked the aircraft to the left and down to the south.

"Heading one-six-zero, climb to 12,000 feet, Skip. Bombaimer let me know as we cross Beachy Head."

Cowan acknowledged the course and about forty-five minutes later Beavers reported that they were over the coast. Ominously he said that it was as clear as daylight with the moon casting a bright light around them.

The gunners had already said that they could see other aircraft and Clarke began to get a bad feeling that this could be a Nuremberg encore. He checked their progress to the target using GEE and then H2S and he began to realise they were going to arrive ahead of time.

"Skip we must have a stronger tailwind than forecast. My estimate is that we shall be about five minutes too early. We could do a dogleg – I've worked out a course."

Cowan altered course, careful to keep a lookout for other bombers and told the gunners to keep their eyes open for fighters.

"Right that should do – back onto course now – steer one-two-zero and descend to 7000 feet. About ten minutes to the holding point. Should be marked by yellow target indicators."

A few minutes later Beavers said he could see the markers but nothing else. They were spot on time and there should have been some red target markers on the target itself.

"Skip I can see the markers now to the south of us."

"Radio operator anyone telling us we can bomb?"

"No Skip. Can't hear a thing because there sounds like some American programme playing on that frequency. Can't quite pick it up but it sounds like dance music. I've tried other frequencies but nothing there either"

"Christ, we will just have to go around. I am going to give those yellow markers a wide berth. They will attract fighters from bloody miles around, like moths to a flame."

Cowan eased the aircraft into a left hand turn and the moonlight allowed him to see that there were aircraft everywhere. F-Freddie was north of the markers when there was a blinding flash below them and Cowan had to fight to get control. Clarke was getting increasingly worried. This was meant to be a straightforward raid. As F-Freddie came around again the rear gunner, White, said he could see several aircraft going down in flames. Cowan looked over towards the target and could see bombs going down.

"Radio anything heard?"

"No Skip just that background programme. Sounds Yank music to me."

"Well you should bloody know. OK I am going in to bomb. We are like fish in a barrel here. Bombaimer can you see the red markers?"

Just then flak started to curl its way up towards them and there was a rattle of shrapnel on the fuselage.

"Right that does it. We're out of here. Bombaimer see where we are going?"

"Yes Skip. Quite clear. Christ I can even see the barracks. Left, left, steady. Bombs gone. Flash gone." At their low altitude the bomb blast threw the aircraft around as Cowan turned southwest and out of the area.

"Course navigator. Get us out of this hole. Don't care what we were given at briefing just get us out."

Clarke had not heard Cowan so worked up before. Clearly there had been a screw-up somewhere and the gunners were still calling out about the aircraft being shot down. They were now near Troyes so going due west seemed about right. They had just got onto the new course when White shouted for a corkscrew. F-Freddie stood on her side as Cowan dived away and there was a rattle of guns.

"Missed the bugger. No here he comes again. Corkscrew starboard."

The aircraft shuddered as it was hit and there was a smell of cordite.

"Everyone alright?" Cowan asked. All replied but Clarke was feeling as scared as he could remember. They quickly came to the coast near to Le Havre and once again flak came up to meet them but Cowan dived the aircraft to skim over the sea.

"Skip we've got company. It looks like a 110. He's gaining on us. Here he comes."

White opened fire as the fighter came in to attack but the cannon shells ripped into the rear turret killing him instantly.

"Rear gunner, rear gunner. Mid-upper can you see what's happened?"

"I think Chalky bought it Skip. That bastard hasn't finished with us yet. Here he comes again."

More shells ripped into the aircraft as Cowan weaved the aircraft in an attempt to escape.

"I can see the coast." Beavers shouted.

Cowan took the aircraft right down so they were just above the sea and as they got to the coast climbed just in time to clear the cliffs.

"See that 110 now, gunner?"

"No, he's had enough by looks of things. I can see some holes in the wing on the starboard side Skip. Looks like we could be losing fuel."

"Engineer, what's our fuel position. Have we enough to make base. Yes or no."

"Yes, but I will keep an eye on the numbers Skip. How far to base?"

Somehow Clarke managed to pull himself together. "About 40 minutes."

"That's alright. Should be enough."

They climbed to 10,000 feet to clear London and, spot on time, Beavers reported seeing the East Kirkby beacon and Cowan brought them in for a perfect landing.

Once the engines shut down the weary crew climbed down and walked to the rear of the aircraft where the crash crews were trying to extricate White's body from the turret which had been peppered with cannon fire.

"Not exactly a bloody milk run then!" Cowan remarked quietly as they waited for the truck to take them to debriefing. "And no one light up. There's still fuel dripping out of the starboard wing. That would certainly end the night with a bang."

Clarke felt exhausted as they got back onto the truck and he even struggled to get up over the tailgate.

"You OK Nobby?" Beavers asked. "You look all in."

"I'll be fine Ray, thanks. Feel a bit rough. Probably not helped by being led astray by you lot last night."

But he actually felt sick with fear. He had been shaken by the Nuremberg raid and although this outing had been much shorter it felt again that there had been a major foul up. They got down and walked into the debriefing room, collected their mugs of tea laced with rum and went over to the cheery face of the Intelligence Officer.

"Hallo chaps. Sit down. How did that go then? Nothing too tricky?"

Clarke thought that Cowan was about to explode and he thumped the table as he spoke.

"It was a fucking cock up. What else do you need to know?"

"Well in what way?" the IO asked quietly as he licked the end of his pencil.

"Every bloody way. We never heard the MC, just bloody dance music from America. The delay allowed the Kraut fighters to get all over us whilst we waited to start bombing. And the beautiful moonlit night made it nice and easy for them to see us. Bloody shambles, please take that pencil out of your mouth and write that down. Oh, and the bonus is that our rear gunner was made into mincemeat and his birthday was yesterday. Perhaps you would like to write the letter to his mother?"

Cowan was standing now and Clarke was shocked to see him so upset and angry. The Station Commander, Wing Commander Squires came over and put a hand on Cowan's shoulder.

"Sit down Cowan" he said gently. "Something did go wrong tonight but shouting at the IO won't help. It wasn't anything to do with him. Just so you know, it sounds like the raid was completely successful. I suggest you pack up here and go and get a drink and some sleep."

Cowan stood slowly back up.

"I apologise sir and to you too" he said looking at the Intelligence Officer. "Feeling a bit up-tight. Come on everyone let's get out of here."

CHAPTER 25

Thursday 4ᵗʰ May

When Clarke woke up at nearly ten o'clock, he felt as if the stuffing had been knocked out of him. He lay on his back looking up at the ceiling trying to recall the events of the previous night. If it had not been for Cowan, he was sure they would have died along with all the others just milling around like that. Bloody Germans must have thought it was Christmas come early. He looked across at the others and most were still asleep although Hank was sitting on his bed reading a letter.

"Not bad news Hank?"

"Gee no, man. It's from my gal back home. We all live in Minnesota and she's just talking about how her folk's farm is getting going after winter. It's good to hear about something coming to life rather than dying. Shame about Chalky – he was a nice guy."

"Do your parents run a farm as well?"

"Yep, we're the next one along to Madge's -that's my gal – my younger brothers are helping pa just now. Madge and I are going to get wed when I get home. What about your folk Nobby?"

"Oh we don't own a farm. My dad was a teacher. He's not so well at the moment."

"Oh, that reminds me. There was a telegram on the noticeboard for you. Hell, sorry I forgot."

Clarke rolled out of bed, dressed and set off to the Flight Office. His immediate thought was about his father as he tore open the envelope.

'Father very ill. Please call as soon as you can. Love mother.'

The nearest phone was in the mess which at this time of the morning was nearly always empty. He lifted the receiver and asked to be put through to his home and after a while his mother answered.

"Thank goodness you are alright, dear. I'm afraid your father has taken a turn for the worst. He was not doing too badly until a couple of days ago when he started to complain that he was having difficulty walking and that his legs felt funny. And gradually he seems to be becoming paralysed. Oh, John it's terrible to see. I've called the doctor and he should be here sometime today. I suppose there is no chance of you coming home dear? We still haven't heard from Richard." Clarke could hear her voice break and he knew she was crying.

"Mother, I will try to get away today or tomorrow at the latest. Let me know if anything changes."

Clarke walked out of the mess feeling more down than he could ever remember. Last night, and now this. He made his way back to the Flight Office ready for a fight. If they would not let him go then he would just walk out. They could stuff their commission up their backsides for all he cared.

Flight Lieutenant Granger was sitting at his desk, pipe in mouth, when Clarke walked in.

"Hallo Nobby. Last night was a bloody shambles wasn't it? I think they found out that the sodding music was from some American transmitter that crashed our frequency. What a fuck up? Anyway, what can I do for you?"

"Well sir. Just had a telegram from my mother. My father sounds as if he might be dying and I need to go back home to see what is going on. She is completely on her own."

"Not a problem old boy. Sorry to hear about your father, of course. Station is stood down for five days but you and your crew have leave in any case over that time. So, I suggest you pack your bags and get your arse out of here as soon as you can."

Clarke remained standing in front of Granger. He had been so certain that leave would be refused and that he would have to go into battle to get it, that he couldn't quite take in that he was free to go. The last twenty-four hours had taken its toll and Clarke realised he really wasn't thinking clearly anymore.

"Well get going then. Out of here by midday and that's an order."

Clarke saluted and without speaking, turned and walked out of the door and into the sunshine.

He walked over to the billet and met Hank James coming out of the hut.

"Your father?"

Clarke nodded. "Apparently we have leave for five days so I will head off to see how things are at home. What about you?"

"Well if we can get out of here, I will go down and see some buddies on the base at Bassingbourn. Then I might just look around. Get to know your funny country a bit better. You have a safe drive now."

Clarke started getting his things together and then thought he would call Anne before he left. As usual she was hard to find so he decided that he would ring her once he got home and, with that thought, he headed off.

The roads seemed particularly busy and the drive took a long time so that it was past ten o'clock in the evening when Clarke arrived home. His mother came to the door and walked out to the car. Clarke could tell she had been crying again and he put his arms around her.

"How are you mother?"

"John, your father. I think he may be slipping away. The doctor came this afternoon. Says your father has something called creeping paralysis. Sometimes it gets better but he's having trouble breathing and the doctor has given him a sedative."

Clarke dropped his bags in the hallway and ran upstairs to his parent's bedroom which was dimly lit. His father was propped up on his pillow and he seemed to be hardly breathing.

"Father can you hear me?" he said gently as he sat on the chair beside the bed. "It's John. Managed to get some leave to come home to see how you were."

His father's hands were freezing cold and he was obviously near to death but his eyelids flickered open and he was clearly trying to say something. Clarke leaned close to hear him.

"John. I'm a goner. Look after mother best you can. Have a drink in the Stag for me when you have a moment."

His head lolled sideways and Clarke leaned across to support him but he realised his father had died.

"Mother" he called, "Come up here."

"I think he was waiting for you to come back John." His mother's swollen, reddened eyes stared down at her husband and Clarke covered his father with a sheet, put his arm round her and led her downstairs.

"Well at least he didn't suffer for long mother. I'm pleased that I got back before the end. Any news about Richard at all?"

The crying started again and through the tears she said that Richard had been posted missing. He had been in the battle for Monte Cassino and his unit had been out of touch for some time.

"I didn't want to worry you, John. I'm sure you are having a bad time too."

"I'll make us some tea mother. Why don't you sit down? You look exhausted. I'll sort out things about father in the morning but you need a cuppa and a good rest. Did the doctor leave anything for you?"

"Yes, some little blue tablets. He did say they would help me sleep."

"Well let's take your tea upstairs to the spare bedroom, you swallow your tablets and let's get you off to sleep."

It was gone midnight by the time he had got his mother settled and he sat in the kitchen, poured himself a large whisky and reflected on the last twenty-four hours. The trip to Mailly, Chalky's death, his brother's possible death and now this. He felt peculiarly passive about things, as if the emotional energy had been sucked out of him and that nothing much seemed to matter anymore. He was just getting around to thinking that life really wasn't worth the living when he suddenly remembered Anne and that he had been going to ring her. He looked at his watch – three in the morning, probably wouldn't make him popular to try now! He finished his drink and went upstairs, peeped in to see that his mother was asleep and then went to see his father. He lifted the sheet and thought how peaceful he looked – no pain now dad, he thought, kissed his forehead and took himself wearily to bed.

CHAPTER 26

Friday 12th May 1944

The drive back up from home had been relatively easy for once and he had arrived at East Kirkby about eight o'clock on Thursday night. By some miracle, he had managed to arrange his father's funeral on the Tuesday. It had been a rainy, miserable day but the little churchyard had been filled with local people – his father had been very well known in the area partly because he had been a teacher but also because he had sat on the parish council. His mother had borne up pretty well during the funeral but once it was all over and they got home she became very upset and cried almost endlessly. Clarke rang Flight Lieutenant Granger and managed to get his leave extended so he could wait for his mother's sister to come over from Winchester. One bit of good news that they had received was that Richard was alive although seriously wounded and presumably would return home in the not too distant future.

It had not been until after the funeral that Clarke had managed to get through to Anne and after talking about his father they agreed to meet as soon as possible once he got back. Anne had said that there was a concert to be held in Lincoln cathedral which she was planning to go to and that perhaps, Clarke would like to join her.

When Clarke returned to his billet, he was relieved to see that all the crew of F-Freddie were still in one piece. They had had two short trips since they returned from leave both to targets in France but their "odd bod" navigator had managed to get them lost on the second outing.

"Gee, glad to see you back. Last nav was bloody hopeless. Looked about fifteen years old and from where I was sitting seemed to spend most of his time picking his nose!"

"Thanks Hank it's nice to be appreciated! Did you meet up with your chums?"

"Yeh, sure did. Had a great time. Did some exploring too. Pretty neat little country you have here, you know that? Sorry to hear about your pa. How are things? Your ma on her own an' all?"

"Her sister's there now. She'll be OK. My brother was badly wounded in Italy but at least he's alive– we thought at one stage that he was dead. So, he'll be back sometime."

"Christ, you've been through it a bit eh Nobby? Incidentally there's a party on for tomorrow night. You could bring your gal along."

"God I'd forgotten that I was meant to ring her. Thanks Hank I'll go and try and speak to her now. We are meeting the Boss this afternoon is that right?"

He managed to get through to Anne at the first attempt. "Hi Anne. Sorry to ring a bit late but I have just got back. Any luck with the concert? Apparently, there is a dance up here tomorrow?"

"Well, the concert is tomorrow evening. Would you rather go to the dance?"

"Anne I would just rather spend time with you to be honest. I would sooner go to hear the music than jig about crushing your feet and not able to hear what you are saying?"

Anne laughed. "So what time shall we meet tomorrow then?"

"I will need to check. Things seem rather quiet just now and we have been told that there will be no flying at least 'til next week. I will see if I can get into town by five o'clock. Perhaps we could have something to eat before the concert?"

* * *

The briefing room was full when Group Captain Brookes entered with his entourage.

"Sit down chaps. Now I want to indicate to you that we are entering a new phase of the war and that over the next few months we will be taking the war to Jerry on the ground. In other words, a second front. You will already have realised that the type of targets we are going for has changed and the bombing raids are into France and Belgium with the occasional one to the heart of Germany just so they don't forget us. The aim of this strategy is to disrupt communications so when our armies get over to France the enemy will not be able to move reinforcements easily. I have been instructed that the squadrons will be stood down until Monday 15th May although I remind you that there is no leave. And I also have to tell you that all leave is cancelled from then onwards for the foreseeable future."

Cheers were followed by boos but the thought that possibly this was, at least, the beginning of the end left everyone feeling happier than they had been for some time.

"Now, what has become apparent to us all is that these shorter raids into France are not necessarily any less dangerous than the ones to Germany. We experienced that in the Mailly raid and the one a couple of days ago to Lille, in which we were not involved, resulted in significant casualties. I am pleased to announce, therefore, that the half rate for a short trip is being discontinued forthwith, and all trips will count fully towards a completed tour."

As far as most of the men were concerned this was the icing on the cake and the resulting cheer could probably have been heard in Germany.

"Well that's a turn up for the books Nobby, me lad."

"It certainly is Jerry. What do you think about that, sir?" Clarke asked Cowan.

"I think it's a reason for a celebration. How about the Red Lion tonight?"

As the crew filed out of the briefing room the adjutant came up to speak to Clarke.

"I see you haven't got your stripe on yet Clarke. Problem with needle and thread is it?"

"Ah no sir, sorry. I have had to be down at my parents. My father died last week."

"God yes. I'm sorry Clarke. Stupid of me to forget. My condolences. But do get your stripe fixed there's a good chap and there is now a bunk for you in the Officers' quarters. I suggest you move there immediately."

Clarke felt a certain reluctance to move away from the others in his crew but Charlie Barton was the only one left that he had known since they started training and Charlie had never understood why Clarke was still with them in any case. It took him about an hour to gather his bits and pieces and move to the officers' quarters– his new room had four beds, the other three occupied by pilot officers like himself but to him they looked like kids. Cowan called by and they went to the Officers' Mess for a drink.

"Glad you made the change Nobby. You're a bloody good navigator you know. I've had some over the years that would get lost in a broom cupboard."

"Well I'm glad to have you as the driver I can tell you. Your predecessor would have had us dead by now!"

"Are you going to the dance tomorrow?"

"No Paul. I have met this very special lady and we are going to a concert at the cathedral. I'm not sure where it will all end. Her fiancé was killed just before Christmas, Matt White, he was B flight commander here. I feel slightly uncomfortable it being so soon after his death but we get on really well."

"In this bloody war Nobby nothing can be "too soon" believe me. If she's up for it, good luck. Let's have another and then get down to the Lion. You are coming there aren't you?"

* * *

Clarke slept well after a fairly riotous evening in the Red Lion and if his new hut-mates snored he certainly did not hear them. His headache wasn't too bad either once he had got going. The morning dragged by and Clarke was tempted just to head off to Lincoln but he had a few things to do, including some sewing! It was a lovely, early summer day and after lunch he walked out of the base, along one of the nearby lanes and out into the country. The trees were looking very beautiful in their fresh, multiple, shades of green and the May trees were now covered in blossom, the scent from which always reminded him of home and childhood for some reason. The last few weeks had been very bleak and difficult, but he felt that he might have turned a corner and that things were on the change for the better. He walked for a while, the gentle breeze wafting the scents of springtime over him and it was a while before he turned back to the base anticipating, with great pleasure, the next few hours with Anne.

The car started at the first attempt and driving through the lanes he found himself singing out loud something he had not felt like doing for many weeks.

Anne was waiting for him on the hospital steps looking lovely with her long hair falling over her shoulders and her pink blouse and white floral skirt. Clarke's heart was already thumping as he got out of the car and they kissed.

"Good afternoon pilot officer" she said laughing and pointing at his new stripe. "When did this happen?"

Clarke explained what had been going on as they walked along to the restaurant. Anne had booked a table and they each had the lamb pie which, they both agreed, was delicious. Anne did not mention Matt once and compared with their last time together she seemed very relaxed and genuinely enjoying herself.

The cathedral was filling up when they got there and they found a place at the back of the nave.

"I hope you like the music" Anne whispered. "It's Handel's Messiah."

"Wonderful. I used to sing in a choir you know?"

"When you were still in shorts? I can see you dressed up as a choirboy!" she laughed.

"No, no much more recently in fact. Manchester university had a choir and I sang regularly. We used to go all over giving concerts."

"I am impressed" and she squeezed his hand gently. "I used to play an oboe at school but haven't done much since. Maybe I should take it up again. I think it's still at home somewhere."

"You should. I play the piano – we could do duets."

Clarke found the atmosphere in the cathedral especially comforting after the trauma of the last few weeks but as the music soared so did Clarke's emotions and he found himself thinking of his father, his brother and all those killed in the squadron. Looking up at the vaulted ceiling of the nave, built hundreds of years ago, he knew that against the constancy and beauty of this place, Hitler and his henchmen really counted for very little and they and Germany would be crushed sooner or later. He quickly wiped away a tear and felt Anne gently squeeze his hand.

"That was wonderful" Clarke said as they walked out. "Would you like to find somewhere for a drink before I take you back to the hospital?"

"You know John I would rather just walk back with you."
She took his hand as they walked along.

"What are you doing tomorrow Anne? It looks like we are
not going to get any leave for a while after tomorrow. It would
be lovely if we could get out – perhaps another walk. It looks like
the weather will be fine.

Anne turned to look at him. "John, I would love to. Let's do
that." She reached up to kiss him, this time on the lips, and he
put his arms around her and held her closely to him.

CHAPTER 27

Sunday 14th May 1944

Clearly quite a few of the aircrews were planning to head off somewhere, mostly into Lincoln, realising that this might be their last chance of a break for some time. Clarke felt excited by the fact that this wretched war might be entering its last stages, but even happier at the prospect of spending a day with Anne. The morning was beautiful, blue sky with a few feathery clouds. He had got together a small hamper and had even blagged a bottle of wine from the mess steward.

The car seemed almost as keen as he was and they roared through the lanes and into the hospital grounds where Anne was waiting. Even in her walking gear she looked gorgeous and as he helped her into the car, he got a whiff of her perfume.

"Well, where to navigator?" she said laughing. "Where are you going to take me to this time?"

"I was thinking about going back to the Wolds – it should be lovely up there now."

She leant over to kiss him "Maybe not quite so far as last time?"

"Right, OK then" he replied feeling slightly flustered. "What I thought we might do is walk a little way and try and find somewhere quiet where we could have lunch. I've even brought a hamper."

"John, that sounds lovely. Actually, anywhere would be OK just now" she smiled at him.

Clarke put the car in gear and they raced off through the countryside. Everything looked lovely in the warm sunshine and in no time at all they got to Donington, the village they had walked to all those weeks ago. People were coming out of the church as they arrived in the village and as Clarke drove slowly by, he noticed that the Black Horse pub was just about to open.

"Fancy a quick drink, Anne? It was good here before wasn't it?"

"What about that walk?" she replied smiling. "Just teasing, I would love a drink. Thank you."

They sat down outside the pub to wait until the landlord was ready. It was really warm in the sun and Anne leant her head against Clarke's shoulder.

"Do we need to walk John. I feel really sleepy sitting here."

"Of course, we don't. Let's have a drink and then drive off and see if we can find somewhere quiet to have our lunch."

They finished their drinks and got back in the car and Clarke drove through the village and a little further on they came upon a stream running through some woods.

"This looks OK. I'll park here and then we can walk a little way over to where those woods run alongside the stream."

He picked up the hamper and a rug from the car and they walked into the cool of the woods.

"Here OK?"

"Perfect. Here let me help with the rug. I must say you seem to have come very well prepared!"

Clarke knew that he was blushing. "Well I haven't had any practice at this I can assure you."

Anne kissed him and then took the hamper.

"Come along slow coach. I'm feeling very hungry. I hope you have put enough in."

They sat on the rug and Clarke opened the hamper.

"You do the food. It's really all I could get. I'll get this bottle open."

Anne spread out the food and they tucked in, sipping the wine as they went along. After they had eaten Anne lay down and loosened her hair which had been up in a bun.

"Lie down here with me, John. Thank you for lunch it was delicious if, perhaps, a little spartan" she smiled.

Clarke put his arm round her and as they kissed deeply, he loosened the buttons on her blouse and felt the fullness of her breast under his hand. After a while he felt her undo his belt and trousers and he quivered slightly as he felt her take him in her cool hand.

"Shall we?" he asked her gently.

"Yes, I think we should. Just let me get things organised down below"

John rolled over and into her and came almost immediately.

"Sorry Annie. It has been a very long time."

She looked at him tenderly "That's alright, I'm sure there will be another time. Come here and let's just lie down for a while. That sun is so lovely and warm."

He lay with Anne in his arms. It felt almost perfect to Clarke. He could hear her soft breathing, the sigh of the wind in the trees around them and the birds twittering in the branches. So quiet and far away from the roar of the aircraft's engines, the clatter of flak on the fuselage and the rattle of the guns as they tried to fend off near certain death. After a while Anne turned towards him and began kissing him again.

"I think I like being called Annie. When do you finish John? Have you long to go?"

"Well, I have completed sixteen and a half, an odd number but that is because until now trips over France only counted as a half. Unbelievable really but now the powers that be have decided to let our French trips count fully. The good thing is that they are relatively short and they send us nearly every night so the numbers are mounting up fairly quickly. That will make a big difference. There is something big coming along Annie. We all think that there will be an invasion perhaps in the next month or two. Who knows maybe it will all be over sooner than we think."

"What will you do afterwards?"

"Back to my old job in Manchester I suppose. I might look in to becoming a doctor although I'm a bit old now and goodness knows how I could fund it. What about you?"

"Oh I'll keep on nursing. I might move back nearer to my parents. But that's quite near to Manchester isn't it?"

She kissed him again and lay on her side looking at him. The sun had gone behind some clouds and she shivered slightly.

"Just get myself back together John. Look at me all in bits."

They laughed and Clarke pulled his trousers up and put his jacket back on.

"This has been wonderful Annie. We must do it again, probably now it will be when the war is over."

"Do you think it could end so soon?"

"Hard to say but when we get ashore Jerry might just crap himself and give up. Here's hoping. It's going pretty badly for them just about everywhere you know?"

They folded up the blanket and tidied everything away and slowly walked back to the car.

"John, you will keep in touch won't you and if you get time, let's meet whenever we can."

"Oh don't you worry old girl. I don't intend to let you out of my sight. You are the best thing that has happened to me for years."

The drive back to the hospital was certainly more restrained than when they had come. It had been an exquisite time but for

Clarke there was the lurking dread of going back in the air and for Anne the dreadful thought of losing someone else she was fond of. They kissed as Anne walked back into the hospital and this time, she did look back to wave goodbye.

Clarke drove quickly back to the base thinking of what had happened today rather than what was in front of them tomorrow. The first person he met was Cowan.

"Hallo Nobby. Where have you been to then? No, don't answer that, I think it shows in your face you old rascal. Any way the fun starts tomorrow for sure. We need to do an air test in the morning. I think they are going to work us pretty hard from now on. Better get a beer down your neck whilst you have the chance."

CHAPTER 28

Friday 19th May 1944

The last few days had been difficult for the crews. They were in limbo – everyone knew that something of enormous importance was coming but not when. Cowan's crew had their old aircraft T-Tommy back after it had been patched up and they spent time flying over the bombing range as well as doing a couple of night navigation exercises just to keep themselves on their toes. After one of the daytime outings Cowan suggested they all went down to the Red Lion for an evening's serious drinking and they were there in force when the pub opened.

"Nobby's in the chair" Cowan called out. "He's been promoted, got himself a girlfriend and managed to get us home last night in the rain."

"My pleasure. Couldn't buy a drink for a more deadbeat crew" Clarke laughed. "Pints all round."

There was a cheer and the evening had begun. After a while Cowan eased Clarke to one side.

"You OK Nobby? I sensed you weren't quite as sharp last night. Anything wrong? Not this girl is it?"

"To be honest Paul that Mailly camp fiasco shook me up quite a bit. I came as near to crapping myself as I ever have. I am finding it a bit difficult to concentrate because once we are near the target, I just feel so bloody scared."

Cowan paused for a while and then put his hand on Clarke's shoulder.

"Not love then?" Cowan smiled.

"Oh, I think that might be a factor too. Anne has become a very special person to me. Maybe there is also something about feeling that we can see an end in sight for this bloody war."

"Want some advice, Nobby? Never think like that unless you want to end up in a coffin. The "light at the end of the tunnel syndrome" has killed a lot of good blokes, believe me. We will have to fight these bastards to the death. Personally, I don't think that they will give up until Hitler's dead and buried. And that won't happen unless he can be assassinated or when we overrun Berlin. No, we've got a long way to go yet, take it from me old boy. Maybe this is the beginning of the end but it could still take years to finish them off. Now let's have another pint?"

The evening followed the usual course of steady drinking and singing and Clarke had to agree that he felt a good deal better about things as they walked home. The new rear gunner was called Ernie Stark and was quite a comedian, indeed, had been in the music hall for several years before joining up. Wasn't a bad pianist either and he had led the assembled host on most of the songs that night.

However, Cowan's pep-talk had struck home and after he had mulled it over in his mind, Clarke felt much less confident that the end of the war was anywhere close. He had written a couple of letters to Anne since Sunday and had tried to call her several times but she had been busy. He was desperate to see her again but knew that just wasn't going to happen unless some how she could come up to the Red Lion – girlfriends sometimes did.

As he walked back to the camp, he thought about what Cowan had said and realised that he was dead right. Victory would only result from grinding Germany down, the Russians from the east and a second front from the west. It was never going to be easy.

And no doubt they would soon be back to battering German cities – this was just a short but welcome, break.

* * *

Friday dawned cloudy with a fairly stiff westerly breeze and Clarke joined Cowan in the officers' mess.

"We're on for tonight Nobby. Rumour is that Bomber Command is hitting a number of targets tonight but we will just have to wait to see which one they have selected for us. How do you feel now?"

"OK, thanks Paul. And thanks for the chat last night. You are right and I need to get a grip."

"Let's do an air test this morning and get that out of the way. Briefing is not until seven o'clock so almost certainly it will be a shortish trip."

As the crew gathered for the air test, Clarke reckoned they had become quite a close-knit group, maybe one benefit from that dreadful Mailly raid. They had been petrified together!

"You OK Nobby? Got your pencils all sharpened up for this evening?"

"Yes, thanks Ernie. Hope you have cleaned out those gun barrels of yours. You never know. Hank you look a bit worse for wear. Please tell me you didn't go back to the mess after last night?"

"Gee you guys just don't know when to stop do you? Once we got on to the whisky that was me finished. Don't even remember going to bed."

"Just a matter of training, Hank. Another few weeks and you'll be fine."

"So you bloody say Ernie but Christ knows whether I can last that long at this rate. Feels like I'm going to die of alcohol poisoning rather than at the hands of some Kraut pilot!" They all laughed and clambered aboard T-Tommy.

* * *

The air test had gone without a hitch and the crews gathered in the briefing room to hear of their fate for the night. Wing Commander Squires walked in with his team and everyone stood up.

"Sit. As some of you may have heard there will be a number of raids tonight – we are off to Tours, southwest of Paris. Our job is to destroy the railway yards. It is not the first time bomber command has paid a visit there but we would like it to be the last. Make sure your bombs find their mark. As usual with this type of target, accuracy is of paramount importance."

He handed over to the rest of the team. The squadron bombaimer made it clear that they would need to wait until their Master Bomber was satisfied that the marking was perfect and that might involve holding off. There were groans around the room as the memory of the last time that happened flooded back into their minds.

"The good news chaps" Squires summed up, "Is that it is not very far to go and you should be back here before you know it. Good luck to you." And with that the officers all trooped out leaving the crews to talk amongst themselves.

"Well navigator I reckon that it's all down to you."

"Thanks Skip. If you can keep the aircraft flying then I think we'll be alright."

The night was very dark as they waited for the truck to take them out to T-Tommy and as they reached the aircraft it started to rain.

"Lovely, I don't remember the bloody met man saying anything about rain."

"Well Ray he did mention clouds and that often means rain as I recall."

"Don't be smart arse Nobby. You and you bloody pencils under that hood. Could be a blizzard outside as far as you are concerned. Just don't ask me to tell you when we cross the coast!"

They all chuckled as they climbed into the aircraft.

Cowan switched into his skipper's role as they all went through their checks.

"Right everyone, I know this is just to France but remember Jerry doesn't want us there and he will stop us if he can. Don't let our guard drop for a second. Navigator, toys all working?"

"Yes, Skip all OK."

"Right here we go then. It's rather blowy out there so could be pretty bumpy until we get above the cloud."

T-Tommy taxied out to the runway two-six and after the pre-flight checks Cowan opened the throttles and they roared into the night. They were relatively lightly laden with fuel and after a short run into the westerly wind they lifted off lurching this way and that until they were at about 5000 feet.

"Climb to 20,000 feet and heading one-seven-zero. We cross the coast at Eastbourne in about an hour."

They were above the clouds now and, joined by about a hundred other Lancasters, they made their way steadily south until Clarke noticed on H2S that they were crossing the French coast.

"About fifty minutes to the target Skip. We are over France now. Start to descend to 10,000 feet"

"Right everyone eyes peeled. Bombaimer everything ready up front?"

"Yes Skip. And it all looks quiet as well."

"Don't be fooled. They could be there, we just can't see them."

They droned on until Clarke said they were five minutes from the target and on time.

"Radio – anything heard?"

"No Skip. All quiet."

"Bombaimer anything?"

Beavers peered out into the black night. The cloud had broken up quite a bit, but in the darkness he could see nothing.

"Skip, MC says hold for now. They are trying to be certain that the markers are on target."

Clarke felt his guts squirm at the thought of being delayed again.

"I can see markers Skip. Shall we go for those?"

"No wait until we are given the Go Ahead."

"We are over time now Skip."

"Just wait Navigator. Those are French down there, not Germans. Tail and mid keep your eyes outside. Anything radio?"

"No Skip. We have been told to hold off. And there is no music to listen to this time either."

Clarke felt sweat break out despite the intense cold around him and fear was beginning to gnaw at him.

"That's it Skip. We can go in now. MC says aim for the green markers."

Cowan banked T-Tommy steeply to the left to bring the markers in front of them.

"Got them bombaimer?"

"Yes Skip. Come left, left again steady. Left, steady, steady. Coming up. Bombs gone. Flash gone"

Cowan pulled the aircraft round to the right and climbed hard to get away from the others.

"Course navigator?"

"Three-zero-five. We cross the coast at St Malo. Bombaimer you may be able to see when we do that." He felt huge relief that they were on their way home.

"Well the clouds have gone so I'll do my best. The bombing looked pretty tight Skip."

"Good. Now, we know there are flak batteries all along the coast here so watch out."

Almost as he finished speaking searchlights started probing the sky and as they got closer to St Malo the flak started its slow path towards them but they were soon past.

"Course for home navigator?"

"Three-four-five to Weymouth. About forty-five minutes."

The coast appeared and they turned on their final course for home. That it had been an uneventful trip made Clarke feel lucky rather than relieved. There would be plenty more trips like this that was for sure but he doubted they would be so without incident.

CHAPTER 29

Tuesday 23rd May 1944

The trip to Duisburg on Monday night had been a big raid involving over five hundred Lancasters and had been complicated by cloud covering the target. Nevertheless, a lot of damage had been done and although all the Lancasters from East Kirkby had returned safely, many other aircraft had been shot down. For T-Tommy and her crew, it had been a fairly uneventful run and apart from a shower of shrapnel when they were near the target, they were unscathed. An added pleasure, and something of a surprise, was the news that they were to have leave from now until Friday night. After the debriefing Clarke went straight to the phone to call Anne praying that she would be able to get some time off as well.

"Annie, it's John. Amazingly they have given us some leave. Probably the last for a while but is there any chance you could get off?"

"Well, you know, I think I can. I'm owed loads of time. I'll go and speak to the dragon and get back to you. It would have to be after I finish today though."

"Annie any time would be good. Do I need to speak to said dragon do you think? I mean a pilot officer rank should cut some ice!"

"No, I'll sort her out" Anne replied laughing. "What shall we do?"

"Well" he said hesitatingly "I wonder if you would like to meet my mother. I need to go down and see how she is in any case, and my brother is home as well. What do you think?"

"Do you think that would be a good idea? I mean we haven't known one another for very long have we? She might prefer to see you on your own."

"Nonsense, she would love to meet you. I did talk to her about you when I was last down."

"Oh you did, did you? Bit presumptive wasn't it?" She smiled imagining Clarke blushing to his hair roots.

"No, not at all" he stammered. "I mean, I said I had found a wonderful lady."

Anne had to stop herself laughing "Let me go and see John. I would love to meet your mum. I was just teasing."

"Annie you are naughty and you know that I fall for it every time. Hear from you soon."

Clarke went off to tell Cowan that he was heading off to see his mother to check how she was.

"On your own?" he asked raising his eyebrows.

"Hopefully not Paul. I tell you, this girl could be the one. Never felt like this before."

"That's what they all say. You get off and enjoy yourself. I think Bomber Command are playing a game. Apparently quite a few squadrons have been stood down, I reckon on the basis that this will get out and fool Jerry into thinking the invasion is still some way off."

"You think it's close then?"

"I'm sure it is, then we can get over there and give those blighters what for, just like the Reds are doing. We'll squeeze them 'til the pips squeak. Now off you go before the boss finds you a job."

Anne rang the mess after lunch with the good news that she could get off when her shift ended at four o'clock and Clarke arranged to meet her in front of the hospital.

He made sure that the car was ready and managed to scrounge some extra petrol from the fuel bowser before setting off to the hospital at least two hours earlier than he needed to. He had rung his mother and told her they were coming down the next day realising that somehow, they would need to find somewhere to stay that night. Anne looked lovely as she walked down the hospital steps but was sensibly dressed for the coming trip and only had a small suitcase.

"Ready for the off then?"

"I certainly am. How long will it take?"

"Well to be honest Annie we will have to stop somewhere on the way down. It can take up to ten hours to get home from here."

"Have you somewhere in mind then?" she said smiling.

"Er, well there are inns all the way down. We could stop somewhere for dinner and get some rooms."

"That sounds like a good idea. I'm looking forward to the drive and I very much want to meet your mother. Is she nice like you?" she said leaning over and kissed him.

Although the morning had been sunny the sky gradually clouded over and by the time they had reached Leamington Spa it was raining quite hard and Clarke pulled into a pub set back from the road. They both got out and once they were in the pub and had ordered some food, they started to feel a little more relaxed.

"This is nice John. Great food too. Do they have rooms do you know?"

"I think they do but I'll go and see what they can do. I don't think we want to go on much further. It has become a filthy night out there."

The inn keeper said that they had a couple of rooms left and Clarke snapped them up before anyone else could.

"They have two single rooms if that is alright?"

"Well done. Perfect. Shall we have another drink. I still feel quite thirsty."

Clarke got the drinks and they sat down in a corner of the pub.

"How's it going? I hear there were some more raids in Germany?"

"Yes, we were on one last night. Pretty straightforward really. A wizard prang I think is the RAF term, whatever that means. The leave has come as a bit of a surprise I can tell you."

"Maybe they think you all need a rest. Talking of which John, I am feeling pretty sleepy – it's been a long day."

"Me too. Let's go up. Still a bit of a way to go tomorrow I'm afraid."

They said their goodnights and went to their respective bedrooms. Clarke undressed and got into his bed feeling tired but happy. He realised that he was really very fond of Anne who was so different to his other girlfriends. She was such good company. He fell soundly asleep thinking of her and woke at about five o'clock. The pub was very quiet and he thought about going to see Anne. Would she mind? Would she object? He thought it would probably be OK and he had to visit the toilet in any case so he would just tap her door on the way back.

"Come in" a sleepy voice from within. Clarke opened the door quietly and went over to Anne's bed and as he did so she pulled back the bedclothes for him to join her. "Couldn't you sleep?"

"Thinking about you. Did you sleep?"

"Well, until I was woken by someone knocking on my door! Come here John."

She pulled him down towards her and kissed him gently on the lips.

"Not much wriggle room I'm afraid. But I am sure we can manage."

She was wearing a dark blue satin nightdress which she lifted up to her waist and they lay kissing for a while before they made love gently and slowly.

"Oh, that was nice John. Can we do it again sometime?"

He kissed her "I was hoping so. Let's stay like this for a while? I don't ever want to forget this moment."

"John, promise you won't do anything silly. I don't think I could stand losing someone else who I love. I hope to God that this war will be over soon."

Clarke lay quietly for a while, listening to the cacophony of the dawn chorus. There was a tree just outside the bedroom window which obviously served as a bandstand for the blackbirds, thrushes, robins and chaffinches vying with one another.

Anne had fallen asleep and Clarke eased himself out of bed kissing her forehead as he left to go back to his room. It was six o'clock and he felt that he was unlikely to get any further sleep so he dressed and went outside for a walk. He had some serious thinking to do.

Last night's rain had stopped, to leave a lovely sunny morning. There was a wood behind the pub and he could see a path leading through it to the hill beyond. As he walked along he found himself thinking about his relationship with Anne. He felt that he could love her for ever but it seemed like they were doing things back to front. He hardly knew her, after all, but here they were making love as if they were married. It was this bloody war, he thought. It turns everything upside down. He could be dead next week for all he knew, but somehow the way things were working with Anne made him feel uneasy.

He walked through the wood and soon the path led him to the top of the hill. The sun was well up now and the smells of the warm, damp soil, for some reason brought thoughts of his father and the times they used to walk together through the countryside around Leckhampstead when he was a young boy. He suddenly felt a great sadness and a longing for a life uncomplicated by war. The view from the hill was a little obscured by the early morning mist but the spire of a nearby church could be seen poking out almost like a symbol of peace. The whole thing had an almost mystical feel, made more so by the silence of an early morning, broken only by birdsong. He stood still for a while trying to absorb the sights and sounds before, somewhat reluctantly, he walked slowly back to the pub to find that Anne was already down in the bar waiting for breakfast.

"Are you alright John? I checked in your room and found you had gone."

"Yes, I'm fine, Annie. I just needed to get outside for a think. Anyway, it's a lovely morning and you look lovely too."

"Was it this morning? I thought it seemed the right thing to do."

"Well it was right Annie. It's just me. I'm feeling that everything is happening rather quickly I suppose. And if I'm honest we've had a couple of dodgy trips which have shaken me up quite a bit." Anne put her arms round him and they stood there for a while and when she looked at him, she saw that there were tears in his eyes.

"Do you still want me to come home with you John? I can easily go back to Lincoln if you would rather. Maybe me being here just puts too much pressure on you."

"No, silly. I love you being here and I really want you to meet my mother. Maybe we just need to pace ourselves a bit, although most men would think that I was completely mad not to want to make love to you all the time."

Anne smiled, "I understand what you mean. Maybe the war makes us all get the feeling that everything has to be done at a hundred miles an hour." She kissed him gently but she felt fearful that, maybe, Clarke was beginning to show the early signs that she had seen in Matt as the stress and tension of the endless trips began their toll.

"How about breakfast? Then off to your mother's?"

* * *

The rest of the journey was tedious in the extreme. The roads were cluttered with both US and British army trucks, tank carriers and jeeps all seemingly making their way south.

"You know Annie. I think the invasion is just around the corner. I have never seen anything like this before. Certainly, when I came down for father's funeral a few weeks ago there was quite a bit of traffic but nothing like this."

"Well here's hoping. Sooner the better and then we can all go back to our normal lives."

"But together, yes?" Clarke darted a sideways glance and saw her nodding and she reached over and touched his hand.

They left the old road at Abingdon and made their way towards Wantage before turning off the Great Shefford road to Leckhampstead. It was a little after one thirty when they reached the house and as he pulled up, his mother came out to meet them.

"And you must be Anne. I'm so pleased that you could come down. Hallo dear" she said putting her arms round Clarke. "Lunch is ready if you would like to eat now. John, show Anne up to her room, it's the one at the back, and then we can start."

"Where's Richard?" Clarke asked. His mother lifted her eyes.

"Down at the pub. John, he's not well. You will notice a big change in him I'm afraid. He was terribly injured. Come along let's sit down and Anne you can tell me all about yourself."

They finished lunch just as Richard came in, obviously drunk.

"Ah, my kid brother. And how's little Johnny today?" Clarke was stunned by Richard's appearance. He had a livid scar down the right side of his face, his eye socket was clearly empty and two fingers of his right hand were missing.

"Not a pretty sight eh? That's what happens when you are a real soldier, not swanning about in big aeroplanes three miles above Germany like you boys in blue. Oh, sorry who's this lovely lady? Surely not someone who thinks very much of you brother?"

"Do you want something to eat, dear?"

"No thanks, ma. I'll just get myself another drink." He strode out of the room leaving the three of them looking at one another.

"How long has he been like this?" Clarke asked quietly. He was conscious that Anne had gone pale after Richard's outburst.

"Since he came back. They are going to invalid him out of the Army apparently so maybe that's what has caused him to be so upset? He's doing a bit of work down on the Culper's farm but usually spends most of his time in the pub or drinking here."

"I'll go and speak to him. You and mum can have a talk."

He found Richard emptying the contents of a whisky bottle into his glass.

"What the hell was that all about Richard? Not very nice in front of Anne whose fiancé, incidentally, was killed in a bomber raid just before Christmas Day. And whilst we are about it, we are regularly losing chaps night after night, so don't come the bloody hero with me." He was shouting now, something he almost never did. "And what about mother? She's still upset about father's death and here you are drinking yourself into the ground with no thought for anyone else. Just bloody well pull yourself together. When you have done that come and apologise to Anne and at least say hallo to her. You're a bloody disgrace."

With that he turned on his heel and walked back to the dining room where Anne and his mother seemed to be deep in conversation. Anne looked up anxiously as he came in but carried on talking to his mother. She had never seen Clarke look so angry and it almost frightened her.

"Is everything alright, dear?"

"Well not really mother but hopefully he can buck his ideas up a bit. He has been through the mill, you know – needs help, doesn't he? Anne and I will pop out for a walk around the village mother if that's alright. I'll show her the sights of the town" he said laughing trying to lighten the tense atmosphere.

Once they were well away from the house Clarke turned to Anne.

"I'm so sorry about that – he was completely out of order. The Richard I remember was a delightful brother full of energy, yes, but also love. Oh, what is this bloody war doing to us all? It's just tearing everything and everyone apart." He turned away and his shoulders slumped and Anne could tell he was crying. She put her arms round him and they stood for a minute whilst he got himself back together.

"You did well in there darling. Don't worry for me. He didn't mean any harm. He's ill and you are right, he needs help. Doesn't the army have some way of assisting him. Surely they can't just leave him on a rubbish dump?"

"Oh I wouldn't be so sure – they probably have enough to worry about just now without the likes of Richard. Annie are you happy to stay? I could understand if you didn't want to, you know. I could take you to Oxford for the train."

"Not on your life. In any case your mother and I have several stories about you that we need to talk about" and with that she kissed him on the cheek. They walked in the warm afternoon sun over to the village of Chaddleworth and Clarke pointed out that the swallows had started to arrive.

"Bit early to be honest and listen, there's the cuckoo as well. At least they don't seem to care that there is a war on!"

"You and your birds, John? You seem to know so much."

"Well, as I said, my father taught me most of what I know about them."

It took them about an hour to reach the village and they arrived in time to see the pub opening.

"Let's have a quick drink and then head back. It has been good to get out of the house even though we have only just arrived!"

"I like your mother very much John. She's been through so much recently and she must be worried to death about you and yet she seems to take it all in her stride."

Clarke smiled "I reckon it was because she came from farming stock. In fact, her father used to own the farm we passed on the way here. He sold up years ago but it always strikes me that she would have been a natural as a farmer's wife."

By the time they got back home Clarke's mother had some supper ready but Richard had gone back to the pub. After dinner the three of them sat and chatted and Clarke was pleased to see how well Anne was getting on with his mother. Eventually he and Anne excused themselves and went upstairs to bed, Clarke making it clear they were in separate rooms.

It was around midnight when Clarke was awoken by the front door slamming and the sound of a very drunk Richard trying to sing some bawdy song. He got up and put his dressing gown on to go downstairs.

"What the hell are you doing making so much noise at this time of night? Don't you have any consideration?"

"Oh, sorry John I wouldn't want to disturb your beauty sleep or that of the lovely Anne."

"Actually I was thinking more of mother. Don't you think that she has had enough to put up with lately?"

He did not see the fist that smacked into the side of his head and he fell, dazed, to the ground. When he turned, he saw that

Richard was charging towards him with a kitchen knife in his hand and although he swung round lashing out with his arms to defend himself, he felt the slash of the knife as it tore into his arm. He fell on to his back and as Richard attacked him again, he kicked as hard as he could aiming the blow for the crutch. Richard screamed with pain and doubled over just long enough for Clarke to pick up a nearby bottle and hit him on the head as hard as he could. Richard crumpled on to the ground and at that moment his mother, followed closely by Anne, came into the room.

"Whatever is going on?"

"I'm surprised you didn't hear the racket as he came in. I came down to tell him to keep quiet and he went for me. I think that his next move was to kill me mother. It's not safe for you to be here with him alone. He needs urgent help."

"What shall I do dear?"

"You had better ring PC Summers. Richard needs to be taken into custody. God knows what he will be like when he comes round."

"That arm is bleeding quite badly. Let me have look at it. And you are going to have a real shiner."

"Thanks Annie. I might sit down, I'm feeling a bit woozy" and he dropped on to the nearest chair. Clarke's mother came back in to say that she had called the police. Richard's problem was no surprise in the village and they were sending a couple of policemen from Newbury to take him in. She got some towels and Anne skilfully dressed Clarke's arm which she said was only a flesh wound. Richard's head looked a bit of a mess but they left him where he was until the police arrived.

"Cup of tea might help?" Clarke's mother said and went away to the kitchen.

"God, John do you think he would have killed you?"

"I reckon so Annie. I'm not sure he really knew it was me and he was just lashing out at anything and anybody. He'll have to go to a hospital. He must have really bad shellshock don't you think?"

Anne nodded in agreement and at that moment the tea arrived followed closely by two burly policemen.

"Blimey looks like a war zone" one of them said.

"Not really, I can assure you" Clarke replied. "I had to hit him pretty hard or you would have been collecting a body."

"You bringing charges, sir?"

"No, of course not, he's my brother but he is a very sick man and needs treatment. He has only just got back home after being wounded."

Oh, I see, sorry sir. Well we'll pack him up and see what the police doctor can make of him. He stinks of booze though, doesn't he?"

"Part of the problem constable. I'll pop down to the station in the morning."

"We'll pop down constable" Anne said quickly.

CHAPTER 30

Wednesday 24th May 1944

When Clarke awoke, he found that Anne was sitting on his bed wrapped up in a blanket.

"How do you feel sweetheart? That eye is pretty well closed now."

"Christ, Annie my head feels as if a bloody elephant has sat on it."

"Well it rather looks as if one has" she giggled nervously. "How's the arm?"

"Arm? What's wrong with that?"

"Quite a slice. I'll have another look – I don't think it needs stitches but we better check. In fact, I think we should get you round to your doctor's this morning. He hit you pretty hard."

"God what an irony – managed to survive the Luftwaffe only to be stabbed to death by your own brother. Have you been sitting there all night?"

"It's what nurses do isn't it?" she leaned over and kissed him. "Can you get up. It's about eight o'clock. Maybe we should go and see how your mother is faring. Poor thing looked stupefied last night after we had got you into bed."

Clarke levered himself up slowly but it took a while because of the pain in his arm and together they went slowly downstairs.

His mother looked up as they came into the kitchen and she gasped when she saw him.

"Oh, John what a mess you are in. Anne thank you for looking after him. I don't know how I would have coped without you. Would you like a cup of tea? May be plenty of sugar in it will help?"

"I'll be fine mother don't you worry. How about yourself? It must have been quite a shock for you too. Annie and I will go into Newbury this morning to see what has happened to Richard. I think they will take him away you know?"

She nodded as she brought the tea over and sat down next to them.

"Maybe for the best I suppose. I'm a bit frightened with him here with me alone, dear. Maybe especially after what has happened." And with that she started crying in long, pitiful sobs. Anne put her arm around her and it was sometime before she stopped and wiped her eyes.

"I'm sorry. Oh, Anne what must you think of us. Not a very nice welcome for your first trip here. I really hope it won't be your last. I am sure we could do better next time" and she smiled wanly from her tear-soaked face.

"There will be a next time Mrs Clarke don't you worry" and she looked up at Clarke and winked.

"Anne why don't you call me Dora – I'd like that very much" and she bent over to kiss her on the cheek.

Fortunately, Clarke had put the car hood up after they had arrived yesterday because now it was pouring with rain. Clarke drove first to the see the doctor for a check up and when he had pronounced that there was nothing broken and had put a few stitches in his arm, they set off to Newbury police station.

"Good morning" Clarke spoke to the desk sergeant. "We have come to see how my brother, Richard Clarke, is doing. He was brought in last night."

"Had a bit of fight did you sir? Not exactly brotherly love looking at you and him. The police surgeon said he'd never seen someone such a mess top and bottom. Come to think of it you don't look so good yourself."

"If he's still here we'd like to speak to him if possible," trying to ignore the sergeant's comments.

"Well, how shall I put it. He was here but he became pretty violent again and because we don't really have the manpower just now, we rang up the army to come and get him. You just missed them actually – the MPs took him away about half an hour ago sir."

"But where to? Presumably you know where he went."

"Aldershot – the army hospital at Aldershot sir. Sorry but he could have hurt himself if he had stayed here."

"Aldershot. OK thanks sergeant."

He turned to Anne "What now? Not much point trailing off to Aldershot. Let's go back home – I'm beginning to feel a bit rough myself. Incidentally sergeant, do you know who we should speak to, to find out how my brother is getting on? I have to be back to my squadron by Friday evening and I need to be able to let my mother know what she should do."

"Just a minute – they left a docket – here we are; he's under the care of a Major Simpson. Sorry that's all they gave me."

Clarke thanked the sergeant and they made their way back to the car. The rain had eased off but the clouds were hanging low and, altogether, the weather rather reflected how Clarke felt. He had a thumping headache and his left eye had closed up almost completely so he had to drive carefully back to Leckhampstead. When they got back, they found that Clarke's mother had cleaned up the house so that all signs of the night's events were nowhere to be seen.

"Richard's in hospital in Aldershot, mother. I have a name to call. Probably best after lunch when they have got him settled in. The problem is I have to get back on Friday."

"Surely they won't expect you to do anything with your eye like that, dear?"

"Mother to be honest I think they would consider that death itself a poor excuse not to go on flying operations – I have to get back" and he smiled as he put his arms round her. "Actually, I think I will lie down for an hour if that's alright. I'll take some aspirin for this headache."

"I'll stay here and talk to your mother John – sorry, Dora – I'll come up and check how you are later" and she kissed him as he went past.

Clarke felt better after he had slept for a while and went down stairs to find Anne and his mother still chatting.

"Pretty poor care in this hospital" he joked. "Man could have died waiting for the nurse to do her rounds."

"Lunch is ready dear. How are you feeling?"

"Better thanks mother. We'll try and sort out Aldershot later."

It took a long time to track down where Richard was but eventually Clarke was put through to his ward and spoke to the sister in charge. She said that he had been sedated and was sleeping and she described him as being in the "shell shock" ward. At least they had found out where he was.

Dinner that evening was subdued and Clarke noticed that his mother picked away at her food.

"Come on mother. At least we know that Richard is safe and Anne and I will be down as soon as possible, won't we Annie?"

She nodded but Clarke could tell that she was not happy either – the last few days had been difficult but she realised that she had fallen in love with Clarke and that after Friday not only would the war take him away from his mother but from her as well. After dinner they walked to the Stag for a quick drink before bed and on the way back, Clarke put his arm round Anne and pulled her gently towards him for a kiss.

"What's that for then?" she smiled.

"Because Annie I love you and I want you to marry me. After the last few days I realise you may not be too keen to join a crazy family like ours but to be honest I won't take no for an answer."

"I thought you had to ask my father first. Can't possibly agree without his say so" she said giggling.

They walked on back to the house and saying their goodnights went upstairs.

"I'll come and tuck you up if you promise to be good" Anne whispered. "No hanky panky with that face of yours."

Clarke had only been a bed a few minutes when Anne came in wearing her nightgown. She looked lovely with her hair hanging down over her shoulders and as she sat on the side of the bed they kissed gently and eventually she slipped under the covers to cuddle him.

"Is this a service you provide for all your patients, nurse?"

"Only the very, very special ones. Now you get some sleep. Oh, and the answer to the earlier question is yes. I would love to become Mrs Clarke." She kissed him and left Clarke lying looking at the ceiling wondering what the next few weeks would bring until he drifted off.

Parting at the hospital had been difficult for them both but the problems over the last few days with Richard had helped forge a close bond not only of love but also from the realisation that they had worked well together to sort things out. Clarke had no doubt that she was the one for him and once the war was over they would marry and live together forever of that he was sure. Just this bloody war to fix first.

When he returned to East Kirkby, Clarke received many suggestions about how he had acquired his black eye and bruised face, from the wife's husband coming back unexpectedly, to being rat-arsed and walking into a wall. The MO declared that he was fit to fly after he checked him over on the Saturday and it was only over a pint in the Mess with Cowan that he revealed what had really gone on.

"Blimey, Nobby that sounds bad. Have the redcaps still got him then?"

"No, he's in a military hospital just now but God knows what the future holds for him. Not good I reckon."

"How are you feeling in any case. Couldn't have been much of a leave."

"Well actually Paul it was fantastic because Anne and I have decided to get hitched. Well, after the war at least. She was tremendous about Richard but particularly good with my mother who, what with father dying a couple of weeks ago and then the problems with Richard, looked as if she had been run over by a bus."

"I'm pleased for you Nobby. You old chaps need to start thinking about settling down somewhere – slippers by the fire, pipe in the mouth, little woman making tea. Fits you like a glove!!"

"Bugger off. Another pint? In any case what's the buzz around here?"

"Well it looks like the invasion will happen somewhere in France probably within the next month. General feeling is that it will be the Pas de Calais but we are bombing all along the coast all the way down to St Malo, so who knows. But it sounds like something will happen soon."

"Sooner the better as far as I'm concerned. Stop that little shit in his tracks, that's what we need to do."

CHAPTER 31

Sunday 4ᵗʰ June 1944

Over the next few days the crew were busy bombing French railway yards and had several visits to the coastal batteries but the big difference, compared with trips to Germany, was that by and large there were few fighters or flak batteries trying to kill them. They had all been confined to their base, leave cancelled and no phone calls outside so it was a difficult time for everyone and not that easy for those outside either. The main complaint from the crew of T-Tommy was that they couldn't even get down to the Red Lion!

Clarke wandered over to the Flight Office to see that the list for the night's raid was long and seemed to involve all the crews. As they filed into the briefing room at five o'clock that afternoon there was a buzz of excitement that may be this was, at last, the start of the finish and the importance of the raid seemed to be emphasised by the fact the briefing was led by the boss, Group Captain Brookes.

"Right chaps sit down. I have some very important news for you. The invasion is scheduled for tomorrow although some unseasonably bad weather may delay things." Once the cheering died away he continued. "Our job tonight and probably for several nights to come will be vital to the success of the invasion.

We have been detailed to bomb batteries on the Normandy coast. Another group are off to bomb shore batteries around the Pas de Calais. The weather doesn't look too good but there will be markers put down by the Pathfinders. It is vital that these coastal guns are put out of action."

The other specialist officers followed ending with the meteorologist. "It's going to be rainy and windy from the south west. Can't say more" and he sat down to the usual jeering which continued until Brookes stood up and called for silence.

"Right, so it won't be easy to see the target but you must hit it. I can't emphasise that enough. Any questions?"

"Do we know where the invasion will land, sir?"

"No. That is classified. We need to keep Jerry guessing for as long as possible and maybe for at least another forty-eight hours. Then we nail him."

The crews were in good spirits as they walked out of the briefing.

"This might be it then Skip?" Stark said to Cowan. "Hope it doesn't end too soon. I'm only just getting to know you lot."

"Can't end soon enough for me, Ernie. Fed up flying around never knowing what's going to happen and thinking the next moment is your last."

"Gee man, it's not that bad Ray. At least you're in your own country and used to the crappy weather and food."

They went to their separate messes to eat and after a sleep met up in the crew room. They all felt remarkably relaxed since, although this was an important op, it was only to France and back and generally they had met little resistance. But, as they geared up, Cowan made it clear this would be no cake walk and they needed to be at their best as usual. No slacking.

Ernie was telling one of his endless stories when the truck came to take them to T-Tommy.

"OK here we go lads" Cowan said. "All aboard."

They arrived at the aircraft and whilst Cowan, Clarke and Beavers got on board the others lit cigarettes for one last smoke before they left. It was a nasty night with rain and a gusty wind so even the smokers did not stay out too long and the remaining four levered themselves up into the aircraft and closed the rear door.

Clarke shuffled his papers and charts and checked that all the electronic gear was working and was ready when Cowan asked for his report.

"Right everyone. We are set to go. Let's make this a successful trip as if the invasion depends on it. Green flare. Ready for engine start flight engineer?"

"Yes, Skip, all set. Starboard inner prop turning and engine firing."

They went through the usual routine and soon all four engines were running smoothly.

"Control, T-Tommy ready to taxi."

"Taxi to the hold runway two-zero."

Eventually they could line up and the throttles were opened and the aircraft, quite lightly laden this time, seemed to leap into the sky. There was a lot of turbulence as they climbed away and Clarke had to hold things down on his desk as T-Tommy shook violently."

"Blimey, Skip pretty rough back here" Stark called over the intercom. "Like a bloody bucking bronco. You'd know about those Hank."

"Cut it out Stark. Just concentrate on your job. It'll get better once we get above this bloody cloud."

"Sorry Skip, but I had just smacked my face on the gun breech."

"You OK?"

"Yes, not bleeding too much. Any case feels a bit smoother now."

"Course navigator?"

"One-nine-zero climb to 15,000 feet. We cross the coast at Selsey Bill in forty-five minutes"

"Don't ask me to tell you when. Can't see a thing with this cloud."

"Don't worry Ray. I can do without you tonight. Toys are all working. Just crossing the coast, Skip. This wind is pretty strong from the west about sixty miles an hour at this height. More than forecast for a change! Time to target thirty minutes."

"Skip there are some breaks in the cloud. Even from this height the sea looks pretty rough. Can't see anything else down there."

"OK just keep your eyes peeled for any markers. This isn't going to be easy with that wind."

"About ten minutes to target, Skip. We are dead on time so we should be able to see something soon."

"Yes, Skip, dead ahead I can see some flak. Maybe they are shooting at the Pathfinders. I don't think they want us in there."

"I see the flak bombaimer. Time now navigator?"

"Two minutes Skip. We are bang on target and on time."

"I can see markers over to starboard Skip, quite close now."

"Yep, I've got them. Gunners watch out for fighters just in case. OK heading towards the markers. Quite a lot of flak and searchlights. Hold tight everyone."

Cowan could see the sky markers quite clearly but there was cloud all over the target.

"Bombaimer all yours."

"Left Skip. Left, steady. Jesus, Skip there is an aircraft right below us."

"What the fuck is he doing there. We are going around, shut the bomb doors." Cowan heaved T-Tommy round to starboard and eventually aimed for the markers once more. "OK let's line ourselves up again. No problem. Navigator take us in."

Clarke guided them around on to another bombing run and although most of the other aircraft had left, the target was obvious from the presence of a huge fire.

"Bomb on that blaze bombaimer. That has to be the area. In we go."

"Right, right, steady. Bombs gone, flash gone."

Flak was curling up towards them again but was some way off and for once it did not feel at all threatening.

"Home we go, course navigator."

"Zero-one-zero Skip. Maintain our height at 15000 feet until we get to Peterborough then we can descend."

"Well spotted Ray. God knows what that Lanc was doing there. Was it one of ours I wonder? Guess we'll never know, will we?"

"I was sure we were bang on time and at the right height Skip. I don't think it was our mistake."

"No, of course not. Some erk not sure what they were doing. It's always a risk isn't it?"

* * *

"Invasion on then?" Cowan asked the IO when they went for the debrief.

"Nope. Weather not good enough for landing craft."

"I can believe that" replied Beavers. "From what I could see, the sea looked bloody rough."

"Maybe tomorrow" the IO said. "It's all down to the met man."

"God help them then" Clarke smiled. "Beer, Paul?"

"Good plan. See you in the morning chaps. Well done tonight. Looked like a good show."

* * *

By all accounts the targets from the previous night had been hit hard and there was excited anticipation as the crews gathered for their briefing the next evening.

"Well everyone, we did well last night and I am now allowed to tell you that the invasion of Europe, the second front, is underway."

There was cheering and clapping, and several crews stood up and slapped one another on the back.

"The code name is Overlord and troops will be landing early tomorrow morning. The next few days will be crucial if the operation is to succeed and the RAF will be playing a big part in trying to ensure that troops get established ashore. Now your target for tonight is the town of Ouistreham and once again the bombing must be accurate. This town is just behind one of the assault beaches and is thought to be heavily armed."

After the others had made their presentations and the briefing was drawn to a close, the crew of T-Tommy made their way outside and for a while stood around not quite knowing what to do or say. They had all been waiting for this moment for so long and it seemed unreal now that it was here.

"Well everyone" Cowan began "Looks like it's the real thing this time. It would be nice to think that Jerry will just give in but, unfortunately, I don't think that is very likely."

"I agree with you Paul. They'll fight to the death. Just hope our lot get ashore OK. Makes me pleased to be flying for a change. Feels like we are making a real contribution instead of just flattening houses"

"You're right Nobby. Bastards won't give in until they have to. What you reckon Charlie?"

"Yeh, be a while yet. I bet we finish our tour before the bloody war comes to an end that's for sure. I mean we're well over half way through now and these tiddlers to France are mounting up pretty quickly now."

"Don't count your bloody eggs too soon Charlie." Stark said shaking his head. "Bad omen" and with that he walked away from the others.

"What's got into Ernie – not like him."

"I think we all feel it might be tempting fate saying we are nearly finished. Let's get off to have something to eat. See you in the crew room." And with that Cowan and Clarke walked off to the Mess.

"To be honest Nobby I'm a bit worried about Charlie talking like that. It's understandable but sodding dangerous. Never over 'til the fat lady sings, as they say."

"Well, that was the point you made to me Paul and I agree with you but wouldn't it be great if it happened? Anne and I could get married for a start. We certainly aren't going to do it before it's over."

"Maybe you shouldn't wait. What if the war goes on for another five years?"

"God don't say that, Paul. I mean Hitler's getting his balls squeezed by the Reds, things aren't going too badly in Italy for us now Cassino has been overrun and if we get ashore alright tonight, I reckon things are beginning look pretty black for the Krauts."

The crew met again in the Crew Room and some light-hearted banter continued between the two gunners.

"How many are you going shoot down tonight then Ernie?"

"You know what, I feel like letting them bloody Germans off tonight. Them have got enough to worry about I reckon. What about you."

"Nah. If I see one, I'm bloody letting him have it. Too many of them around as it is."

They struggled into their flying kit and one by one picked up their parachutes and made their way outside to the waiting trucks. The night was quite clear and Clarke reckoned that he could just see the last glimmer of dusk. They climbed up into the truck driven by their usual WAAF.

"Hallo luv" Stark said, "Where are you taking us tonight then? They tell me there's a good film on at the Odeon in town. Even buy you an ice cream."

"Cor, you know how to treat a girl that's for sure. Can't make it tonight love, got another date."

"That's what they all bloody say" Stark replied whilst the others laughed.

They followed the usual ritual and eventually all got aboard T-Tommy. Engines were started and as they taxied out Cowan wished them all good luck.

"This could be an historic night," he said "Maybe one you will remember for ever," and with that he opened the throttles and in no time at all they were airborne.

It was much clearer than the previous night and when they were about half way across on their way to the Normandy coast Beavers called the others to look outside. There, far below them it was possible to see, through the breaks in the clouds, a vast armada streaming towards France.

"There you are" Cowan said "I told you today would be important. Take a look at that. Something to tell your kids. And navigator how long to the target?"

"Twenty minutes. We need to descend to 10,000 feet."

"I can see a lot of action up front. The whole length of the coast looks to be alight."

"Thanks bombaimer, I see that too. Course from here?"

"Steer one-eight-five"

"I can see the target area Skip, slightly over to the right. It looks very clear just now. Quite a bit of flak coming up to the leading aircraft."

"I see it too now. Bombaimer you take from here. Bomb doors open. Christ more flak than we have seen for a while. They don't look very pleased to see us."

"OK Skip. Come left, steady. Right a touch. Steady. Bombs gone."

They flew on for five minutes and then turned for home.

CHAPTER 32

Monday 12ᵗʰ June 1944

The raid on the 5ᵗʰ June was the first of a series of trips across the Channel to bomb coastal batteries, railways and airfields. A couple of the coastal raids were just after dawn and the crew could clearly see the progress of the invasion which at least initially seemed to get held up even though a substantial bridgehead had been established. The allies appeared to have almost complete dominance in the air over Normandy and this was made certain by the fighter patrols which accompanied the bombers.

When Clarke had last spoken to Anne they had discussed going away when he next got some leave which, rumour had it, was likely to be at the end of the month. Anne hesitated to suggest that they maybe could go to Scotland because that brought back memories about what she and Matt had planned to do before he was killed, but she had set her heart on going there sometime, so why not now?

The invasion had brought a different atmosphere to the squadrons and between the raids the crew talked excitedly about the war ending and, at last, they started turning their minds from just surviving to actually having a future. They spent their evenings in the Red Lion yarning, laughing but mostly hoping.

On the morning of the 12th Clarke noticed that once again they were on the board for operations that evening.

"Another milk run eh, Nobby?"

"Well here's hoping Ernie. It certainly seems a good way to pile up the op numbers doesn't it?"

"Can't go on. I reckon they'll get us back into Germany soon you see if they don't."

"Blimey, Charlie you're a right Job's comforter you are and no mistake. I mean we've got to keep banging away at those defences for a while I would think."

"Nah, Butch Harris will want to get back at the Kraut cities. Bloody hates them he does."

The briefing was ominously held at four o'clock and the crews had noticed more fuel being poured into the aircraft than had been the case for quite a while.

Once again Group Captain Brookes led the way in and all stood. It looked like a big raid and twelve aircraft were listed.

"Well chaps. You have done well over the last week but it has been decided that we need to attack the synthetic fuel factories to try and dry up the German's fuel supplies. We are therefore tasked with destroying their factory at Gelsenkirchen and this is the start of a series of such raids. As you see from the chart it is in the northern part of the Ruhr – not quite Happy Valley but not far from it. You can anticipate a warm reception." He handed over to the Station Navigator.

As they made their way outside Ernie said "You bloody psychic or something Charlie? How'd you know?"

"Stands to reason don't it? Germans will think we've bloody well run out of aircraft soon if we don't get back over there. In any case I bet Harris won't be satisfied with something like this. Sooner or later we'll be off to bloody Berlin as well you see."

"Christ and I thought we might even make it through just with these Frenchy trips. I bet the Krauts have just been saving up their ammo for when we get there tonight."

"Come on chaps. There is a rumour that we are going to get some leave soon. Who knows, maybe even after tonight."

"They're always saying that, Skip. I think that it's just to keep us going, the bloody twisters."

"OK, everyone get your heads down. It has been a busy few days and we need to be in good shape for tonight. See you in the Crew Room twenty-one hundred hours," Cowan said to them all and as they walked away, he asked Clarke about a beer in the Mess.

The evening was warm as they all gathered together to get their flying kit on. It had been a lovely June day with warm sunshine and a gentle breeze and as they got into T-Tommy the fuselage still felt warm from the heat of the sun and once the checks were completed and the engines started, they were on their way.

The aircraft lifted off into the night sky and climbed steadily to 15,000 feet heading towards Great Yarmouth to cross the coast.

"Coast in sight navigator."

"Thanks. Skip come on to one-one-zero – it is thirty-nine minutes to the Dutch coast."

"Right everyone, eyes peeled. They will pick us up pretty soon and probably realise we are going to Happy Valley. Check your guns. Bombaimer let us know when you first see the coast."

It seemed no time at all before Beavers called and as they crossed the coast, searchlights probed the sky with their silvery fingers and flak curved its way towards them.

"We are slightly south of track. Come to one-zero-five – forty minutes to target."

"One-zero-five." Cowan's calm voice repeated. "Bombaimer call if you see anything up front. Gunners keep really sharp now. The bastards are bound to be out there."

They were about ten minutes from the target when Beavers shouted that he could see what looked like a huge fire ahead and before they knew it, they were on their bomb run. The flak was all around them and the aircraft was flung about with the explosions.

"Can you see the target markers bombaimer?"

"No Skip but it looks like Hell itself down there – smoke and flames everywhere."

"OK let's aim for the brightest flames."

"Skip come right, keep coming right, OK steady now, left, steady bombs gone – flash gone." Just at that moment flak burst close to them rattling against the fuselage and Clarke heard a ripping sound followed by an agonising pain in his left arm. He looked over towards James and saw him clutching his head with blood running over his gloves.

"Everyone alright?" Cowan asked as he tried to control the aircraft which was turning steeply to the left and losing height.

"Skip, Hank and I have both been hit. Hank looks pretty bad and I can't move my arm. There's a small fire here which I'm just about to deal with. And the port inner looks on fire as well."

Cowan did not reply as he fought to get control of T-Tommy which seemed to be just falling out of the sky. Clarke picked up the extinguisher and with one hand managed to point it at the flames and set it off before Beavers came back from the front of the aircraft and took over. Clarke had a look at James who was conscious but bleeding heavily from a deep wound on his forehead.

Between them Cowan and Barton got control of the aircraft and although they were on three engines, they managed to gain some height and steal away into the darkness.

"Navigator can you give me a course?"

"It's only a single-handed one just for the moment Skip. What shape is T-Tommy in?"

"OK for now. How's fuel engineer?"

"We are still losing some. About three hours remaining."

"I'll bring us in over Kent then. Steer two-six-five."

The pain in his arm was now severe and he sat down heavily on his stool and put his head in his hands.

"You OK Nobby?" Beavers was standing next to him trying to examine his arm. "Looks a bit bloody matey. I'll tie a bandage round and see if that helps. Poor old Hank doesn't look too good neither."

"Had a quick look earlier. I think it's a flesh wound – they always bleed like stink from the head but he's probably a bit concussed as well."

"Well that's you done. I'll bandage up his head."

"Thanks Ray. If I rest my arm on the desk, I can still just about still use my hand." Clarke checked GEE and H2S and found they had both been knocked out.

"Skip we are down to one-handed dead reckoning. Everything's US back here. We should be coming up to the coast in about thirty minutes may be less. Over the Scheldt so it could be lively."

"Thanks. You OK?"

"Not bad!"

As they approached the coast the searchlights and flak intensified but the guns never got their height and they were away and over the sea before anyone could latch on to them.

The English coast slowly came closer and clearer with the first glimmers of dawn.

"We are getting low on fuel Skip. They must have hit the tanks" Barton said.

"That and our wounded. Nobby you still there? Do we know where we are? I guess Manston is nearest?"

The pain in Clarke's arm had settled whilst he rested but as soon as he moved it became intense and he caught his breath as he spoke almost inaudibly.

"Ray can you identify the coast at all?"

"Looks like Deal to me. I can see the pier. You OK Nobby you sound like shit?"

"Skip. Turn right and follow the coast. You should be able to see Manston if we're right."

Clarke suddenly felt very sick and before he knew it, he vomited all over the navigation desk.

"Yes, I see it. Can anyone get to the radio and tell them we are on our way in?"

Beavers was on his way back to check on Clarke and James but realised the radio had been hit and was useless.

"OK Ray get the flares out. We will just have to make them realise we are here and in trouble."

Beavers found the flare handbook and as they approached Manston fired the appropriate flare for the day as they flew down the runway. Cowan turned the aircraft downwind and as he did so saw the answering flare – green – they were cleared to land. He turned onto their base leg and then finals.

The aircraft bounced slightly and the jarring produced agonising pain for Clarke and he vomited again and held tight until they stopped and had shut down the engines. Cowan came back quickly to see what had happened.

"Christ, this is a mess."

"Sorry old chap I just felt really unwell."

"No, not that you clot. You and James and this whole area. You're lucky to be alive. It's a complete bloody shambles. Look you can see out through the fuselage the holes are so big."

By this time the ground crew had arrived and Cowan shouted at them.

"We need a blood wagon here smartish. Two badly injured crew. Look sharp now."

James was conscious now and the others helped to lift him out and in no time, he was smoking a cigarette inhaling deeply as if his life depended on it. Clarke walked slowly to the main spar and Beavers and Cowan gently eased him across it towards

Barton and Stark. By the time they got to the rear door the ambulance had arrived and he was lifted down to their waiting arms.

As the ambulance raced away with Clarke and James, Cowan and the others walked around T-Tommy to look at the damage in the cold light of dawn. The left wing was full of holes from the flak and the fuselage next to the navigation and radio station had been ripped apart.

"Blimey Skip, just like the old times?"

"Somewhat reminiscent Ernie, I agree" he replied with a wry smile. "Let's go and see if they've got some breakfast for us, shall we? Poor old T-Tommy won't be flying again for a while. Everyone else alright? You look a bit washed out Jerry?"

"Just trying to get over Nobby and Hank, Skip. Never seen nobody bashed up like them was?"

"They'll be OK. Few scratches, nothing too serious. And we should have some leave don't forget?"

"S'pose so Skip. Shook me up a bit that's all."

Cowan put his arm on the young lad's shoulder. "They'll be fine, you see. We'll get back today and get down the Red Lion tonight for a good old booze up. Set us up a treat it will."

By the time Cowan had got over to the sickbay Clarke and James were looking better and they each greeted him with a smile.

"You two swinging the lead I see! Glad to see you are surviving. We are being picked up about seventeen hundred. Will you be fit to come with us or are you going to stay here ogling the nurses?"

"I think we will be OK, don't you Hank? They took a chunk of shrapnel out of my arm and it feels much better now. It was resting near to a nerve apparently and that's what made it so painful when I moved. Hank's just got a headache haven't you buddy?"

Hank nodded – he was clearly not that good and had concussion but nothing a beer wouldn't fix.

"East Kirkby say the raid was a success and the refinery was blown to kingdom come. Oh, and the Wingco confirmed we are off now for ten days at least. Whole squadron stood down. You chaps rest here and don't misbehave with the nurses and I'll let you know when we are ready to go."

CHAPTER 33

Tuesday 13th June 1944

Clarke was dozing in the sickbay when he heard someone coughing at the bedside and he realised that Wing Commander Squires was standing there.

"Morning Clarke. How's the arm? You chaps did well last night. Raid a complete success, losses not too bad." Before Clarke could answer Squires continued "Hear from Flight Lieutenant Cowan that you did damn well, kept at the job though wounded, that sort of thing. I'm putting you up for a gong, DFC. Well done. Some bad news for you though Clarke. Sorry couldn't let you know sooner but communication blackout just now as you know. Heard from your mother yesterday that your brother Richard is dead. Very sorry. Ring your mother when you can, there's a good chap."

With this he turned on his heel and walked out of the ward leaving Clarke struggling to understand everything that had been said. How could Richard be dead if he was in hospital? He got out of bed, dressed and walked over to the nurses' station to ask for the nearest phone.

When he got through to his mother she immediately started to cry and for a while it was impossible to understand what she was saying.

"Thank God you are alright, dear. I tried to ring but they said I couldn't speak to you and then I thought that you had gone too. Oh, John it has been terrible."

"What happened, mother? How did he die?"

There was a long pause and through the sobs he made out that he had hung himself in his room at the hospital.

"John apart from losing him, it's such a dreadful disgrace him dying like that. Just think what your father would have said? He must be turning in his grave" and she started to cry again and eventually she continued "I don't feel I can talk to anyone else about how he died, I just feel so lonely and lost, dear. Is there any chance you could come home even for a day or two? I'm sorry to ask, I know you are so busy. I've got to talk to the vicar to see if we can have him buried properly." She was crying bitterly again and Clarke had to wait for the weeping to stop before he could reply.

"I'll come as soon as I can mother. Leave the vicar to me, I am sure we can sort something out don't worry. Must go. I will try and get down tomorrow."

He replaced the receiver and sat heavily down and put his head in his hands.

"You alright, sir?" one of the nurses asked. "You look a bit pale. Not bad news I hope?"

"My brother has died. I need to get home as soon as I can. I just have another call to make first."

Amazingly he got through to Anne straight away.

"I was beginning to get worried. Is everything alright?"

"Yes and no. We got caught last night and I have got a bit of scratch but I'm OK otherwise. Just spoken to my mother and found out that Richard is dead."

Anne was silent for a while "How did that happen? He was still in hospital, wasn't he?"

Clarke lowered his voice. "He committed suicide in the ward."

"Oh my God John. Your poor mother, well you too. What are you going to do?"

"Get down there as soon as possible. Annie, I have something to ask you. Is there any chance at all that you could take some leave? I have two weeks leave now – perhaps we could go away once I have sorted out things at home?"

"As you know, I'm owed lots of time off. I can ask our old battle-axe matron if I can go. No, actually I'll just tell her I'm going. When will you go to your mother's?"

"This afternoon if I can get out of here."

"What do you mean. I thought you said you were free to go."

"Well I am but I need the doctor to say so."

You're not in hospital too, are you?"

"Just a little bit. I'll meet you front of the hospital about two-ish."

* * *

Anne was quiet as they drove away from the hospital and it was nearly half an hour before she spoke.

"What happened John? Is your arm very sore?" She felt cross that he had said nothing and his injury brought to mind that Matt, too, had been hurt and, similarly, had said nothing.

"Bit of flak. Nothing really. It was better after they had fished out whatever it was."

"Are you alright to drive.? It still looks pretty sore from where I'm sitting."

"No it's fine, old thing. Wonderful you could get away."

"Oh, I just walked out. Told them I had some urgent family problem to sort out and that I was taking leave. Talking of which, this is terrible news about Richard?"

"It is, and mother feels it brings disgrace on the family. Suicide in the Clarke family will never do you know!"

"But he was so sick, John. Think how he was when we last saw him."

"I know, I know but suicide is frowned on especially in the Forces. Stiff upper lip and all that. In any case I have said to mother I will go and negotiate with the vicar to see if he can have a proper burial. Next to father I suppose."

Anne went to touch his arm and then drew back realising it would be sore. They drove along for a while before Clarke pulled into a pub.

"Let's have some grub. I think it is going to be a long trip, the roads seem completely choked with trucks and tanks. Anyone would think there's a war on!" he smiled.

It was late by the time they arrived home but Clarke's mother was waiting at the gate for them. She hugged Clarke and he held her tightly before letting her go to embrace Anne.

"Thank you so much for coming" she said through her tears. "You must be exhausted, both of you. Come on in and let's have some tea."

Once they were in the house, she noticed Clarke's injured arm. "Oh, John what has happened to you? You see. I knew you would get hurt eventually."

"It's alright mother I've brought my own nurse along you know?"

"Well it's just as well isn't it Anne? Are you alright dear? You look very tired. Have you been working very hard?"

"Not too bad Mrs Clarke, Dora. But it has been nice to get away even though it is so sad about Richard."

"Oh, I can't believe it, dear. Will you go and see the vicar tomorrow John? He was sympathetic but said suicide was a mortal sin and he couldn't possibly bury him in our church graveyard."

"Bloody ridiculous mother. I'll go around there first thing so we can get this sorted out. Now I'm afraid I need to sleep or I will just keel over."

"Your rooms are upstairs dear. There are towels on the beds.

I am so relieved you are here dear, well you too Anne. It's such a relief. Maybe even I will sleep tonight."

Clarke went around to the vicar first thing in the morning leaving Anne talking to his mother.

"Oh, hallo John. Do come in. It's about your poor brother I suspect?" He knew the family well and had baptized both John and Richard.

"Well actually it's about my poor mother," Clarke replied sharply as he walked into the old vicarage preparing for a fight. "What with father dying just a few weeks ago and now this with Richard, she is in a dreadful state."

"Would you like some tea? Elizabeth will make us some and then we can sit down and talk."

"To be honest vicar I'm not sure a cup of tea will fix it. Whilst I completely understand how sinful the church regards suicide Richard, in effect, gave his life for this country. He was seriously injured fighting in Italy. You probably haven't realised how sick he was when he came home." Clarke was shouting now. "All that and my father dying as well. Have you any idea how hard my mother is finding all this? And, of course, I'm away too – you may have noticed my arm?"

"John, John, please try and calm down. Let's sit and have a civilised chat, shall we? I really think a cup of tea will help. It often does."

Clarke sank into a nearby chair and before he knew it, he was crying bitterly and the vicar was standing at his side with a hand on his shoulder.

"John" he said quietly "You, too, are near the edge, aren't you?"

Clarke looked up into the vicar's kindly and troubled face and nodded silently.

"Do you have some leave? Can you get a break?" he asked gently.

Clarke nodded "But it's not about me vicar. It's my mother I'm concerned for."

"Of course, you are but I think it is also about you, John. You have had enough – I saw it myself in 1917. Trouble is you have to keep on, have to keep going. Then things like Richard's suicide become almost the final straw."

Clarke nodded in agreement as the vicar put a cup of tea in his hand.

"But what can we do vicar? It will destroy mother if Richard can't get a proper burial. She's already too ashamed to talk to neighbours. And Richard's death was part of his illness. You must have heard how he was, over the last few weeks?" His anger had gone now and he felt drained and exhausted.

"Well maybe I can get a special dispensation from the bishop, I will certainly try."

"But when? I only have a few days of leave."

"I'll ring this morning John and will come and see you all this afternoon. You being here will be a great comfort to your mother in the meantime. And I hear that you have a young lady?"

"Yes, I have. She's very nice. We look forward to seeing you this afternoon vicar." He rose to leave. "Please do all you can to help us won't you?"

CHAPTER 34

Tuesday 20th June 1944

Richard got his funeral and was duly buried next to his father and although Clarke's mother was tearful, her composure reflected the relief she felt that everything had worked out for the best in the end.

Eventually Clarke and Anne managed to get on their way to Scotland, somewhere Anne had always wanted to visit. It was a long, slow trip and by the end of the first day they had only reached the outskirts of Manchester. The pub they stopped at was set back from the road and the bedroom looked out over a deep valley from which drifted the warm smells of a June evening. Dinner had been basic but nice and after sharing a bottle of wine Clarke was feeling decidedly sleepy.

"I think I'll hit the sack. Last few days have been pretty full on."

"Let's have another look at that arm?"

"Yes, nurse."

"It's very bruised John, and the wound where the metal went in is inflamed. Is it very sore?"

"It's OK if I don't touch it or come to that if you don't touch it!" he said wincing.

"Let's just get some sleep. You must be exhausted and we have a long drive tomorrow."

She slipped his shirt and trousers off and got him into bed before undressing and joining him. They kissed and she snuggled her head on to his chest and within minutes they were both asleep.

As they drove further north, they noticed that the roads gradually got less and less busy and they eventually arrived at the hotel on the banks of Loch Lomond. Clarke felt that at last he was beginning to leave his problems behind him. His arm was still sore but he was sure that once the swelling had settled, he would be fighting fit.

The silence that met them as they got out of the car, was difficult to comprehend. It had recently rained and the unsullied smells of wet earth, flowers and the nearby pine trees was almost overwhelming. They were shown to their room which overlooked the loch and once the door was shut, they held each other closely.

"I had always wanted to come here John. Matt and I had planned to, you know?"

"Well now we are here, Annie. It feels so peaceful after all that has happened."

They kissed again, this time more passionately.

"John can we make love. I promise to be very careful with your arm" she chuckled. "Let me help you out of those things." She undressed him and then herself but left her silk petticoat on and got into bed beside him.

"Me on top I think, with your arm". They made love slowly and when they had finished, she lay on top of him her long hair falling over her shoulders whilst they both slept.

It was still light when Clarke woke and as he sat up, he saw that Anne was sitting by the window looking out across Loch Lomond.

"What time is it. Feels that I have been asleep for hours?"

"Well you have been sweetheart. It's nearly ten o'clock. Are you hungry?"

"I am and of course it's still light because this is June in Scotland."

"It looks beautiful out there. Can we walk tomorrow? Are you up to it?"

"Darling they got my arm, not my leg. Of course, I am. Let's go and find food. I could even eat haggis if necessary!"

* * *

The next day was beautifully sunny and Clarke had arranged for the hotel car to take them around the loch to Balmaha so that they could climb Ben Lomond. They walked along the road by the side of the loch to Rowardennan and they began the climb leaving Coille Mhor on their right. After a while they stopped to catch their breath and turned to look over Loch Lomond.

"John, this is wonderful. The water in the loch is so still you can see a perfect reflection of the mountains on the surface."

"Should be even better from the top. It's a Munro you know?"

"I don't – what's that?"

"Munro is the name given to all mountains over 3000 feet in Scotland. Named by a chap, in the late 1800's, unsurprisingly called Munro. Ben Lomond just makes it!"

They continued climbing until they reached the top. There was a gentle breeze blowing that wafted the smells from the valley below towards them. The views all around were spectacular and Clarke named the mountains that they could see away to the north. They gazed in awe at the sight before them and it was some time before Anne spoke.

"Let's sit down John. What did the hotel give us to eat? All that climbing has made me hungry."

They ate and drank in silence until Anne suggested they lie down. They kissed tenderly and after they had made love, she lay her head down on Clarke's chest and they rested there listening to the world around them.

To Clarke it was as if he had arrived in heaven. The warm afternoon air was carrying the sweet smell of the gorse up the mountain to them and apart from the mewing of the golden eagles soaring above them, nothing else could be heard. The war, Richard's death and his lucky escape during their last outing seemed a million miles away and they lay together for a while before Clarke spoke.

"We better get going, sweetheart. We have to get back down to the loch for the ferry to Inveruglas. They were going to send the car for us about five o'clock."

Anne eased herself off him and brushed her hair back with her hands.

"I could stay here for ever. Can we come back to Scotland one day when the world has more sense?"

"Of course we can. Annie, I had an idea. Why don't we get married?"

"I thought we were going to?"

"No, I mean, now. While we are in Scotland."

"Are you worried my father will say no?" she giggled. "I mean you're not much of a catch. Lecturer in Manchester, pilot officer navigator in the RAF!"

"No, be serious, in any case it's the RAAF" Clarke said as they started walking down towards the loch. "Of course, I realise that I will need to speak to your father eventually but they have a telephone, don't they? I was thinking that we could tie the knot in Gretna Green on our way back. At the old anvil, that sort of thing."

"Gosh, you are a romantic, aren't you? Well I don't think my parents will be very happy about that you know. Mummy had always wanted me to have a big wedding. On the other hand, it would be jolly cheap for daddy wouldn't it?" She laughed again.

They were above the loch now and the path was steep and Clarke turned to help Anne down and as he did, she put her arms around him.

"I think Gretna sounds a wonderful idea, darling" and she kissed him tenderly. "Shall we see if we can speak to mummy and daddy tonight?"

Clarke nodded and he held her hand as they worked their way down to the path along the loch.

The phone call was not an easy one. Anne's parents were firmly against the marriage saying that it was far too soon after Matt's death and, in any case, she could end up losing someone else she loved. Clarke was impressed how stubborn Anne could get and in the end she and her parents agreed to differ. Gretna it was.

They drank champagne before dinner and in their minds their dinner was their wedding breakfast. When they went to bed that night their lovemaking was almost a confirmation of how they felt about one another and in the morning they lay together for a long time Clarke gently stroking Anne's hair.

"Annie" he said "I've been thinking about last night. Perhaps we should wait. I really don't want to hurt your parents' feelings. It wouldn't be a very good start would it?"

Anne lifted her face to him. "You are a very nice man you know, for an RAF officer I mean. I was lying awake worrying about that. It would be terrific to get married just now but I think that it would be a big upset for mummy and daddy. I'll ring them again tonight. She rolled on top of him and resting on her elbows looked into his eyes. "But you must promise me one thing, John. Never leave me. I couldn't stand that happening again."

"Do my best old thing. Things aren't as bad as they were when Matt was flying but it's not exactly a joy ride, even now. Let's go and get some breakfast. Shall we walk again or stay here?"

"What right here, like this?" she smiled. "If you insist Pilot Officer Clarke." She made a salute and rolled off him and got dressed.

After breakfast they got a lift to Inverbeg and walked through Glen Douglas until they overlooked Loch Long. There, the huge barbwire fence clearly built to keep everyone out, was a stark reminder that even here the war was really not very far away and Clarke turned sadly away. It was if the magical enchantment of the last few, precious days had been suddenly broken and they walked in silence back to Inverbeg; and as if to emphasise the gloom that had enveloped them both, it started raining. As Clarke trudged along, he thought about the next day and them starting back to Lincoln, back to the war, back to the death and destruction, back to our side knocking hell out of their side. By the time they reached the hotel Clarke was convinced that Anne's parents were right. It would be crazy for them to marry now. The ghastly reality was that he could be killed at any time and where would that leave Anne? Reality was something they had escaped for a few days but now it was back in their faces and all the more awful for that. The next day they set off back to Lincoln through the rain and never even stopped at Greta Green.

CHAPTER 35

Friday 7th July 1944

After they had returned from Scotland, Clarke saw little of Anne. He had felt a terrible emptiness after he had dropped her off at the hospital and an awareness that somehow their relationship would never be quite the same again. The war had seen to that and he smiled grimly at the thought that, but for that, they might well have eloped and now be married. How strange that it had seemed just the right thing to do on that fateful night, whilst by the next morning it clearly would have been a disaster for everyone.

He had been back to flying two days after they returned and although the air support for the D-Day invasion had eased off for a while, there was now an urgent need to destroy the sites of the flying bombs which had begun to drop on to London in large numbers and the squadron was involved in almost nightly raids in an endeavour to destroy them. Nevertheless, the raids were relatively quiet, the crew seeing little in the way of action and Clarke was surprised how quickly he was clocking up his trips such that he was up to twenty-seven with just three more to go.

The morning of the 7th dawned bright and the blue and cloudless sky presaged another hot summer day. Clarke had breakfast and then went to the Flight Office and, unsurprisingly, found that the crew of T-Tommy were on the operations board for that night's raid. As he left the office, he was nearly bowled over by Cowan rushing in.

"We're on tonight again, Paul."

"Bugger. I thought they might give us a break after these last few nights. I met a rather nice lady a few days ago and I had hoped we might get together for dinner tonight."

"'fraid not Paul. She'll have to wait for another night. Anyway, who is she? Anyone we know?"

"You keep your hands off her young Pilot Officer" he smiled. "She specifically indicated that she wasn't interested in anyone below the rank of Flight Lieutenant. Actually, she works in the control tower. Smashing looking girl as well, I can tell you. Long fair hair, blue eyes and body built in heaven! She just happens to have tonight off and now the bloody war has screwed that up hasn't it? Never stops does it? Ah well, we better organise the chaps for an air test say about elevenish? Charlie thought the starboard outer was running a bit hot so we need to check that the ground crew boys have fixed it."

Clarke eventually ran the others to ground in the sergeants' mess.

"Oi you're not allowed in here now, you know" Barton called from the bar. "Well unless you buy us a bloody drink of course. What's up Nobby?"

"Well just for a change we are on for tonight. Skip wants an air test. All your fault saying there was a problem with that bloody engine."

"Bugger that for a bunch of daisies. We've been up every bloody night since we got back off leave. I thought they would give us a break this time. What d'you think Ernie. You're always complaining."

"Yeh, can't be right. It's bloody difficult getting any sleep in that sodding turret, you know. I'm knackered."

"Well can't be helped I'm afraid, Ernie. Eleven o'clock for a pre-lunch joy ride."

The air test went without problems and Barton was happy that the engine was behaving and they went their separate ways before lunch. Clarke suddenly felt that he needed to try and speak to Anne and he went to the Mess to telephone and to his amazement got through almost immediately.

"Hallo stranger. Guess you have been either busy or have gone off me."

"Annie I'm really sorry. Yes, we have been out every night so far. We are all getting a bit fed up to be honest. How have you been?"

"Oh, working too. I'm going home at the weekend to catch up with mummy and daddy, oh and to see if Scrap is still alright. John what shall I tell them about us? I mean we seemed so close when we were away until that last night. Then everything went a bit odd. You do want us to be together, don't you?"

"Of course I do, sweetheart. If it wasn't for the wretched war we would just have called in to Gretna and got married, wouldn't we? Maybe everything has happened too quickly. And there is Matt still in the background isn't there? You said you and he had always planned to go to Scotland."

There was a pause and Clarke wondered if Anne was still there.

"Annie?"

"I'm here. What do you want to do then?"

"Let's meet when I get a break. Should be soon. Maybe after the weekend when you get back from your parents. It's difficult on the phone isn't it?"

"So, do I tell my parents we are going to get married, yes or no? Simple question really."

"Of course you do. Well, I still love you anyway." He was getting cross. The endless nights of flying were wearing him down and this had not been the conversation he was expecting. Sod this war, it ruins everything. He remembered the wonderful times they had had together and the thought of losing Anne made him feel utterly desolate.

"Annie I'm so sorry. I love you very much and I want us to be together. Please don't let us part like this. I can't take too many more bad things happening in my life. Our love is the only thing that is keeping me going. I can't bear the thought that we might be finished."

There was another pause and when she spoke Anne's voice had lost its softness, "Well you need to make up your mind don't you?"

The phone clicked down and he replaced the receiver and walked away just as Cowan walked in.

"You OK old boy? Not more bad news I hope."

"I think I have just had my last chat with Anne. Everything seemed to be going so well and then suddenly they weren't. Like a switch had been thrown somewhere inside her."

"She'll get over it old boy. Women are very complicated. Probably got a period or something. Try ringing her tomorrow. Probably be as right as rain."

"I'm not so sure Paul. She didn't sound too good at the end. Maybe the shadow of her fiancé is still hanging over her. Easy to understand – they were very close by all accounts, well almost married."

"Mark my words old boy, it will fine when you ring next time. She's probably pining for you – I mean you were together for quite a few days and now you're not. It's hard."

"Maybe Paul. Here's hoping. Let me get you a pint. Briefing at five o'clock isn't it?"

Clarke went back to his room after lunch and started writing a letter to Anne but somehow the words wouldn't come and he only got as far as "Dearest Annie".

The briefing was taken by Group Captain Brookes, a sure sign that the operation was of major importance.

"Good afternoon chaps. You will be aware that Jerry has unleashed these flying bombs on London and we need to put a stop to them. The French underground have found what appears to be a storage dump for the bombs in tunnels around St Leu D' Esserent, north of Paris and we think we can fix them. It is a precision bombing show. Wing Commander Squires is joining you tonight. Now for the Station Navigator."

As the curtain covering the map of France was drawn back Clarke and Cowan looked at one another and Cowan raising a quizzical eyebrow. The route was a simple dogleg but with two long straight runs, one sure way of making it easy to attract attention from Jerry. And this would be one target that they would be keen not to be bombed.

The crews left slowly after the briefing. They were all tired after interminable nights of flying and even though they were less often attacked now than they had been, the tensions of each flight were beginning to have their effect and wear away their resilience.

"Right, this may not be a piece of cake chaps" Cowan said seriously. "Bound to be flak around the target and maybe even some fighters for you to shoot at Jerry, Ernie. So, make sure you stay awake. No sleeping on the job." he smiled as he walked away. It was tough for the gunners all alone in their freezing turrets, usually with nothing to do hour after hour.

Clarke walked slowly back to his room in the Mess. He thought of trying to ring Anne again but he knew that he would be on a charge if he was found making telephone calls after the briefing. He felt sick with despondency and saddened at the thought that he had probably lost someone who had become the love of his life. This trip did not sound too good either but then if he got killed that would be the end of it. What did he care now in any case? He realised that he had never felt like this before and suddenly all that had happened in the past months tumbled on top of him and his life felt of little importance. He went quietly to his room and sat alone, head in hands. Maybe Tucker had the right idea and just blew his brains out. Or Richard hanging himself. Why not, he thought. Who would care?

He eventually got up and made his way to meet the others in the crew room getting their kit together. Everyone seemed remarkably subdued, probably just tired, he thought. He hoped they didn't feel like he did. Cowan walked over to him.

"You alright Nobby? No news on the woman front?"

"No, I think I've had it Paul. She didn't sound very friendly when we said goodbye. Anyway, how about you? Have you sorted out your popsie?"

"I certainly have, old boy. The lady in question is off tomorrow night as well. I'm sure they can't give us another job tomorrow so I've already booked a table on a promise for a romantic evening."

They clambered into the truck and were dropped off at the dispersal area, T-Tommy standing alone in the gathering darkness.

They taxied out to the runway and with the green flare, Cowan opened the throttles and they set off on yet another trip. With a light fuel load the aircraft lifted easily into the night sky and turned south towards their crossing point at Hastings. After a while Beavers said that he could see the coast coming up and as they crossed it, Clarke gave their course to the target. It was a clear night and Cowan could see other aircraft around them, gently rising and falling on the summer thermals.

"Ten minutes to target Skipper."

"Thanks navigator. Keep your eyes peeled everyone. Jerry will definitely not be pleased to see us tonight."

"Come to one-two-zero. Starting our bombing run now."

"Markers are going down Skip just off to the left."

"I've got them bombaimer. Heading that way."

"Corkscrew port" Stark shouted and Cowan threw the aircraft into a dive as Stark opened fire.

The aircraft turned quickly back on to its course to the target and was nearly there when cannon fire ripped into the fuselage.

"Drop those bloody bombs" Cowan called and turned the aircraft away and into the surrounding darkness.

Clarke could see flames licking around the aircraft's fuselage just behind James who was clearly dead with blood pouring from what remained of his head and almost at once Cowan shouted to them. "Bale out, bale out, get out everyone. I'll hold her for as long as I can."

Clarke picked up his parachute and ran forward to the front hatch which Beavers had already opened.

As Clarke went past Cowan, he threw him his parachute but Cowan just mouthed 'Get Out'.

Clarke looked back again as he moved forward and his last sight of Cowan was of his grim face as he tried to control the aircraft. Then he was down to the hatch and out into the blackness below.

The cold hit him as he fell, praying that his parachute would open when he pulled the rip cord. The silence after the noise of the aircraft was extraordinary and as he descended, he could see their aircraft steadily falling, trailing flames and smoke and, just before it hit the ground, exploding in a shower of sparks.

CHAPTER 36

Saturday 8ᵗʰ July 1944

As the sun came up Flight Lieutenant Granger wearily pushed open the Flight Office door to begin the task of writing even more letters to relatives and loved ones. Three aircraft had failed to return last night, twenty-one men for whom, likely or not, there would be no tomorrow.

Author's Note

Bomber Command lost 55,573 aircrew during the Second World War out of the 125,000 personnel who volunteered.

Also by the same author

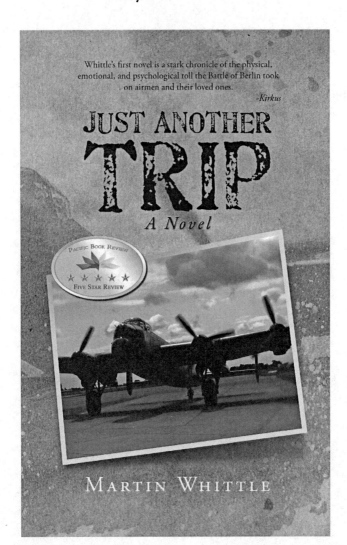

Whittle's first novel is a stark chronicle of the physical, emotional, and psychological toll the Battle of Berlin took on airmen and their loved ones.
-Kirkus

JUST ANOTHER
TRIP
A Novel

PACIFIC BOOK REVIEW
★★★★★
FIVE STAR REVIEW

MARTIN WHITTLE